"DO YOU EVER DREAM ABOUT US LIKE THIS, SHANNON?"

"Every night, Ash," she whispered. "I..."

He didn't want her to talk anymore, afraid of her power over him. His mouth cut off her next words as his fingers sought out all the hidden places she once loved to be touched.

Lost! He was lost in her, lost to himself. Her wet heat surrounded him like a custom-made glove, and he shared her excitement, the beat of her heart, her very breath. It was a moment of surrender for them both, and they were one once again.

The pure perfection of their joining was suddenly too much. Ash jerked away—and knocked his head against the doorframe.

He'd been dreaming, watching her sleep. Sweat made a fine sheen on his bare skin as he stood there alone. *He'd been dreaming.*

Fool! he thought. Nothing could have been that perfect...not even Shannon.

ABOUT THE AUTHOR

Although Evelyn Crowe lives in Houston and has
made Texas the setting for all of her previous
Superromances, for her sixth novel she's ventured
outside her home state to Montana. On a research
trip north, Evelyn fell in love with Montana's
rugged ranches and snowcapped mountains, and
she is looking forward to a return visit some day
soon to the Big Sky country.

Books by Evelyn A. Crowe

HARLEQUIN SUPERROMANCE
112–SUMMER BALLAD
160–CHARADE
186–MOMENT OF MADNESS
233–FINAL PAYMENT
262–TWICE SHY

Don't miss any of our special offers. Write to us at the
following address for information on our newest releases.

Harlequin Reader Service
901 Fuhrmann Blvd., P.O. Box 1397, Buffalo, NY 14240
Canadian address: P.O. Box 603,
Fort Erie, Ont. L2A 5X3

For my mother,
Marianne J. Crowe

Even a baby vulture is a beautiful,
majestic eagle in its own mother's eyes.

I soar among the clouds.

E.A.C.

Evelyn A. Crowe

A WILD WIND

Harlequin Books

TORONTO • NEW YORK • LONDON
AMSTERDAM • PARIS • SYDNEY • HAMBURG
STOCKHOLM • ATHENS • TOKYO • MILAN

Published February 1988

First printing December 1987

ISBN 0-373-70294-9

CHAPTER ONE

"SHE'S BACK!"

The statement preceded the speaker into the Cattleman's Café in Bartlet, Montana. At six o'clock in the morning the few customers scattered among the tables and in the booths, drinking their coffee and waiting for the local feed store down the road to open, glanced up. Those who were disturbed by the open door, the chilly breeze and the blowhorn voice frowned. Those who were all too familiar with that voice simply ignored it.

"She's back!"

"Who's back?" a female voice full of curiosity called out from the kitchen.

"Shannon! Shannon's come back."

The glass door, decorated with advertising decals, swooped shut on the patched backside of a scrawny, bent, elderly man. Chester Fawnsworth shifted a bulge from one side of his cheek to the other, then puckered his lips to spit a stream of tobacco juice in the styrofoam cup he held in one knotted hand. But he paused, his bright gaze suddenly searching out the proprietor of the café before he made a horrible face, swallowed hard, then grimaced.

Stella Hopkins gave the old geezer at the door a speaking glance from under finely plucked eyebrows and spiky lashes thick with mascara, then she swayed down the long counter, wiping absently at the clean surface, alternating her strokes to the movement of the swivel stools as she made her way toward him.

She loved this place, and sometimes the memories of her mother and father were so strong she could still see them behind the counter. Oh, there were bad memories, too, but running the Cattleman's Café kept the painful ones at bay, allowing her time to remember only the happier moments. The old place was sure a dinosaur, she mused, all hunkered down in the midst of a town that had been remodeled and modernized and had grown all out of proportion as far as she was concerned. She turned away from the foot-shifting old man and glanced around the café proudly.

Red vinyl booths lined one long mirrored wall, each with its own jukebox selector. Stout tables with spotless red and white checkered cloths formed a row down the middle of the room, and at the back, on a minute dance floor, squatted a mammoth jukebox. Of course the ancient box was an attraction in itself, a never ending source of conversation and awe. When a quarter was dropped in and the mellow tunes began to play, the rounded top with its rainbow of colors would light up and begin to pulse in time to the beat.

The old-timers came early for coffee, breakfast and gossip. The youngsters came after school and the café jumped with their music as they ate hamburgers, drank cokes and chattered endlessly. Evenings at the café were a little more sedate with the dinner crowd, unless it was a Saturday night and there was a local dance or a new band playing at one of the rowdy nightclubs. Then, although she normally closed at ten o'clock, Stella would stay open until one in the morning to be sure those who needed food and coffee got it. Ranch country made for long drives home.

"Chester, how many times a day do you come in here for a cup of coffee?" She pursed her pink mouth, trying to show her disapproval, but her chipmunk cheeks stained with two circles of red rouge ruined the censorious look she gave him.

"Every morning for the last twenty years, you know that." He stuffed his scarred, work-roughened cowboy hands in the grimy pockets of his blue jeans jacket and scowled. "But listen, Stella..."

Stella moved behind the counter and stared at the town gossip, enjoying herself thoroughly. It was obvious from the way he kept shifting from one foot to the other and touching his hearing aid to make sure it was working that Chester had a juicy tidbit to pass on. She loved needling the old pest. Leaning against the counter, she asked, "And how many times have I told you I don't allow no chewing and no spitting in my place?"

Chester's scowl grew deeper as he cast furtive little glances around the café to see who was interested in his humiliation once again.

Stella raised a dimpled arm and pointed toward the door. Her freshly starched white uniform with its tiny red handkerchief pinned neatly to the pocket stretched and pulled even tighter over her ample bosom as she moved. "You just march out that door and get rid of that disgusting stuff 'fore you come back in here and get your coffee."

"Damn Hitler," Chester wheezed, but he did as he was ordered, still grumbling under his breath as the door swung shut behind him. Any other time he'd have known better, except this morning was special and in his excitement he'd forgotten the rules. But hell and damnation, his news was sure going to rock this town on its ear. Once he'd heard it he could barely contain himself, so he'd taken off for the nearest place where he knew he'd find a captive audience. Now the lovely Stella was acting uppity. Women! They'd been the bane of his existence since he could remember.

Chester spit the last of his tobacco into the cup and without thinking pitched it in the nearest trash can beside the curb. He muttered a favorite four-letter obscenity and immediately felt better. Just as he clasped the door handle and was about to reenter the café, he glanced back over his shoulder toward the north and the rugged mountains far beyond the town.

Indigo clouds ribboned a suspiciously clear sky and seemed to hover over the high ridges. He knew, without the benefit of any newfangled, space age weather report, that Bartlet was in for a storm. His aching bones told him a cold spell was moving this way, a freak storm far worse than the television predicted, too. Suddenly he shivered inside his thin denim jacket, wishing he'd paid more heed to his bones and worn a flannel shirt underneath.

He shivered again as he tightened his grip on the door handle, but this time the trembling wasn't from the cold but from excitement. His tired eyes hadn't lost any of their sharpness and they hadn't missed the man sitting alone at a booth toward the back of the café. Maybe the look on Ash Bartlet's face would warm him as he related his juicy piece of gossip.

Chester gave the handle a tug, then smiled with anticipation before pulling open the heavy glass door and swaggering back into the café, sure this time there would be no interruptions. Hitching himself up on a stool, he nodded a thank-you to Stella for the cup of steaming coffee waiting for him. He picked up the cup, poured some of the scalding hot liquid onto the saucer, set the cup back down, then blew hard on the coffee before slurping a steady stream into his mouth. With an audible thud he set the saucer down and gazed steadily at Stella.

"You remember the Reed girl, don't you, Stella?" He didn't give her time to answer, knowing she never forgot anyone. But he didn't want any interference while he savored the telling of his news. "Shannon Reed—the girl that ran wild with Ash Bartlet and Dean Wayne all her young life. You'd think she wouldn't have the nerve to show her face around here even if it has been ten years since she and that fancy Wayne boy ran off and got hitched." A cough from behind him brought a smirk to his leathery, seamed face. He had everyone's attention now, by God.

"'Course most folks hereabouts knew after what Shannon did, she wasn't never going to be welcome around these parts—not her or that half-foreign husband of hers. He never fit in nowhere, even though his mama was born and bred here in Bartlet. I tell you, Stella, a woman, no matter how special, just can't deliberately kill a man's prize race horse that he'd pinned all his ranch's hopes and future on, break his heart in pieces, then run off with his best friend and marry him. Though old Ash must have sighed with relief once those stories of how she drank and whored her way around Europe started drifting back here."

Chester shook his head sadly, feeling the tension in the café building to a peak. Good, he told himself. This might teach the Bartlets not to be so high and mighty. Maybe next time he asked for a job out at the Bar B ranch he wouldn't be turned down and told it was because he couldn't keep his nose out of other people's business and his mouth shut. It would do that uppity bunch good, he thought, to bring them down a peg or two.

With a sly movement, his eyes rolled toward the rear of the café, then came bouncing back as they collided with a steady winter-green gaze. Gnarled fingers tightened around his coffee cup as he turned back to Stella and his eyes clashed with her angry stare. Daunted a little, yet determined to go on, he took a shallow breath.

"Todd Hands down at the sporting goods store told me that Clyde Hanks told Rex Smithers from over at the county office that Shannon and Dean won the draw for a tag on a bighorn sheep. They flew their own plane in a couple days ago just for the hunt. Wonder how Ash's going to like having that trash around?"

Stella leaned forward, her billowing bosom taking up a considerable amount of space on the counter in front of Chester. She lifted a plump arm and swiped his coffee cup onto the floor as she yanked the saucer out of his hand. "Why don't you ask him, you spineless old goat? You're nothing but a damn loose-mouth troublemaker, Chester. Now get out of my place and don't come back till I say you're welcome."

He grumbled something under his breath and was just about to slip off the stool when he sensed the tension in the room. It was as if everyone was holding their breath. Chester turned in time to see Ash Bartlet climb slowly to his feet, pick up his gray Stetson and place it on his head.

Ash dug in the front pocket of his jeans, fished out a dollar bill, then set his Stetson more securely on his head, pulling the brim down over his brow, shadowing his face. He could feel the eyes on him, but it didn't bother him. Hell, he was used to it, or so he told himself.

As he walked past the counter he flipped the money to Stella, nodded, then left without a word or a sideways look at anyone. He had to get out of the place, fast, before he suffocated from the lack of air. Chester's news had been like a punch to his chest—worse, in a way. This particular punch had gone straight to the heart. Ash shoved the door open and inhaled deeply, trying to calm his racing pulse with a gulp of biting air. He closed his eyes for a second, wanting only to block out the pictures her name conjured up, but it wasn't any use. They were there, branded for eternity. The heels of his boots tapped out a nagging question on the sidewalk, and no matter how fast he walked it was always the same. *Why, Shannon? Why?* But the answers never came, no matter how hard he searched for them.

Stella followed Ash to the door, wanting to say something to help ease the pain she saw in his eyes before he'd had time to mask it, yet what could she possibly say that would comfort without embarrassing the boy. She stopped herself for a moment. Ash was thirty-two. She could hardly think of him as a boy. She'd known him all his life; known his dad, the senator, and his mom, God rest her soul. She'd known and loved Shannon too, as had everyone who'd come within a few feet of that wild, unpredictable imp.

Damn, she moaned, life just wasn't fair. Ash had loved that gal since the day she was born, everyone knew that. It was a shock, even to this day, to look up and see Ash and not find Shannon tagging along right behind him. Then there was the other one—Dean Wayne. What was it her mother had nicknamed those kids? The Three Musketeers. And just when the town was bracing itself for a wedding between Ash and Shannon, all hell had broke loose.

Stella shook her head sadly. Ash hadn't spoken Shannon or Dean's name in ten years. Even when he was around others and Shannon's name was mentioned, she could never catch so much as a nerve twitch in his face—until today.

She sensed a dormant volcano just under the surface of that controlled exterior. An icy finger touched the back of her neck and she shivered. Poor Shannon. Stella prayed to God that she and Dean stayed out of Ash's way. Ten years was a long time to harbor so much hate. Who would ever have thought things would come to pass the way they had?

ASH STEERED THE TRUCK past the town square with its massive two-story, white stone courthouse and the life-size bronze statues of the town's founders, Zeb and Anna Bartlet, his great-grandparents. He passed the feed store without a backward glance as Cal Young, a Bar B ranch hand, watched in puzzlement while the boss's truck sped by.

Ash's grip tightened on the wheel and his boot seemed to weigh a ton as it pressed heavily on the gas pedal. Once on the open highway, the scenery nothing but a colorful blur, he allowed himself to think. She was back! Something painful caught in his chest and he couldn't catch his breath. He made a small noise deep in the back of his throat, determined that the news wasn't going to get the better of him.

As if on its own accord, the truck slowed and turned off the main highway. Suddenly he was on one of the Bar B's back roads. Tall trees, green yet thin of foliage, marked the route. With a jerk the truck came to a stop, spraying dirt in its wake as the tires chewed into the ground.

With an angry shove the door opened and he was out. Huge boulders from some ancient eruptions formed a half circle around an old oak tree. A cool breeze whipped the leaves and tugged at the brim of his hat as he squatted down, using one of the tumbled rocks as a backrest.

Absently he searched the inside pocket of his sheepskin coat and pulled out a crumpled pack of cigarettes and an ornate silver lighter worn smooth with use. He shook a cigarette out and placed it between his lips. Then, cupping his hands around the flame to protect it from the wind, he inhaled. Bitter smoke bit deep in his lungs, making him cough at the unaccustomed invasion. Looking down at the cigarette trembling between his fingers like a dry leaf in a light breeze, he frowned. Goddammit, he wasn't going to let her do this to him. With an angry gesture he threw the cigarette down and crushed its burning ember out beneath the toe of his boot.

Shannon was home!

His shoulders stiffened as if to ward off a blow. The words pounded behind his eyes until he squeezed them tightly shut. Hope ran through him like fire, then quickly died as a lifetime of memories came flooding back. She'd been like the very blood in his veins, the beat of his heart. Even after ten years he hadn't forgotten the sweet scent of her as she lay in his arms, nor had he ever felt the utter contentment he had then. She had been the sun and the stars and the future for him. Then one day fate had taken a hand and turned his perfect world upside down. Where there once had been warmth and laughter, there was now only ice and bitterness.

Shannon was home. And with her, her husband.

Just what the hell was he supposed to do? Ash climbed slowly to his feet, checking to make sure the cigarette was out before he returned to the truck.

The drive to the ranch was a painful one as he fought to keep the memories at bay. As he topped the ridge and caught sight of the house, a sigh of relief passed through the straight line of his lips. Here was safety, the familiar. A solid foundation to rely on. His home, the home of four generations, rose out of the earth like the mountains far beyond. Built of natural rock, the two-story structure sprawled in a meadow of gentle rolling grass, nestled in the shade from the trees that spotted the land. Home, his haven—his prison.

Rounding the bend in the road, he turned into the horseshoe-curved driveway in front of the house and pulled to a stop behind the sheriff's car. Peace, he surmised, was far from being his. "Damn," he muttered.

The crushed rock of the drive crunched like dry bones under his boots as he approached the official car. Jeff Hall was one of his best friends, but he wasn't expecting a visit, official or otherwise, from the local law today. Ash's steps lagged as he headed for the front door. When a familiar voice called out, he stopped, feeling ridiculously relieved at the delay.

"Hey, Boss," Bob Young shouted as he jogged around the side of the house. "You decide to dump that good-for-nothing brother of mine?" The adolescent ranch hand reached the truck, glanced in the long empty bed and frowned. "Where's the feed?"

Ash whipped off his hat and ran his fingers through thick, wavy blond hair. Squinting from the glare of the morning sun, he stared off in the distance for a moment deep in thought. Then he cursed, slapped his hat against his thigh a couple of times in anger and turned his attention to the puzzled but eager youth. "Take the truck and go pick up Cal at the feed store." Still the kid stood

looking at him, and he added defensively, "I got sidetracked and forgot, that's all. Go on, move."

Bob climbed into the cab of the truck, his long shrill
whistle covered by the roar of the engine. He was old
enough to know only a woman could make men do such
stupid things. He just wondered who the boss had tangled with—and so damn early, too.

FRAGRANT AROMAS as familiar as life itself surrounded
and soothed him as he quietly entered the house. He'd
always had a keen sense of smell, and from early childhood he would close his eyes, separate each scent and
identify its source. Today the air was filled with the
wonderful smell of hot homemade bread—it was Saturday, the day Bridget, his cook and housekeeper,
baked. He strolled by the living room with its bright
lively colors and caught a whiff of fresh flowers, cut that
morning by his stepsister, Jeri. But he didn't stop to en-
joy the heady fragrance. The sound of raised voices had
reached him, and he tossed his hat on a hall table and
quickened his stride toward the study.

Sharp scents assaulted him as he came to a halt in the
doorway; wood smoke, worn leather, gun oil, tobacco
and a distinct, rather pungent odor of age that per-
meated the room itself. The study was the original house,
a big room with a high ceiling crisscrossed by broad
smoke-darkened beams, smooth wood walls with a pa-
tina of satin and numerous hunting trophies, stuffed
heads of local and exotic animals that vied for wall space
with the many oil paintings.

Over the years the study had become the hub of the
house, and though Ash used it for his office and tried to
discourage everyone from perching like birds here, they
still migrated toward the room whenever they pleased.

He guessed he couldn't blame them. With its monstrous fireplace and the books and paintings that represented a long history of the Bartlet family and Montana, the room seemed to draw people like a magnet.

A shrill voice cut through his thoughts, jerking him back to the present and to the scene taking place in the study. His presence hadn't been noticed yet and he stood perfectly still, the harsh lines around his mouth melting into a grin and the hardness of his gaze softening to the summer green of new grass. Propping a shoulder against the door frame, he savored the predicament of his friend and Bartlet's sheriff, Jeff Hall, as Jeri gave him hell, her head of curly hair tilted sharply back and her turned-up nose stuck even higher.

His amusement was hard to contain at the sight of Jeff's discomfort. Six foot three and built on the lines of an all-pro tackle, Jeff listened solemnly, his gaze planted on the tips of his boots, motionless except for his big hands, which worried his hat, rolling it round and round in a circle by its brim. It wasn't until Jeff raised his eyes and glanced over Jeri's head at his friend that Ash caught what was being said.

"Jeri!" Paula snapped.

"Well, for heaven's sake, mother. I'm right."

"That's beside the point, dear." Paula Bartlet ran a newly manicured hand through her shoulder-length blond hair, fluffing out the sides in a gesture of agitation. "Leave the poor man alone. You've done all you could to protect Ash."

"But it's not fair," she wailed, and turned toward her mother, furious and red-cheeked. "I've run myself ragged this week and now Jeff is going to ruin all my efforts." She whipped her head around, her hand making a jerky swipe at a mink-brown curl as it dropped in one eye, then she glared at the quiet man standing so close. Hazel eyes that usually gazed up at Jeff so adoringly now shot daggers, and his hat made the circle in his big hands once again. "You just can't tell him, Jeff."

"Nonsense," Paula said. "Ash is a grown man and able to take care of himself. What happened, happened ten years ago. Besides, Jeri, it's not your place to protect him anyway."

"Thank you, Paula." Ash spoke, startling them all but Jeff. He pushed away from the doorframe. "I'm quite capable of taking care of myself." He caught them each with a direct stare, and both women looked away. Jeff, however, was a different matter. He might be shy and reserved in the company of ladies, but he backed down from neither man nor beast.

Ash studied the four hairlike scars that showed white on his friend's left cheek. A vision of a sudden snow storm and four kids trying to stay warm in a makeshift shelter flashed through his mind. He could still see the wounded grizzly charging them and Jeff throwing himself in its path while he, Shannon and Dean worked frantically at the frozen bolt on the rifle. Jeff had that same hard glint of determination in his eyes now as he did long ago when he shoved his three friends out of his way so he could tangle with that bear.

"I'm sorry, Ash, but I need your help."

"Why sorry?"

Jeff shot a disgruntled glance at the two women, wishing they'd either leave the room or offer some assistance. He cleared his throat, at a loss how to break the the news to Ash gently. "Shannon's come back with Dean this trip. They flew in the first of the week."

Ash acknowledged the statement with a grunt of admiration for his friends and family for keeping the news from him so long. This was Saturday, which meant Shannon and Dean had been in town for six days without him knowing. Of course he hadn't left the ranch either—not until that morning. "What's the problem, Jeff?" He was a little amused to see the big, tough man relax and throw a meaningful glance at Jeri.

Ash's long legs ate up the distance from the door to the desk chair and he eased down, trying to hide the sudden weakness in his legs. He had a strong premonition, an aching awareness deep in his gut that a confrontation with Shannon was going to be unavoidable. "Go on, Jeff."

"The Waynes's housekeeper called me at home around dawn. Seems Shannon and Dean packed up for their bighorn sheep hunt early Monday morning. They were only supposed to be gone three days, four at the most. Now it's been six with no word. But what really panicked her was when she was on her way up to the big house and saw Dean's two pack mules grazing not too far away. One of the animals was carrying part of a pack, the other was in bad shape, Ash. It looked like he'd been jumped by a mountain lion and barely got away. Dean's foreman waited until I got a good look at the animal before he put him down." Jeff paused before he went on. "There's a good possibility that the big cat could have injured one or both of them, Ash."

They were all watching Ash closely, so he was careful to keep his expression neutral. "What about their saddle horses?"

Jeff shook his head. "If they were spooked like the mules they haven't made it back yet. Or maybe they weren't as lucky as the mules and ended up dinner for a vicious hungry cat. God knows what the hell has happened." He shifted his gaze from Ash's set face and looked out the picture window at the sweeping panorama of the mountains beyond. ''There's a storm coming, Ash. Light flurries have already been reported in the high country.'' An ominous chill crawled up his spine. He knew all too well the consequences of getting caught in a surprise snow storm. Death was a constant companion in this country and could take its toll of even the most experienced. ''I'd like to have some of your men for a search party, Ash. They're the best in the state for this sort of work and they know the area.''

''What about me, Jeff? Don't you trust me to help find them? Or do you think if I did I'd be more than a little inclined to just shoot them and leave them there?''

The two women sucked in audible breaths.

''Ah hell, Ash.'' Jeff shot his friend a killing glance. ''You know damn well I never thought anything of the kind. I just thought you'd rather not...you know?...see her again, that's all.''

Ash rose sharply to his feet, startling them all with his violent movement. ''You're right. I don't have the faintest wish to see Shannon—or Dean—again, but I don't want them dead, either.'' A strangled sound drew his attention. For the first time since entering the room he took a good look at his stepmother and noticed that she looked every one of her fifty-four years.

Today her pale beauty seemed marred by an even paler complexion. She appeared haggard, drawn. There was a haunted cast in her eyes that troubled him. He wondered briefly if once again she'd overspent her allowance, then decided money wasn't the problem. But it was obvious something had upset her deeply, and now that he thought about it he realized she'd been like this ever since she and Jeri had come back from Europe a month ago. Silently he promised himself that after the Shannon business was over with he'd look into it.

Jeff coughed and Ash realized he'd been somewhat lost in thought and they were all waiting for his decision. "Jeri, go tell Tom to pick out eight hands and have them saddle up."

Jeri glanced at Jeff with a mixture of anger and longing, then darted out of the room.

"Paula, please have Bridget put together enough food for ten men for a couple of days." She hesitated as if she wanted to say something, but she only opened her mouth then snapped it shut as if she had abruptly changed her mind. Ash watched her leave the room then shrugged and turned his attention back to Jeff. "Do you want to go back to town and get your horse or are you willing to ride one of mine?"

Jeff grinned, his solemn face alight with laughter. "Depends on which one you decide to give me, pal. Not, I hope, one of the half-broken, half-wild ones you've been working with?"

Ash chuckled and shook his head. "Would I do that to you?"

"Hell, yes. If you had the chance. I better go check with Tom. Your foreman's a little more thoughtful to the comfort of my backside than you are." He was at the door, then stopped and looked back over his shoulder. "I know you've heard all the things that seem to have filtered back here about her wild doings in Europe, but to be honest with you, Ash, I never believed any of them. They just didn't sound like Shannon. What are you going to do when you see her?"

"Beats the hell out of me, Jeff." He turned away from his friend and stared out at the snowcapped mountains. She was out there somewhere, she and Dean. Maybe hurt, maybe... He couldn't even let himself think of death. Shannon could take care of herself. But Dean was a different matter. He had only lived in Bartlet with his mother during the school year. His summers were spent with his father in France or touring Europe. Dean had never truly faced the hardships of one of Montana's unrelenting storms, nor had he ever been dependent on the land to survive. Shannon had, though.

Ash moved away from the window and stopped before a wall map of Western Montana on which the boundaries of the Bar B were clearly marked. The ranch was divided into three ranches really, and the family holdings stretched from the Flathead Range to the farthest southwestern border of the state that nuzzled up against the Yellowstone Rockies. But it was in Bartlet that his great-grandfather had decided to make his home. A valley that was typical of the great Montana's ever-changing country—vast canyons for grazing cattle, skyscraper mountain ranges, hot springs and waterfalls. The land was like a woman, ornery, loving and deadly.

He studied the map a moment longer, nodded to himself then turned away. He knew where Shannon and Dean were. They had to be on Devil's Leap at a campsite his family had always used before they ventured up beyond the timberline for the bighorn sheep.

He walked over to his desk and sat down. Pulling out a drawer, he rummaged around in the back till his fingers touched cold metal. The silver picture frame had turned dark with tarnish and the glass was a little smoky with dust, but he could still make out the features of the young girl holding the bridle of a black stallion named Ashland's Fire. Smiling amber eyes full of mischief and shining with love stared out at him and he looked deeply into them, trying to figure out how it had all happened.

A cool mountain breeze and the sharp, crisp scent of a summer day filled his head as if it was yesterday. A vision of the old line shack where they'd first made love rose from the graveyard of his thoughts like a cherished photograph worn around the edges from years of handling. The sight of the log shack, and the outline of the mountain ridge shadowed by tall pines were forever imprinted on the canvas of his brain. He'd made love to Shannon there, taking her innocence and sweetness.

Ironically, he'd made love to her there the last time too. God help him! Would he never forget her or the way the moon had captured her nakedness and held him spellbound with her perfection. She'd come to him, tall, lithesome, her long legs firm and supple from years of straddling a horse, holding him as easily. There was the first kiss taken with pursed lips and giggles, and the last one given with loving passion and promises that would never come to be.

Ash swallowed audibly. He'd been her teacher, her lover, then he'd become her pupil and…her fool. In just a matter of hours he'd lost everything. Anger replaced nostalgia as it had done a million times over the years. Reaching out, he snatched up the picture and slammed it down on the desk, fracturing the glass in a myriad of spider webs.

She'd been his—once.

CHAPTER TWO

FLURRIES OF SNOW, always at her back, chased her down the mountain, dogging every carefully placed step she took, biting through her thick flannel shirt and jeans as if they didn't exist. As she came to a sparse patch of tall pines and the sky became visible through the thin branches, the relentless wind turned brittle and brought on a new set of bone-racking chills.

She had to find shelter.

The wind rushed through the attic of the trees, howling like a banshee.

"Ash, where are you? Why haven't you come to get me?" Shannon wrapped her arms around a young tree, hugging it close as another set of chills shook her body. "Happy," she sobbed, "I didn't mean it, really I didn't. Please forgive me, Happy." Then she said, "Dean," and the sound of her husband's name brought her to her senses. Squeezing her eyes tightly shut, she tried to remember something, something important. But an inborn instinct for survival set off warning bells and blocked out all coherent thoughts but one. She had to find shelter.

Snowflakes touched her face, and she licked her lips thirstily. Much heavier now, the snowfall began to blanket the hard, freezing ground.

"Where am I?" she screamed. Her only answer was the wind and snow. She thumped her forehead on the tree in frustration and fear, thankful that she could still feel the pain. Then she threw her head back, tilted her face to the sky and yelled at the top of her voice as if she were summoning a mythical god, "Ash!"

With a reluctance born of panic, she prized her arms from around the tree and began her trek down the mountain once more. After only twenty or so steps, her booted foot slipped on a wet rock, then suddenly she was flat on her back with the breath knocked out of her.

When she finally regained use of her lungs, she covered her eyes with her arm and began to cry. She was lost. Her ankle throbbed like the devil, so she finally gave in and sobbed her heart out. *If Ash finds out you're crying like a baby instead of doing something to get yourself out of this mess, he'll never let you live it down.*

She had to find shelter.

A thin layer of snow covered the ground and the frigid air was actually painful to breathe. A bird trilled in the distance. The limbs of the trees, now weighted with a veil of ice, moaned as the wind shook them. Above her the sky was getting darker as the full force of the storm began to move down from the high mountain peaks toward the valley.

Shannon dragged herself to the nearest boulder, used the flat surface for support then slowly stood. She shifted her weight to her injured foot, testing the damage, and hissed as a shaft of hot pain shot up her leg. "Damn, damn, damn, damn!" She *had* to go on. Gathering her strength, she pushed away from the boulder and hobbled off.

The rocky ground fought her every step and it wasn't long before she stumbled and fell, got up and fell again. For a moment she lay there, breathing hard, wanting nothing but to give up and go to sleep, but she knew she couldn't. Ash would never forgive her for being a coward. She rose on her elbows and looked around. Suddenly she was furiously angry with everything that had happened to her, not only in the last few days but the last ten years. She crawled to a nearby tree, grasped a low limb, pulled herself to her feet and started off once more.

Flurries of thick snow half blinded her, slowing her progress. Somewhere in the distance, above the shrieking wind, she heard a strange sound, an animal sound that scared her so badly she automatically hurried her steps, careless of her footing.

As she weaved from one tree to another, shivering harder with each step, the only clear thought she had was to get out of the wind and the cold. She was knowledgeable enough, and still rational enough, to realize she was beginning to suffer from hypothermia. A series of chills racked her body, lasting far longer than any of the previous ones, leaving her shaken and weak when they finally subsided.

She was going to die. Die without seeing Ash again, without telling him she had never stopped loving him. *If only I could take back those ten years. Ten wasted, lonely years without him.* "Ash, remember how every day was a new adventure for us. The laughter that blessed us in everything we did together. Even the bad times were good. Weren't they, Ash? Weren't they?" She threw back her head and wailed his name above the wind like a bereft animal who has lost its mate.

Her attention strayed; her thoughts became confused and she began to wander aimlessly, losing the trail she'd worked out in her mind. A fresh gust of blinding snow struck her in the face and snapped her back to reality, but it was too late. She lost her footing, slipped and fell. Then, before she knew what was happening, or the danger she was in, she began to slide down the rocky incline. As the mountain slope grew steeper she picked up momentum and her body shot downward. She rolled onto her back, fighting to grab hold of anything that would break her speed.

Fear of broken bones, fear of being knocked unconscious and freezing to death lent her a new strength. Once again she wrestled with the ground to slow her fall, to halt her slide down the mountain. Seconds felt like hours as each pebble, twig, even each blade of grass seemed to make harsh contact with her body.

With horror she caught sight of a thick pine tree looming directly in her path. She began clawing frantically at the ground in an effort to stop, but as hard as she fought, she couldn't manage to roll herself out of the way. Just before her midsection connected painfully with the trunk, she screamed. Then she was struggling with the blackness that crept over her. All too quickly oblivion enveloped her, dragging her down into its dark pit.

Shannon came to, groaned, rolled over and opened her eyes. She moved experimentally, testing each limb, relieved to realize that the only damage was the sore ankle she'd injured earlier. After several deep breaths she glanced down at herself, and for the areas she couldn't see, she used her hands as her eyes.

A thin crust of ice covered her clothes, her hair was matted with twigs and wet with snow, and her lips, she suspected, were blue. Then another chill hit and she began trembling so hard she could barely breathe. Her vision blurred, then miraculously cleared after a few sharp shakes of her head. She saw a log cabin no more than ten feet away and began to cry at the sight. She squeezed her eyes shut then opened them again. Surely she was

dreaming. But with hope giving her strength, she began
to crawl toward the door.

Once there she managed to reach up and push the
handle. When nothing happened, she whimpered like a
small wounded creature. But she wasn't an animal, she
reminded herself, and tried again. This time the door
swung inward and she pulled herself up on her hands
and knees and scrambled in, slamming the door shut
behind her.

"Ash," she whispered in a voice choked with emotion. As sure as she'd made it to their cabin, he had
somehow led her there. Shannon tried to steady her
shaking limbs so that she could crawl to the black hole
of the fireplace. After only a few feet her head began to
swim and her body finally gave up. She collapsed into
unconsciousness.

ASH REINED IN the big bay gelding, fighting the horse's
nervous movements. When he had calmed him down
enough he pulled back the cuff of his sheepskin coat and
checked his watch. The search party had been strung out
in a long line all day and still no luck. They had swept
the valley in a wide arc hours ago, regrouped, discussed
strategy then begun the treacherous climb up the far
slope of Devil's Hump. Their goal: the ridge and campsite. Though on Bartlet land, the site was ideal for access to the timberline and was frequently utilized by the
neighboring families. Ash was sure Shannon and Dean
had used it as a home base for their hunt.

A thick blanket of snow covered the ground, obscuring any trail they might have taken. But Ash knew
Shannon, and gut instinct told him that if she were
looking for shelter she'd head for the line shack. An icy
wind whipped around him, making the horse stomp his

hooves then dance sideways. Ash jerked down the bandanna that covered the lower half of his face then pulled off his sunglasses. Night was creeping over the horizon far too quickly, a false darkness brought on by the approaching storm.

He'd called off the search an hour ago, found shelter for the men then left them there setting up camp for the night. But he couldn't stay, nor could he explain to Jeff the feeling of urgency that pulled at him to move on. Yet his friend seemed to understand and let him set off alone with the promise that if he got into trouble before he reached the line shack, or if he found Shannon and Dean, he would let them know with their prearranged signal.

Now, no more than a hundred yards from the shack, Ash reached around and dug out a pair of binoculars and examined the area. A deep dread settled over him, making his heart pound in his ears and his mouth turn as dry as dust. The place looked deserted. There was no plume of smoke from the crooked brick chimney, no horses in the lean-to attached to the side…no sign of life at all.

He nudged the bay forward, his eyes automatically scanning the ground for signs—a human foot print, horses' hoof prints, a depletion of the firewood that was stacked beside the front door. Maybe they were asleep, he told himself, and accidentally let the fire burn itself out. Oversight? Neglect? But he knew better. Shannon would never let something so important happen.

Unless…

Unless she was injured.

And Dean, being Dean, was too stupid to keep the fire fed. That had been a bone of contention for as long as he could remember. Dean had been pampered and waited on all his life. There was always someone around to do his bidding. Someone to take the blame when he screwed up.

A swirl of leaves and snow blew across the horse's line of vision and he shied then stumbled in the snow, forcing Ash's attention back to the hidden path he followed strictly from memory now. His patience worn thin from the unseasonal weather and a nervous horse that jumped at its own shadow, Ash set his heels hard against the bay's sides. Yet he knew the reason for his sudden savage mood and it had nothing to do with a skittish horse or the elements. Shannon haunted him—and this place was where they had found such joy and love.

He'd managed to stay away from the line shack, always sending one of his ranch hands there when they worked the ridge for stray cattle. He lifted the binoculars to his eyes once more before stuffing them back in his pack.

Ten years and the place refused to change, as though it was waiting for their return. Ash clamped his lips together in a straight line. If it wasn't a vital location for their work, he would have burned the damn place down to its foundations years ago. He pulled the bandanna up over his mouth and nose, took a firm hold on the reins and forced the horse to plow through the deep drifts of snow.

Darkness had turned the glare of the snow into a gray void by the time he reached the shack. He dismounted, pulled a flashlight from his saddlebags, and led the horse around to the lean-to. The leather girth seemed frozen stiff, and he fumbled with the strap before it loosened. Leaving the bay with a slap on the rump, he followed the beam of light to the front door.

The wind wailed in mournful gusts, tree limbs creaked beneath their load of snow, and the bay stamped and whinnied—sounds of beast and nature, but nothing human reached his ears. He placed his gloved hand on the latch, then stopped. He had to face the truth. If they weren't here, chances were they were dead. He was surprised at the pain the thought caused. Hadn't he forgotten her?

Ash's fingers clenched around the wooden latch, yanked it upward and shoved the door open.

Please, God.

An eerie quiet greeted him, and a black hole yawned before him. He squeezed his eyes shut and swallowed hard as a heaviness settled in his chest. There was an unbearable pain behind his eyelids. Rather than face the emptiness and the obvious truth, Ash thought, he could make it back to the camp even though it was pitch-black outside now.

Hell, he could find his way blindfolded. In fact he'd done just that once, a long time ago, when Shannon had dared him to try. Anything was better than spending the night in this tomb of a cabin, so full of voices from the past that he thought for a second he'd actually heard his name called. *The wind—just the damn wind.*

He stepped back and began pulling the door closed when something stopped him, paralyzing every muscle. A whisper...a whimper of his name. *Ghost? Wishful thinking?* The flashlight that hung loosely in his hand snapped up, and the yellow beam, like a malevolent eye, swept every corner of the room, cutting through the gloom.

A cough, human and female, shattered the quiet.

The light jerked, then frantically zigzagged around the room as Ash stepped over the threshold and closed the door.

"Shannon?" He heard nothing except the echo of his voice and the soft sound of his breathing.

The shaft of light caught a glint of moisture near his feet, then slowly followed its trail to the body lying in a puddle of water.

Hope, elation—and anger—burned through him. He didn't know which one spurred him into action. Or was it the sight of that pale profile, the thick, dark eyelashes throwing shadows on her face, and the mouth so soft, so blue, so still? Ash was suddenly on his knees beside her. He dropped the flashlight, sending it rolling across the uneven floor. The yellow light danced a macabre jig across the hearth, the rough-hewn walls and the two people until it twirled to a stop, throwing his silhouette into a looming shadow that stretched high against the door.

Ash touched her neck and almost recoiled. She was cold and clammy, and when he finally found the artery in her neck, the muscles along his jaw clenched. Her pulse was thready, fast, too fast. Then his shaking hands were on her body, feeling through the wet clothes for any broken bones.

"You're not going to die on me, Shannon. Damn you, do you hear me?" The tight boot leather around her ankle was the only evidence of any damage, so far. Later, with better light, he'd check her more thoroughly. Ash sat back on his heels and let relief sweep over him. "You have a lot to answer for, and by God, *this time* you'll stay and face me." For a second he bowed his head and his shoulders slumped. Then he was up, moving fast, and with a purpose.

Soon a fire snapped and burned brightly, and an oil lamp was lighted. He gathered blankets from the storage closet, pulled the mattress off the bed and threw it in front of the fireplace. Finally he straightened, knowing what had to be done next, but his courage seemed to fail him. How could he touch her without taking her in his arms?

Ash snatched the pint bottle of bourbon that was always kept at the line shack for emergencies, unscrewed the top, grimaced at his cowardice and turned the bottle up. The liquor bit deep, burning a path all the way to his stomach, but still the hard knot remained. Without allowing himself any time to think, he knelt, rolled Shannon over, and began to systematically strip her of her wet clothes.

THE BLACKNESS that had weighed her eyelids down seemed to ease. She felt hands on her, twisting, turning, pulling her body. Something horrible reached out for her, a memory too ugly to recall, yet the horror was all too real. Her mind cleared and she began to fight her assailant, struggling in his hold, mumbling incoherently. Her eyes snapped open and her vision blurred, then focused on Ash.

Years rolled backward to a happier time. In her confused state she didn't see the anger or the set line of Ash's mouth. With all the strength she could muster, she lunged at him, locking her arms around his neck, babbling nonsense.

"Calm down, Shannon. I'm here. You're okay now."

That voice. His words came and went, barely penetrating her clouded thoughts. She only knew Ash had found her. "I knew, I knew... Ash?" A chill shook her body so hard she thought her bones would surely shatter. Suddenly she was more afraid than she'd ever been. She didn't want to die.

Grimly Ash pried her arms away from his neck, grabbed the pile of blankets and quickly wrapped her in them. He gently picked her up, took a few steps and lowered her onto the bed before the fire. A twig that was stuck in her hair had added a fresh scratch on her cheek. After he removed the little stick he pulled out his handkerchief and wiped the trickle of blood from her pale skin. For a few more minutes he just sat there staring, his mind trying to comprehend what he'd seen. Only one thing could explain those dark bruises around her neck and he didn't want to think about what might have happened.

Ash surged to his feet, grabbed his coat and left the cabin, letting the door bang shut behind him. The wild wind whipped at his hair, and the snow, a little less fierce now but still falling, landed on his eyelashes, making him blink rapidly to keep it from mingling with the warm moisture that threatened to leak from his eyes.

Anger burned through him, an anger that had been building for ten years. He wasn't going to turn himself into a stupid sentimental fool again. Whatever had happened to her was *her* problem. He would get her back to the ranch, see to it that she was well taken care of, then his duty was over. Hell, he'd do the same for any human caught out in a blizzard. He stepped off the porch, walked around to the lean-to, unstrapped his saddlebags and pack from behind the saddle, then pulled the rifle from the scabbard.

He flipped the heavy load over his shoulder, freeing both his hands, then lifted the rifle, stepped away from the lean-to and the horse and pointed the barrel skyward, firing three times in quick succession. He counted to ten and fired twice more. It was the signal to Jeff and his men that he'd found their lost hunting party.

But not everyone! For the first time he thought of Shannon's husband. Where the hell was Dean?

CHAPTER THREE

ASH PUSHED OPEN the door of the cabin, relieved that the room was finally warm. He dropped the bedroll and saddlebags on the floor, set the rifle by the door and walked over to where Shannon lay. She shivered pitifully under the heavy pile of blankets, her teeth chattering as she mumbled to herself. It was obvious the blankets and the fire weren't doing the job fast enough.

For a few seconds he watched her, listening to her babbling and recognizing it as delirium. Her movements were uncoordinated, her hands fumbled clumsily as she tried to pull the blanket up high. He had to do something quickly before she slipped into shock.

He made several trips outside bringing in extra firewood, then he opened the storage bin, grabbed a handful of wood chips and lighted the old iron stove. Before long a saucepan with bourbon and a couple of generous spoonfuls of honey warmed on the stove. When the concoction was hot enough but not scalding, he half filled a chipped mug and carried it to the makeshift bed.

Squatting down beside Shannon, Ash paused, a little nonplussed to find her staring at him. How could he have ever thought he could forget those eyes? Large and tilted at the corners, they were the most unusual he'd ever seen. But it was the color that fascinated; neither dark brown nor light, it hovered somewhere in between, amber or maybe golden. Yet they would darken to a deeper hue, almost to the blue-black of her hair, when they made love. He remembered that most of all, the way her eyes changed and the way her hair floated around him like a dark cloud.

A film of moisture popped out on his forehead and he wiped it away with his free hand, bringing his damp fingers before his eyes in astonishment. Without a word he propped her head on his knee and brought the mug to her lips.

Shannon's nose twitched at the strong odor of liquor and she stubbornly clamped her mouth shut.

"Shannon." The rim of the mug nudged her lips again. "Drink."

"No," she croaked, her lips pressed tightly together.

"Shannon."

She tried to move away.

"Drink, damn it."

"Can't."

Her steady gaze, the slightly unfocused eyes, the pale face unnerved him. What was going on behind that vacant stare? Did she even see him? He scowled. God, what had happened to her? "It's for your own good."

"Don't like . . . sick."

Her words were slurred, but at least she was rational. "Sorry it's not champagne, but now is not the time to get finicky."

Shannon rolled her head back and forth trying to get away from the foul smell that hung just under her nose.

Ash clasped her face, his fingers forcing her jaws open, then he poured a small amount of the mixture over her cold, trembling lips. "Come on. I heard you drank and whored your way across Europe. This might only be cheap bourbon, but indulge me and slum a little. Maybe you'll acquire a taste for it, the way you seem to have acquired a taste for everything else.''

Her mouth felt as if it was on fire and she immediately spit the vile stuff out, yanked her head out of his hold and began to cough.

Disgusted, angry, Ash gave up and watched her as another spasm of shivers started. He stood and yanked off his boots, then the rest of his clothes followed. Naked, he pulled back the blankets and slipped between them. After a moment's hesitation he took Shannon's cold body in his arms, pressing her to his warmth. He felt nothing but pity, he told himself sternly, and she snuggled closer.

AN INSISTENT POUNDING in her head forced Shannon awake.

She hurt. Every inch of her body felt as if it had been stomped on. But the fear that had snapped at her heels for what seemed days was now gone. She was warm and safe, and home. The word drifted around in her confused mind and she grabbed on to it like a lifeline. Home—with Ash. Surely she wasn't dreaming? It had to be true. Yet she still refused to open her eyes, afraid if she did reality would shatter the fantasy world she'd made for herself these last few hours. She squeezed her eyelids tighter. *Please let it be him holding me.*

Her eyelashes fluttered as if they too were scared of the truth, then slowly her eyes opened. Her lips formed his name, her features suddenly brilliant with wonder that her wish had actually come true. "Ash", she called to him softly, lovingly. But this wasn't the face from her dreams, nor was it the face she'd left ten years ago. All traces of youth were gone, and in their place were the hard planes of a mature man.

Shannon was filled with sadness and regret as she studied Ash. Tan flesh stretched tautly over high cheekbones. His nose seemed more pronounced, hawkish in profile, and his jaw looked too hard and his chin too square, even with the cleft. His eyes were set deeper now, making the thick lashes throw interesting shadows on his lean cheeks. She knew from the past that when those green eyes were open he could devastate any female with one look.

Finally her gaze slid farther down, and she wanted to cry out in anguish for that beautiful mouth, which even in sleep appeared too stern for his age. His was a face of angles and still unbelievably handsome—sexier than before, if that were possible. She glanced up, pulling her gaze away from his mouth and slamming the door on the seductive view from the past.

A lock of blond hair, darker now without the summer sun to bleach it to a warm golden shade, had fallen over his forehead. A tiny smile touched the corners of her mouth. His hair was thick and curly and achingly touchable. She remembered how he hated it, and how she had loved to tease him and call him Goldilocks.

Suddenly the memories that came crashing over her were too much. They swamped her, overwhelming her with pictures of her and Ash together. Tears pooled in the corners of her eyes and spilled down her cheeks. Hell had to be like this. To be so close and know that this, though seemingly real, was in truth only an illusion. Still, she savored the memories, the familiar touch of his skin, warm and smooth against hers. He needed a shave and her fingers traced the shadow line of his beard without actually touching him. He slept on his side, the way he always had, and held her next to his heart. His hands, his mouth, the way he walked, his easy stride, the broad shoulders, straight back and long legs....

She hadn't forgotten one detail in ten years, nor had time stopped her hunger for him. It was like waking up and finding time had turned backward. Except that it hadn't. She and Ash had always thought alike, and she knew he would never forgive her for what she'd done—she would never forgive herself.

He'd been hers . . . once.

SOMETIME DURING THE NIGHT the storm passed and the wind died, leaving a cathedrallike hush over the land. Tree limbs drooped with the heavy accumulation of snow and deep drifts piled against the walls of the line shack. The big bay horse stamped his hoofs on the hard cold ground of his shelter then knocked his rump against the cabin impatiently. Inside, the bright flames of the fire had burned down to hot embers, throwing a golden glow over the room.

Shannon awoke with the feeling of being watched. She opened her eyes and met Ash's dark green gaze. Words stuck in her throat. She could only watch him, waiting for him to make the first move.

Ash didn't want to think of the way her breast pressed against his chest or the way one of her long legs had insinuated itself between his, pressing her knee against his manhood. As if it was the most natural thing on earth to wake and find her in his arms, he brushed his mouth back and forth across hers, slowly savoring its sweetness. Then with a savage movement he claimed what was rightfully his.

There was never a question of not responding to his kiss. She accepted the first tenderness then the savagery

as reality returned. Only when he was through did she
open her eyes and meet Ash's wintry stare.

He unclasped her arms from around his neck, threw
back the covers and almost vaulted from the bed. A
lifetime of habits die hard even after ten years' absence,
so his nakedness was neither an embarrassment nor a
deterrent for what he had to say—but hers was. She sat
up when he left the bed and the sheet had dropped to her
waist, leaving the full small breasts a feast to his gaze.

"Goddammit, cover yourself," She flinched, but he
didn't see as he turned away to gather his clothes and put
them on.

"Ash."

"You would have let me go on, wouldn't you? Never
let a little thing like morality get in the way. Is adultery
just second nature to you?" He'd managed to pull on his
long johns and jeans and turned to look around for his
boots. "By the way, Shannon, where's your husband?
Where's Dean?" He stared at her with eyes as hard as
emeralds, his expression cold as a carved mask. "What
the hell happened to you?"

Things were moving too fast. The total lack of emotion in his harsh and sarcastic voice formed a vise around
her heart and made her want to cry.

It was the mention of Dean's name that drew a re-
sponse from her. One Ash never expected. The blood
drained from her face, leaving the delicate features white
and as blank as death. Ash took a step forward before
he caught himself and stopped. "Where's Dean, Shannon?"

"I don't know."

"What happened to you?"

"I don't know." Her voice trailed off into nothing-
ness. She stared at Ash without really seeing him.

The wind, always the wind, humming in her head, snatching words from her memory... the feeling of anger followed by disgust and hate... and finally a blood-red rose opening, its petals unfolding in slow motion... then uncontrollable terror....

She shook with the fragmented ghosts of conversation that made no sense and the distorted impressions of visions that were like a dream.

"Shannon." He leaned over, clasped her bare shoulders and shook her gently. "Shannon." When she didn't respond he sat down beside her and took her into his arms. In the light of day the ugly bruises curved around her neck were more prominent, bruises that were the imprint of a man's hands. He touched the darkest ones over her windpipe and shook his head. It looked to him as if someone had tried to choke her to death. "Did Dean do this, Shannon? Shannon, look at me."

She dragged her thoughts back to the present, wanting to remember but afraid to see what lay beyond the nightmare. She collapsed against his chest and began to shiver and tremble. "I want to go home," she whispered.

"Is Dean still up on the mountain or did he leave you and go down the other side?"

"Please, take me home, Ash."

"I will, but, Shannon, I—we have to know about Dean."

"I don't know."

"Sure you do."

"No." She tipped her head back, looking at the deep frown of his puzzled expression. "I don't know what happened to Dean. I don't know where he is, or if he's alive or dead. You see, Ash, I don't remember anything about the trip at all."

His eyes widened then narrowed. "Shannon, a man's life could be at stake here. I know you're tired and sick, but you have to remember." He decided to change tactics. "Where did you get these?" His fingers brushed the dark discoloration around her neck, stopping only when she cringed from his touch. "And these?" His fingers moved to her shoulders and the tops of her arms. Hell, she was covered with scratches and bruises from head to toe, but the ones he'd pointed out obviously bore the imprint of human hands. "You have to tell me what happened."

"I don't know, I don't know." She burst into tears.

Tears were so foreign to the Shannon he had known that he drew her closer. He didn't understand what the hell was going on. He looked out the window to the jagged snow-covered peaks. What had happened up there? His fingers tangled in the thick, blue-black hair, kneading her scalp absently as he tried to think things out. If he found out that Dean, running true to form as the coward and weakling he'd always been, had gone off and left her up on that mountain to die, he'd kill him with the utmost satisfaction. "Listen to me, Shannon. You have to tell me what you're talking about. You have to explain."

She sniffed and shivered, exhausted by just the little conversation they'd had. "I wish I knew. But, Ash, I truly don't remember anything. Please, take me home."

He realized she was in no shape to talk much less explain what had happened. He had to get her down off the mountain soon or there was the real possibility of her getting pneumonia. She needed a doctor, and he had to reach Jeff, then they would decide what to do about Dean's disappearance. He began to dress her in the clothes he'd hung beside the fire to dry, then he wrapped her in a cocoon of blankets. All the while he watched her closely, afraid she might be slipping into shock.

"FOOL WOMAN. Damn horse." He forcefully tapped the sides of the bay, trying to maneuver him around once more to where Shannon sat on the porch railing. One quick glance at her and a deep well of tenderness washed over him. She was balanced on the wooden rail, bundled in blankets, his red bandanna covering the lower half of her face so that only her eyes and one hand encased in one of his extra socks were showing. "Come on, you spawn of Satan. Another one of your tricks and you're liable to end up dog food."

As if the horse understood the angry man on his back, it turned and calmly walked to the edge of the porch. Ash nudged the animal closer, freed one foot from the stirrup, leaned over and grabbed Shannon around her waist. He gave a loud grunt, struggled for a moment to keep his seat in the saddle, then hauled her up in front of him. "Put your arm under mine." She mumbled behind the bandanna. "And shut up." He made the mistake of looking down into her dancing amber eyes and caught his breath. Goddamn woman.

With another hard kick the bay moved away from the line shack, and as it did Ash swooped down and retrieved the unzipped sleeping bag. For a few minutes he fought the overeager, prancing horse, the trailing sleeping bag, Shannon's weight and his balance before he regained control of all four. Sweat beaded his forehead as he struggled with the thermal bag until he finally managed to get it wrapped around him and the part of Shannon's arms and shoulders that were exposed to the brittle morning air. "Jeff's camp is only two hours away, but in these deep drifts we'll be twice as long. Try to get some rest."

It was easier said than done. She was warm enough but her mind wouldn't rest. Wasn't there an old saying that you couldn't go home again? She should never have come here. How had she let Dean bully her into coming back to Montana? Why, after ten years of deliberate absence, had she allowed his constant tormenting to make her change her mind and accompany him on one of his quarterly visits?

Deep down she knew the answer—Ash. It had always been Ash, and with the end of her marriage so near she wanted to be home. Shannon reached up and pulled down the bandanna from her nose and mouth, her breath a visible cloud on the crisp air. "Ash. How's Happy? Is he well?"

Ash's jaw tightened. "Your grandfather is fine. Older and a little slower, but managing just like he always has."

William "Happy" Reed, his facial expression a contradiction to his nickname. Proud and stern, the blood of ancient Irish nobles running thick through his veins, he had an unworldly knowledge of horses. Among Arabian princes, English lords and Kentucky bluebloods, his reputation was universally renowned. The aristocracy of the horse world brought their animals to Happy and the little town of Bartlet so he could train and nurse them back to health. Her grandfather was one with his four-legged beasts. He understood them, talked to them, scolded them when they acted up and loved them. So it was inconceivable that a granddaughter of his, taught to love his ways, could ride a magnificent horse like Ashland's Fire to death.

"Does Happy ever talk about me?"

"No."

"Will he let me come home, do you think?"

"I can't answer that, Shannon. But—I don't think so. I'll take you to the ranch first and get Doc Henry to look you over, then go see Happy."

Her throat ached with suppressed tears and the pain of too many memories. She closed her eyes, giving in to the weakness and exhaustion and an overwhelming sadness that overcame her.

"What about your wife, Ash? She won't mind you bringing me to the ranch?" She felt his arms tighten around her.

"I've been divorced for eight years."

"I see." But she didn't. Dean had taken a maniacal delight in informing her of Ash's marriage, yet he never mentioned the divorce.

"Do you?" He thought about the bruises around her neck. "Maybe we were destined to destroy other people's lives along with our own." He shifted her weight.

She should never have come back. Ten years was a long time to exile herself to a life of the damned. She'd been so young then, younger in some ways than her seventeen years. Then, she had still believed in the goodness of human nature, believed that only good would come her way because she loved Ash and he loved her in return.

How could she have been so naive? She snuggled down in the blankets and gave her weary mind over to memories she'd tried for what seemed an eternity to forget.

IF HER LIFE had been different...

Maybe if her father hadn't died somewhere in the jungles of Vietnam, or her mother in childbirth, and

maybe if she hadn't been left to be raised by her grandfather and he hadn't been so dedicated to his business
and first love, training Thoroughbred horses, she
wouldn't have been able to run so wild and free. She was
born on a modest horse farm situated between two of the
biggest ranches in Montana, the Bar B and the Rocking
W. Fate had set her right down between the two heirs—
both with strong egos—and she seemed destined to be
the only hen in a flock of roosters. And maybe if she
hadn't been such a daredevil nothing would have happened ten years ago.

If things had only been different. Maybe . . .

It had been a hot smothering summer when she was
seventeen, just ready to turn eighteen and become Ash's
bride. God, she could never forget it—never in all her
dreams could she have forseen that *one* day would turn
into a horrible nightmare, changing her life and the lives
of her loved ones forever. . . .

"YOU'RE NOT ANGRY, Dean?" She leaned against the
fence post, watching the man beside her, a little amused
at his sulky expression.

"I'm hurt, Daffy, that you and Ash didn't tell me you
were in love, that's all."

She hated him calling her Daffy. It was Ash's special
name for her, started when she was ten and could imi-
tate Daffy Duck better than anyone, even the boys, and
that was a coup. "It happened so fast, Dean. We didn't
really realize it ourselves until a couple of months ago."
She turned away, not wanting him to see the lie. Her gaze
swept the meadow and lighted on Ashland's Fire, the big
black Thoroughbred that Ash had such high hopes of
winning the Triple Crown with.

"You're sure, Daffy? You can always change your mind and marry me."

"Thanks, Dean." He was making her feel awful. She had known for years that she loved Ash, but he had been older and had hidden so much of himself, it was hard to gauge his emotions and moods. Afraid of humiliation and the pain of rejection, she'd kept quiet. But when the two of them were caught out in a freak thunderstorm and had taken shelter in the line shack, their love had exploded like the early spring.

Dean had been on his usual summer duty visit with his father in France, and they had decided not to call him with the good news. For as long as Shannon could remember, there had been a competitive nature between the boys. As they grew into manhood that competitiveness had grown to a fierce rivalry—usually with her being their bone of contention. Whatever Ash wanted, Dean wanted also, and whatever Ash had, Dean tried to take away.

"Were you two going to invite me to the wedding?"

"Oh, Dean. Don't be like that. Only Happy and the senator are going to be there. Paula and Jeri aren't even coming. Besides, Ash and I are going to Europe for our honeymoon. The trip is the senator's gift and we were going to surprise you."

He looked at her for the first time and his black eyes were full of bitterness. "Are you pregnant?" He placed his finger across her lips to hush her answer. "If you are, I'd still marry you."

"Stop it, Dean." There were tears in her eyes and she couldn't look at him any longer. Maybe she had been wrong and he really did care for her, but deep down she told herself that Dean was a spoiled, selfish, cold fish who only cared for what he couldn't have.

He nodded toward the meadow and the grazing horse. "What's Ashland's Fire doing here? I thought he was with Ash's uncle in Kentucky for training. Is there something wrong with the Bartlets' great white hope?"

"He had a pulled muscle and Byron just thought it best to ship him home and let him recuperate for a while. He's fine now, though."

"Have you ridden him?"

"No."

"Afraid?"

Her chin went out. "Of course not. There's not a horse alive I can't handle."

"I don't know, Daffy. He's pretty fast from what Ash has told me. Hell, he and the senator have bet every cent they have on that fool horse. Land rich and cash poor and they sink everything they have on a horse."

She reached out and pulled his hair. "France has done nothing to lighten that doom-and-gloom disposition of yours."

"Or civilize me, either. Want to have one last race before Ash ties you down? He's going to, you know. You'll never be the same, never be my wild spirit, but an old married woman."

Her eyes lit up with the challenge. "Never." She pushed herself off the fence post and started to walk away, only to be hauled back.

"I mean, do you dare race against me with Ashland's Fire?"

"No!"

"Scared!" he taunted her.

"Don't be ridiculous. But Ash told me not to ride him."

"And you always do everything Ash says? See, he's already made an old woman of you and you're not even married yet. I dare you, Shannon."

She'd never been able to turn down a dare. This time she hesitated, though.

"By God, you are scared." He threw back his head and laughed.

She fumed. He was laughing at *her*.

SHANNON JERKED AWAKE and for a moment was disoriented and dazed at the feeling of swaying back and forth. Her nose was cold, her eyes watered in the frigid air and the only sound above the pounding of her heart was a strange crunching noise. Then she realized she was in Ash's arms, and the swaying motion was from the horse, and the peculiar noise that of the animal's hoofs crunching through the snow.

"Easy," Ash cautioned as he righted her position.

For a minute she watched him, wondering what the past ten years had been like for him. She tried to make up stories in her head, anything to keep the past at bay, but her attempts failed miserably. Suddenly there was a gut-wrenching scream in her head and she wanted only to cover her ears and wish away the nightmare that was going to torment her in broad daylight.

She was in the lead, Ashland's Fire stretching out his long powerful legs, eating up the earth like a machine. The wind slicked her hair back and stung her eyes till tears ran down her cheeks, but still they flew, woman and horse as one. Then, out of nowhere, she saw movement and looked over, realizing that Dean and his horse were actually pulling up beside her. She bent low over the great beast's neck and whispered encouragement, expecting him at any second to take the lead. But something went wrong. She was suddenly airborne, and from the awful shrieking of voices around her she was sure she must have been thrown into the pits of hell.

Somehow she was on her feet beside Ashland's Fire as he thrashed about. She was shouting denials; the horse was screaming in agony; Ash and her grandfather were all yelling for a gun. The whole ranch was there. Paula, even little Jeri, crying pitifully. And Dean—his expression was one of deep regret and sympathy, but his eyes were smiling.

To this day she could never remember much of what happened after that beautiful, graceful animal was put out of his misery. Shannon took a deep shuddering breath.

It was way past time to try to make amends for what she'd done.

THEY RODE INTO CAMP under a noonday sun that burned blindingly bright, reflecting off the white snow, melting the top layer and making it a hard crust that glistened like a newly washed mirror. The bay's head drooped toward the ground with exhaustion from the combined weight of the two people on his back and the long struggle down the mountain slope.

Jeff was checking the row of horses staked out beside his tent when his own mount lifted her head and whinnied a welcome to the bay. He sprinted through a deep powder drift, shouting to the ranch hands crowded shoulder to shoulder around the blazing fire. Managing to reach Ash before the others, he grabbed the bridle and halted the horse's mindless progress.

"We were beginning to worry."

Ash nodded wearily. "Give me a hand with her, Jeff. I'm damn near numb from the waist down."

As if she weighed no more than a small child, Jeff plucked Shannon from Ash's arm and cradled her to his big chest as the others helped their boss from the saddle. Concern furrowed deep lines in his forehead as he watched Ash's legs give out from under him, the helping hands the only thing that kept him from pitching forward onto his face. "You okay?"

Ash straightened, massaging and shaking his cramped cold muscles. "I'll live." When feeling finally returned to his legs he looked up and gave his men a strained, tired grin. "You boys got any hot coffee? About a gallon?" The silent tableau of waiting men was broken and he reached for Shannon. "I'll take her now."

"No need." Jeff looked down at the woman in his arms, caught the welcoming smile in the amber eyes and smiled back. "Not much of a welcome home, is it? Next time you go hunting, check the damn weather reports first." She nodded then turned her head toward Ash.

"Give her to me, Jeff."

The proprietary tone lifted both of Jeff's eyebrows. "Don't be a fool, man. You couldn't carry a flea right now." He strode off, Ash's shaky footsteps behind him. One of the young ranch hands ran ahead of them and folded the tent flap back. Jeff gently lay Shannon on one of the cots, yanked the cold, damp blankets off and immediately wrapped her in a couple of warm ones, then for good measure, he added his own sleeping bag.

"You okay, Shannon?" She mumbled and he laughed, then pulled down the bandanna. "I've never known you to be at a loss for words."

"Hi, Jeff," she managed to whisper huskily. Then she smiled, but her gaze had already shifted to the opening of the tent, seeking out Ash among the crowd that had gathered there.

Jeff scowled at the men hanging around. "Don't you guys have something better to do?"

Bob Young shouldered his way through his friends, a metal cup of steaming coffee in his hand and Ash at his heels. "Yeah. The boss says break camp." He handed the hot brew to Jeff and stepped back out of the way, curiosity making him linger in the corner of the tent.

Ash took the cup from Jeff and squatted down beside Shannon. "Can you hold this? Good. Sip it slowly." He placed both his hands on his thighs, pushed himself up to a standing position and looked over at Jeff. With a motion of his head toward the gaping tent opening, he turned and stepped out into the frigid air.

"Have you been able to reach the ranch?"

Jeff accepted a cup of coffee from Cal, nodded his thanks and answered Ash. "Yeah. Once the damn storm passed we were able to use the radio. Hoyt started out in the truck about nine this morning. He checked in about an hour ago. Roads up here are treacherous, though, and the going's slow. It's a damn good thing he didn't try and follow us yesterday or we'd be making another search-and-rescue trip. It was rough going here last night." Ash silently agreed and sipped his coffee. "What happened, Ash? Where's Dean?"

"You're not going to believe this, but she doesn't know."

"What!"

"She doesn't remember. If he left her, Jeff, I'm going to kill him."

"Come on, man. Would he do that?"

"Yes. If it was to save his own ass."

Jeff cursed softly under his breath. "I have to question her, Ash. We have to know."

"Not now."

"If there's a chance that he's still up there—alive."

"If he's up there, he's not alive. Shannon could have taken care of them, she knows what has to be done to survive. Without her, if he's up there, he's dead for sure." He pulled off the damp Stetson and rubbed his eyes with his forearm. "Something happened."

"What do you mean?"

Ash met Jeff's worried gaze and grimaced. "Have you talked with Dean's foreman? Has he shown up?"

"I haven't contacted the Rocking W."

"Do it. Now."

Jeff ducked back into the tent, stopping a moment as he watched Ash's young ranch hand helping Shannon hold her cup. "Bob, come out here." He gave quick orders for the boy to get on the portable two-way radio and call Dean's ranch, then turned his attention back to Ash.

"Now. Tell me what's wrong. Is she hurt?"

"An ankle that looks badly sprained. I don't think it's broken. Cuts. Bruises. She made it to the line shack, where I found her unconscious and nearly frozen to death. It's a miracle that she found the place."

"Spunky, always was."

Ash took a large gulp of coffee and stamped his cold feet. "She's got..." He cleared his throat. "Her neck is covered in bruises. Looks to me like the bastard tried to strangle her."

"Shit."

"My sentiments exactly."

"You're sure?"

"Go take a look for yourself. You're a better judge at this sort of thing than I am."

Jeff stood, stared at Ash for a long moment, then reentered the tent. Like Ash and Bob before him, he squatted down beside Shannon's cot. "How you doing?"

"It's good to see you again, Jeff." Her voice was raspy and weak.

"Good to see you, too." His head dipped a little in shyness. "Here, let me have that." He took the cup from her, then set it down on the ground. "Feeling better?"

"Yes . . . no. I hurt."

"I know. The truck's on its way and Doc Henry will be waiting when we get you to the ranch. Shannon, may I see your neck?"

She frowned. "Why?" Suddenly she felt afraid, though she had no idea why. "Where's Ash? I need to talk to Ash." Exhaustion was making her voice tremble and her words came out thready. She hated herself for this show of weakness. For ten years she'd held a tight rein on her emotions, careful never to allow Dean to get the upper hand and use it against her.

"Ash will be in in a minute. Now, let's have a look at your neck."

His firm, no-nonsense voice and direct stare worked. Though still puzzled by his request, she reached up and pulled away the blankets.

Jeff sucked in a sharp breath as he studied the black discolorations, definitely the imprint of two hands, a man's hands. "How did this happen, Shannon?"

"What?" Mystified, she crunched her chin down as if trying to see what he was talking about, but the movement sent a white-hot shaft of pain through her neck and head.

"Those bruises?"

She raised a shaking hand, touched the area then winced.

"Did Dean do that? Tell me what happened, Shannon."

Her eyelids squeezed shut. "I don't know, Jeff. I can't seem to remember anything." When she opened her eyes they were glazed with terror. "What's wrong with me?"

"Calm down. You and Dean were up on Devil's Hump, bighorn sheep hunting. You left the Rocking W six days ago. Were you attacked by a mountain lion? One of the pack horses came back all chewed up."

"I . . . don't . . ."

Ash leaned through the opening, taking in Shannon's frightened expression. His mouth thinned into a straight line. "Jeff. Leave her alone and come out here." When Jeff brushed past him, he dropped the flap then motioned for his friend to follow him out of range of Shannon's hearing.

"Dean hasn't shown up yet."

But Jeff was only half listening. "Those bruises, Ash, they're dark and deep."

The two grim-faced, silent men stared at each other, each knowing without a doubt what the other was thinking.

Jeff refused to remain silent. He glanced toward the steep slope of the mountain and Ash did the same. "Whatever went on up there was not pretty nor was it just a family squabble."

"No," Ash agreed.

"She's terrified of something."

Ash nodded.

"If Dean doesn't turn up, there's going to be an investigation."

"Yeah."

"She could simplify things if she'd tell us what happened."

"But she can't."

"Or won't."

Ash turned his gaze back to his lifelong friend, his eyes as hard as polished green stones. "He tried to kill her, Jeff."

"Looks that way, yes."

CHAPTER FOUR

DUSK FELL QUICKLY, sending fingers of darkness creeping across the land, turning the snow-covered ground to a gray drabness until night came along and blotted out the spread of haunting shadows.

The truck pulled up to the rear door of the ranch house just as the last light faded from the sky. Ash got out, then reached back in, positioned Shannon in his arms and lifted her out. Jeff walked ahead of them, nodding to a waiting Paula and Jeri and a white-haired, cherub-faced Doc Henry.

As they all trailed Ash up the curved stairway, Jeri called out, "Mother has the room across from mine ready."

Ash glanced over his shoulder at his stepmother, noting her harassed expression, the wrinkled blouse. He scowled. "Thanks, Paula, but I want her next to me until Doc gives her a clean bill of health."

The house hadn't changed. But the people had.

If it was possible, age had only intensified Paula's immaculate, cold beauty. It had never been a secret that she'd married Ash's father, the senator, for a social position in Washington society, financial security for herself and a future for her little girl. Though she later discovered that the Bartlets were land rich and cash poor, she still enjoyed the benefits of a social standing in the most powerful city in America.

As Jeri grew older, Paula made it known that she intended using her husband's position and influence to assist in finding her daughter a wealthy husband—a man of presence and power, and if she were very lucky, a foreigner with a title.

Everyone close to the Bartlets knew Paula's ambitions, even the senator, but he hadn't seemed to mind. Paula was a brilliant hostess. She could, when called upon, organize and accompany him on the numerous hunting expeditions that were geared to curry favor with his fellow politicians and to sway votes his way.

Shannon caught a brief glance of Jeri and her weary eyes lit with joy. If Paula had become colder, harder, Jeri was the exact opposite—petite, a little chubby with mousy brown hair, sparkling hazel eyes and a smile that once was as beautiful and infectious as the sun shining after a week of rain. But Jeri's gaze wasn't vibrant or welcoming now, she noted. There was something close to loathing in those bright eyes.

When she'd run from Bartlet, Montana, a decade ago, Shannon had abandoned an immature fourteen-year-old girl who had worshiped the ground she had walked on. She'd shattered Jeri's world and the illusion that her idol was perfect. As for Paula, she'd only tolerated Shannon because Ash and the senator had loved her so much.

Shannon's eyes were gritty with fatigue and fever. She wondered sadly why she'd thought things would be the same, her friends and loved ones unchanged.

Fantasies, years of dreams, had kept her sane when she thought only death would release her from the hell she'd made for herself. But now, living just a small fraction of that fairy tale, she knew her dreams had been only illusions, a perfect vision she'd kept in her head to enable her to face the day-to-day life with a man she despised more than she'd thought possible.

She desperately needed a friend. Yet one wasn't likely to be found in this house. The sensation of being lowered and of a firm mattress meeting her back brought her eyes open. She received her first genuine smile.

"Well, Shannon. I see you haven't changed. I've been rooted from my nice warm house, leaving a wonderful dinner my housekeeper slaved over, to patch you up once again." Doc Henry pursed his mouth, his lips as lined as a prune and his rosy cheeks as shiny as polished apples. "Seems like old times, doesn't it?" He leaned closer, holding the dangling stethoscope away so it wouldn't knock her in the head, and whispered for her ears only, "Welcome home, my dear."

Hot tears filled Shannon's eyes, spilling over reddened lids and running unchecked toward her temples.

"There, there. You've had a bad time." The old man coughed, embarrassed at the way his throat ached with tenderness. "Now...now," he said briskly, "let's have none of this. Tears never solved anything." He patted her hand and sat down beside her. "What damage have you done to yourself? Can you wiggle fingers and toes? No frostbite?" The last question was directed at Ash, who stood quietly in the corner watching.

"She's all right as far as I can tell, but you better have a look at her ankle. I think she's got a bad sprain."

The thick head of shocking white hair shook slowly. "Should have been a doctor, Ash, always thought so, even tried to talk the senator into putting you through medical school. Of course that was when you were a small child and that temper and sharp tongue didn't exist. No bedside manners." Without missing a beat, his back still turned to Ash, he snapped, "Put that damn cigarette away! I thought you quit smoking?"

As bad as she felt, Shannon couldn't help laughing. From as far back as she could remember, all the kids had known that old Doc Henry had eyes in the back of his head. When they were about seven and eleven, she and Ash found him asleep on the soft grassy banks of Willow Creek, his fishing line forgotten as the cork bobbed on the mirror surface. They'd both tried to sneak up on him and get a closer look at the back of his head. Of course Doc had only been dozing and jumped up, scaring the daylights out of them by calling out their names before he ever turned around.

Shannon looked at Ash, saw the tiny smile that played around the corners of his mouth, and knew he was remembering, too. Even Doc Henry chuckled as if he'd acquired mind reading over the years and knew exactly what they were thinking.

"You two were always getting into the worst scrapes. I recall the last time I treated you, young lady. Ash had just come home from college for a day to see about one of his horses he was so damn crazy about. Anyway, the two of you had sat up half the night waiting for the animal to drop her foal and decided to drink some scotch that one of the hands had socked away. Later, when I asked why Shannon had done it, she told me you had dared her. Those words have been the bane of your existence my girl. But, Lordy, Lordy," he chuckled, "were you ever sorry you took Ash up on that particular dare." He stopped talking long enough to check her heart and the bruised muscles around her neck. "I've never seen anyone so sick in all my life."

"Doc!"

"I'm sorry, child." There was a twinkle in his eyes that belied the apology. "You swore me to absolute secrecy, but after all these years, surely you don't mind?" He pulled a syringe from his case and plunged it into the rubber stopper of the small bottle he held up. "Ash, you went back to college the next day, but Shannon was laid up for three days. We found out after that little episode that she's violently allergic to alcohol." He filled another syringe, swabbed off a spot on her arm then paused a second. "You haven't acquired any new allergies I should know about, say penicillin—" he held up the syringe "—or vitamin B 12?"

Shannon shook her head and squeezed her eyes shut, but before her eyelids had closed she saw Ash flinch. There would have been a time when that would have sent her into whoops of laughter. The sight of a needle had the power to turn him pale, but now his reaction only brought back too many memories. She let Doc's voice, as he continued his story, wash over her like a healing balm.

"Always had to be extra careful with her medication or any painkillers." He pulled out a bottle of pills and set them down on the bedside table. "Ash, the instructions are one pill every four hours, but since Shannon's system has a low tolerance to drugs, make sure she takes one tablet every six hours instead. This one is for pain for that nasty ankle and the muscle cramps she's going to have. These—" he held up another bottle "—are antibiotics."

Over her protest, he forced her to take one of the painkillers, then set to work wrapping her ankle. When he was through, he shut his black bag with a snap and slowly rose to his feet. "Well, cover that elastic with a plastic bag and have one of the women help you with a hot bath. After a couple of days' rest you'll be better, hobbling around for a few weeks, though, but better. Ash I'd like to speak with you outside."

Ever since Doc's story of her allergy to alcohol, Shannon had been aware of Ash's withdrawal and the puzzled expression that seemed to settle his eyebrows in a straight line across his forehead. "Doc, before you leave, I'd like to talk to you. In private please."

The old man pushed a resisting Ash out the door and returned to her bedside. He picked up her hand and patted it as if to give her strength to say what she wanted to say.

"It looks like I've had six days wiped from my memory and I wanted to know if it's something to seriously worry about. Will I ever remember? I guess that's what I need to know."

"Do you want to remember? By the look of those bruises I'd say you had good reason not to."

"You haven't asked about those?"

"Jeff asked me not to until he and Ash could be present. You've been through enough and I told Jeff to back off until you're feeling up to it. I decided to take my own advice and not ask."

"What if I never remember?"

He squeezed her hand and watched her expression closely. "I delivered you, child, and I've been your doctor for many more years than you've been away. I don't think you could have changed that much."

She gave a strangled, self-mocking laugh.

"Clinically it's probably only a temporary condition—it's obvious you went through a traumatic experience. But as for remembering, it's something I think you'll have to want to do. Let your body heal and your mind will do the same." He climbed to his feet, still

studying her solemn face. Ten years hadn't changed her;
she was as pretty as a new day, but there was so much
sadness in her eyes that it tugged at his old heart. "Rest,
Shannon. Things have a way of working themselves
out."

"Doc. How's Happy?"

"As proud, ornery and butt-headed as ever."

"Do you two still play dominoes on Thursday
nights?"

"Yes, and he still cheats."

He was almost at the door when she swallowed her
pride and asked, "Do you think he'll see me?"

Doc Henry turned the doorknob, then paused before
pulling the door open. "He says no, but ever since he
heard you'd come back with Dean this time, he's been
setting the house to rights. He even got a woman out
from town to clean your room. It's time the two of you
made peace with each other."

The door closed softly on her tears. It was way past
time. She'd let Dean prey upon her pride and use her
own stubborn nature against her. He'd kept her away
from her grandfather, Bartlet and Ash for too long.
Thoughts of Dean brought a feeling of terror and she
began to shiver as if she was still out in the cold.

The wind shrieked in her head.

Shannon clapped her hands over her ears to keep the
sound out.

*Suffocating, she couldn't breathe...Dean's face...
then red...everything covered in red.*

What did it all mean? *Dear God, what had happened?*

"Shannon. What's the matter?" Ash stood at the foot
of the bed, watching her expression slip from confusion

to stark fear, and he wondered what was going on behind that tormented face.

She forced away the odd apparition, like hallucinating while wide awake. The only thing that mattered now was Ash. She smiled tiredly. "I always loved this room. Thank you for putting me here."

He shrugged. "It will be easier for me to keep a watch on you here than having to tramp back and forth down the hall." He held up a plastic bag and a rubber band. "Doc said you wanted a bath."

A jolt of comprehension made her sit up. "You're going to help me to the bathroom?"

"Not exactly. You're too weak to manage on your own and that painkiller Doc gave you will only make it more hazardous."

Was there a hint of unease in his manner? "You're going to bathe me? Where's Paula or Jeri?" When he continued to silently stand there, she understood. "They don't want to help me, is that it?"

"Right."

"Why? I've never done anything to them?"

"Shannon, just forget it. You wanted a bath, Doc says you need one, I'm here to give it to you. That's the end of it."

She watched him move up beside her from the end of the bed, and suddenly he was looming over her. "I can bathe myself, Ash." She gasped when he reached down and picked her up. "Ash. Stop!" He was too close. Even in her tired, disheveled condition she wanted him. After all this time, she marveled, the chemistry between them was still there. She doubted whether Ash would ever admit it, but he wanted her, too. She could feel the tension between them as if it were a bright flame. "I don't think it's a good idea for you to do this, Ash."

"Shannon. I've seen you naked before. Your charms hold nothing new for me." He walked toward the bathroom, kicking the door shut behind him. "If you think I'd take advantage of a sick woman, all I can say is that you've been in some charming company lately." He set her down on the side of the bathtub, hunkered down in front of her, slipped the plastic bag over her foot then eased on the rubber band to hold it tightly in place. "If I get aroused, think nothing of it. It's just a normal male reaction to the sight of a nude woman. Somehow I'll manage to control myself."

He turned on the shower and fiddled with the knobs, adjusting the water until it was at a temperature to his liking. What he was really doing, he acknowledged with disgust, was putting off the inevitable. Twice in less than twelve hours he'd had to touch her smooth warm skin. He inhaled deeply, trying to right a world gone suddenly awry. He'd dreamed about doing this, but in a different manner and under different circumstances.

"I want a bath, Ash, not a shower."

"You're in no position to demand anything. The shape you're in you'd probably fall asleep and drown the minute I turned my back." He glanced at her then wished he hadn't. "Now, help me a little, goddammit, and start taking those clothes off."

The pout that started died with his harsh command, and her heart felt it might break with each callous word. Surely she hadn't been wrong about the feelings that had passed between them a while ago?

She rose shakily and began unbuttoning her flannel shirt, then she staggered, her head as light as a feather, and started to giggle.

"Damn."

Glancing over at Ash she tried to frown. "You never used to curse so much."

"That painkiller has obviously taken effect. You're high as a kite." He was beside her, brushing her hands away, finishing the job her numb fingers couldn't.

"Will you wash my hair, Ash?" She swayed backward and he was forced to grab the front of her shirt. A loud ripping sound made them both look down at the exposed white mound of her breast. Shannon was the first to glance back up. "You didn't used to be so rough. Though I might say..."

"Shut up." He stripped off her jeans and underwear and hurriedly stood her under the warm water. With almost frantic movements he soaped her down, dumped a half bottle of shampoo on her head and scrubbed away, all the while telling himself that her naked flesh, slick with soap and warm to his touch, was not affecting him in the least. When his own shirt and jeans were soaked to the skin, he gave up trying to stay dry and told her firmly to hold on to the railing while he stripped off his clothes. Naked and standing behind her, unable to hide his reaction to her nearness, he let his mind run wild and free with memories.

Shannon melted against his chest, letting the water slide over her, imagining the warmth was Ash's hands caressing her body. She hummed with pleasure, dropping her head back. But the kiss she'd invited never happened. Instead, Ash quickly turned off the water and hauled her out, setting her aside while he gathered towels and began to dry her off as if she were a small child.

Even in her somewhat drugged state, she knew she'd made a major error. She'd mistakenly thought she could break down his resistance with her body, use herself to make amends for what she'd done. She was ashamed, but worst of all she realized that Ash knew what she'd tried to do, though he didn't know why.

"Ash."

"Here, stand up straight so I can finish drying your hair."

"Ash. I'm sorry."

"I am too, Shannon. I never thought I'd see the day that you'd revert to sex games. What is it you want from me? If your ego needs bolstering, then the answer is yes, I want you like hell. But, unlike you, I don't particularly like the title 'adulterer.'"

"It wasn't like that."

"No. Then tell me what you were doing in there? You're a married woman and you were making a pass at me, isn't that right?"

"I've never been married."

The towel halted in its progress. "What the hell are you talking about? Of course you're married."

"Legally yes, but not in my heart."

Ash laughed, a rough sound that made her cringe. "Then that makes screwing around okay? God, you've changed."

The sight of his naked torso was enough to steal her breath away.

Ash quickly wrapped a towel around his waist, tucking in the ends securely. He swung Shannon into his arms then set her down on the bed.

"You don't understand."

"No, and I don't think I want to." He gathered up the damp towels and their clothes and walked toward the door.

"Ash!" She couldn't let him go, not without trying to make amends.

"Shannon." He ran stiff fingers through his wet hair. "Don't do this to either of us."

"Please, Ash. I want to tell you something."

He sighed and dropped his hand. "What?"

"I've..." She didn't know if she had the courage to say what needed to be said. "I love you. I've never stopped loving you."

Ash closed his eyes for a moment. When he opened them they were hard, cold and utterly lifeless. "You had a funny way of showing it, Shannon."

The door slammed shut once more on her dreams. She closed her eyes, wondering where to go from here. Because now, after seeing Ash, she knew she would never, as long as she lived, go back to being Dean's wife. The thought of Dean made her head suddenly hurt as an image of him slid before her mind, his face twisted with hate. Pain stabbed behind her eyes and she rolled over and pounded the pillow. What was happening to her?

CHAPTER FIVE

SLEEP WAS EVANESCENT...the night alive with demons. Like all elusive nightmares, hers was convoluted, mixing past and present.

She was fifteen and miserable, hiding from Ash and Dean. In her idyllic world, change had been thrust upon her and her young heart was breaking. No longer was she one of the boys.

A deep sob racked her chest, snapping her out of the light sleep she'd finally fallen into. As in so many other wakeful moments that night, her eyes fluttered partially open, searching for the man who sat motionless in the chair no more than an arm's length away. The small reading lamp on the bedside table cast his face in shadows, hiding his eyes, darkening his lean cheeks to hollow gauntness, obscuring his lips. Yet at the same time the tiny blush of illumination highlighted his brow, the bridge of his nose and the square chin, making his high cheekbones sharper in contrast. Maturity agreed with Ash, refining his handsome features with a deep masculine sensuality. A lump lodged in Shannon's throat; she'd missed so much.

Ash opened his eyes and met Shannon's amber gaze studying him so seriously. He straightened in the chair, and the book that had fallen onto his leg as he dozed slipped to the floor with a muted thud that broke the spell between them. "What's the matter? Are you in pain?"

"No." But she was. She ached for his touch, a kind word, some understanding. "I was having a dream."

"Another nightmare?"

She rolled over, pulling the covers up to her chin. "A dream this time. Do you remember when I hid from you for three days, and you finally found me at the water-fall crying?"

"No."

She could tell by the tight line of his mouth that he was lying and went on, ignoring the frown that settled between his eyes. "For weeks I wore loose shirts and sweaters to hide the changes of my body. I was angry, confused and scared, but the crowning blow was when I started my period. Happy never told me much. I never had any girlfriends I felt comfortable enough to talk to, and if the truth be known, I really didn't have any interest in girls anyway. You found me and explained everything."

"Yes." As unbidden as a spring snowstorm, the word slipped past his lips in a husky rush.

"But that wasn't the real reason for all those tears. I was afraid I was never going to be one of the boys again. That somehow the changes were going to make a difference in the way you felt about me. You told me then that everything changes at one time or another and we have to accept that and go on from there."

He didn't want to remember the touching scene, burned into his memory with a clarity as if it was only yesterday. She'd been devastated and scared by her newly budding body and the internal changes going on. He'd taken her in his arms that day for their first real embrace, and though he had to hide his embarrassment from Shannon, he awkwardly told her everything he knew about girls and their bodies. Predictably their conversation turned to sex, and she made him explain that too—in detail. Then she had demanded to know how he'd become such an expert, and an argument ensued forcing him to steal his first kiss from her just to shut her up.

As if reading Ash's thoughts, Shannon asked, "You always understood me—my moods, my insecurities. You knew all my secrets. We never lied to each other. What happened, Ash, to trust and faith?"

"You know very well what happened." But he wasn't so sure now. For years he'd never harbored any doubts about the facts, yet now the truth seemed clouded, murky with questions he no longer had the answers to. The turmoil of his thoughts brought him to his feet. He stood for a second looking down at the sad, lovely face.

"Ten years ago you turned your back on me, Ash. Where was the love we shared? The understanding? The trust? Stealing Ashland's Fire and riding him was foolish and wrong, yet what happened later was an accident, a horrible one, yes, but nonetheless an accident. I didn't deliberately kill him, Ash. Where was your understanding and forgiveness then?" She was almost in tears but held them back, knowing how Ash had always hated weepy women. "I know you were hurt by what I did. My God, don't you think I was equally devastated by it? But you turned on me Ash. You and Happy—everyone."

"Stop it, Shannon. It's no use dragging up the past, it's as dead as that goddamn horse." He couldn't listen to any more, not now, not until he had time to think things through.

He was at the door, his back stiff and unyielding. Shannon jerked upright, her breath a long hiss of pain as she put pressure on her ankle. "What happened to the love we shared?"

"You'd know the answer to that better than I would. You tell me."

"Don't leave, Ash. Talk to me."

"No. Go to sleep, Shannon, and try thinking of your husband while you're at it."

The solid thud of the door shutting behind him made her flop back onto the bed. A sickening feeling filled the pit of her stomach. Why wouldn't he talk to her? Surely there was more to what had happened than the death of the horse. And why hadn't she stayed ten years ago? Why had she run? *Dean*. Just thinking of him made her head hurt. She touched her throbbing temples, telling herself that this time, without Dean's interference, she was going to find her answers.

She was afraid to close her eyes again; terrified she'd remember what she was trying so hard to hide from. As she had learned to do so many times in the past when things were unbearable, she cleared her mind and lay there watching the morning light stream through the window, chasing away the gloom that had invaded the room.

When the door opened, she became fully alert, tense and ready to face Ash again. But it wasn't Ash. A smile bloomed across her face as she watched Bridget O'Conner step lightly into the room and shut the door with a firm kick of her foot.

"Well, if it's not herself. Home at last and about time I'd say."

"Bridget." Her mainstay. Proud, tough, strong, independent, with a heart of gold. She'd left Ireland at the age of ten, yet fifty-five years in America hadn't sapped the soft, melodious brogue from her voice.

The plump housekeeper set the tray she carried down on Shannon's lap then jammed her hands on her ample hips. "And who else, I ask you, would have the nerve to venture into the den of such a wicked child?"

"Not you, too?"

"My, yes." Bridget's clear blue eyes twinkled under heavy eyebrows that matched her fire-engine-red hair, now lightly touched with gray at the temples. "And just be looking at yourself, lying up here naked as the day you were born. No shame. I always knew it." She clucked her tongue.

Shannon wanted to laugh and cry at the same time but knew Bridget would have none of it, so she swallowed hard, fighting to control her emotions. "It's good to see a friendly face. I've missed your sharp tongue."

Bridget hurrumped. "Then you should have brought yourself home." With an uncharacteristic gesture she leaned over and kissed Shannon's scratched cheek. "Poor child, all cut and bruised." Her eyebrows gathered together at the sight of Shannon's neck. "Did the snow fairies take a dislike to you and drag you through the bushes?"

Bridget had never allowed anyone to answer her questions, and Shannon let the sweet motherly voice continue, washing over her like a healing balm. When she was able to regain control of her voice, she said, "I think I tangled with a bear."

"A polecat, and a two-legged one, I'd say. Eat your breakfast, child. You're going to need your strength," she added almost as an afterthought.

Shannon glanced down for the first time at the tray on her lap and laughed. "Chicken soup this early?"

Big-boned hands were once more set firmly on wide hips. "You'll not be turning my medicine down."

"Yes, Bridget."

With a nod of approval, Bridget began to plump up the pillows behind Shannon and helped her to sit up straighter without overtaxing herself. Satisfied, Bridget plopped in the chair beside the bed with a gusty sigh.

Shannon knew she couldn't question Bridget. The old woman considered gossip evil, but if a person had the patience Bridget would eventually tell her everything she need to know.

"Where's Ash?"

The housekeeper shot her a mischievous look then immediately sobered. "That one. Why he's as ornery as a wet cat this morning. Stomped around the house snapping at everyone, yelling orders like he was some general on the battlefield. Sure was a relief when Jeffrey called him and he left for town. You and that husband of yours kicked up a real fuss."

Her reference to Dean was said with such loathing that Shannon was instantly alert. Bridget never openly showed her dislike for anyone; she did it in little ways that could easily be missed. "Has Dean turned up yet?"

Bridget's expression went blank, then she crossed herself. "No. And I hope the wood elves have carried that devil off." Her lips firmly compressed into a thin line. "But we'll not be discussing *that* one just yet. Eat!"

Shannon nodded, her gaze glued to Bridget's face, trying to figure out what was going on. When she dipped the spoon in the hot broth and brought it up to her mouth, she looked down for the first time and began to giggle like the little girl she had once been.

"You were always partial to alphabet noodles."

That did it. Shannon dropped the spoon, barely aware of the hot liquid splattering the sheet and soaking through to her skin. Huge tears spilled over and ran unchecked down her cheeks.

"Here now." Alarmed, Bridget sniffed loudly, set the tray aside then pulled Shannon against her ample bosom. "Poor child. You've had a wee spot of trouble, that's all. Trust old Bridget, everything will right itself now that you're home. Hush now, you're still weak and scared. What you went through would even make a crybaby out of me. Why, I remember a fierce, independent little cuss that'd rather die than have anyone seeing her bawling."

Shannon shuddered and forced a smile on her trembling lips. "How's Lynette and Tom?"

The world once again righted, Bridget grinned. "Tom's still a slow dullard, but a good husband, I guess. Ash thinks he's the best foreman the Bar B has ever had, but there's no counting for the taste of men. Lynette has made me a grandmother three times. But that's enough of me, there's trouble on the way. The *queen bee* and her drone will more than likely be sticking their noses in here and we have to set you right. Don't you dare let them see you like this, Shannon Reed."

The reference to Paula and Jeri was not said unkindly but with humor and a twinkle of her blue eyes. Shannon couldn't help but notice Bridget's refusal to recognize her marriage or speak her married name. "You never liked Dean, did you, Bridget?" she called out to the old woman as she disappeared through the bathroom connecting to Ash's room. Shannon could hear her rummaging around the room, and when Bridget came back carrying one of Ash's shirts, she repeated her question.

"Dean was always a sly one. Always wanting what Ash had, though he had more." She screwed her mouth up. "I never understood that situation over at the Rocking W. His parents divorced, his dad leaving him and living in France, his mom fluttering back and forth from Hollywood and New York, barely willing to take the time to stop and see the child. And him raised by servants." Bridget shook her head and clicked her teeth together in distress. "Then when his mom died, everybody thought for sure his father would send for him. But no, he wanted Dean to finish his schooling in America." She fanned herself with her apron as if to sweep the past away. "Maybe that's why the boy turned bad." She shrugged then stared at Shannon. "But I'll tell you, peculiar happenings have gone on around here after you ran off with him." Her lips closed on the gossip, and it was obvious she thought she'd said enough already.

"Please tell me, Bridget. Help me piece together some things that I've learned over the years."

"Here, put this on." She helped Shannon slip into the shirt, threw back the covers and lent a hand for her to stand. "There were some bad rumors about you. You'd think after a few months or a year at the most they would have stopped, but they never did. It was like someone was feeding the gossip to certain big mouths in town."

"Who? What were the stories?"

This time Bridget's mouth clamped shut with an intractable finality. "Ask Ash. Now, let's get you to the bathroom and cleaned up. My you're a mess, child."

After a soothing hot bath, Bridget made Shannon sit down and she began to comb the knots and tangles from the younger woman's hair. The soothing pull and tug brought back memories of other quiet times like this, and Shannon felt her spirit renew itself .

"Now. You're looking almost like yourself again. Brush your teeth while I go and straighten your bed, then I'll help you back."

With the support of the towel rack and the cool tiled walls, Shannon carefully hobbled to the sink. Once she finished her task she felt really human for the first time, and she stiffened her back and slowly raised her eyes to the mirror. Shock widened her gaze when she saw her pale face, the scratches still red, angry marks on one side and a darkening spot that ran high along her cheekbone on the other. There was even a discoloration over her right eyebrow that was turning a sickening shade of pea-green edged with yellow. How could she be such a wreck and not remember what had happened?

Gradually her gaze dropped to her neck. With a detachment, as if her neck belonged to another person, she inspected the mass of bruises.

Without warning a pain shot through her head. An image obliterated her own in the mirror and she squeezed her eyes tightly shut—but not before she'd seen Dean's face, his features all screwed up in an expression of venomous hate.

A fragmented dream, like a scene from another world, played out behind her eyelids. A hideous scene that made no sense, yet made all the sense in the world, if only she could just remember.

He was yelling at her, his mouth twisted and ugly. The wind kept whipping the words away no matter how hard she strained forward to hear. Suddenly there was a splash of red on his shirt and she watched, horrified, as it bloomed like a rose. Slowly, slowly the crimson petals spread against the white material until the color was so glaringly bright it hurt her eyes....

Shannon bowed her head as a barrage of unrelated images flashed inside her mind like lightning spears across an ink-black sky. Little by little she was remembering. Her temples pounded, the bile rose in her throat and she was seized with an unexplainable terror. She began to tremble and sweat.

"Here now..." Bridget grabbed Shannon's sagging body before she hit the floor. "What's this about, child?"

"Sick."

Bridget guided her to the bowl and held her head and shoulders as Shannon heaved and shook. "Poor wee thing," she soothed, and knelt down to wash the damp face, then gave her something to rinse her mouth out with. "Well, you're finished now, let's be getting you back in bed and some of my medicine in you."

Shannon shuddered and groaned at the thought of food.

"I'll be having no argument from you. You need something to fill the empty space."

"But, Bridget, I'll only throw it up again."

"My soup? Never!"

Bridget was right, Shannon concluded later. Once she was warm again and had finished the broth and was sipping the cold Coke over crushed ice—her favorite remedy for an upset stomach—she did indeed feel better.

"You'll do now." The housekeeper patted Shannon's shoulder and for a brief moment they grinned at each other.

Neither Shannon nor Bridget heard the bedroom door open, but simultaneously they became aware they weren't alone, and they looked toward the intruder.

"That will be all, Bridget," Paula said as she strolled past the older woman, the heels of her riding boots causing a loud echo in the room.

Before Bridget left she leaned down and plumped Shannon's pillow, adding under her breath, "Remember, child, bees have stingers."

"That will be *all* Bridget."

The cool blonde was dressed for riding, and her face bore an expression of bitter resentment. Shannon wondered if Paula still refused to ride Western style, preferring the English saddle and the prestige she claimed it gave her.

Paula silently watched the housekeeper leave, making sure she was out of hearing distance before she spoke. "Like the proverbial bad penny...here you are turning up and causing trouble."

"Hello to you, too, Paula."

Red lips, a garish slash against a white face, compressed. "You always had a smart mouth. But I'm not here to spar with you, Shannon. Ash asked me to give you your medicine if he wasn't back in time."

Shannon sighed inwardly. She and Paula had never gotten along. No, that wasn't true, she thought. Paula had never really noticed her unless Jeri managed to get into trouble or disobey her, and then she would blame Shannon for her daughter's misdeeds. Paula acknowledged few outside her sphere of sophisticated friends.

Why was Paula in Montana at this time of year? Shannon wondered. Usually she was at her Georgetown home, planning parties to help bolster her lagging social standing so she could find a rich husband for her daughter. From what Shannon had heard and read in the gossip columns, the senator's death four years ago had done little to curb Paula's social climbing. But what Shannon knew, and obviously Paula hadn't figured out yet, was that a widow, an unattached female, on the Washington political scene was taboo.

The two of them had never been friends, nor had they ever declared open war on each other. So why did Shannon now feel a tension in the woman standing so close, as if she harbored a deep hate for her? Shannon's heart began to pound with unease.

"Here, for land's sake, take these so I can go riding."

"What?"

"Why are you looking at me like that?" Paula demanded.

"Like what?"

"I don't know...strange."

Shannon shook her head as the warning bells went off. She didn't know why she felt so uneasy, but trusted her instincts.

"Ash said you'd lost your memory. I thought maybe you'd remembered something?"

"No." She held out her hand and accepted the pills and the glass of water. "There's nothing there."

"That's a real shame. I hope you get well soon."

"Why, thank you Paula." She should have known better.

"You misunderstand, Shannon. Personally, I couldn't care less what happens to you. You always were disruptive and a bad influence on Jeri. You haven't changed. I think everyone concerned in this new mess you've gotten yourself into will be better off if you get well and return to the Rocking W. You tend to ruin people's lives. Go back to Europe, Shannon. Soon.''

SHE FELT DEAD, leaden with sleep, wishing she could stay in the darkness forever and never have to face reality again, but a voice kept intruding on her safe haven and she was forced to claw her way to the light.

Shannon opened her eyes, blinked and focused on Jeri standing beside the bed. "Good morning." A silent, sullen nod met her greeting. Propping herself up, she tried again. "Is it morning?"

Jeri shrugged. "Mother told me to give you these." She held out a hand holding Shannon's two pills.

Shannon frowned and shook her head groggily. "I don't need them." Her tongue felt funny and the words came out thick and slurred.

"Dammit, take these so I can leave."

Shannon blinked in surprise at the harsh edge to Jeri's voice, so foreign to the young open face. "Jeri, don't be this way."

"What way, Shannon? Bitter? What did you expect, to be welcomed back with open arms? You ruined Ash's life...and mine," she mumbled. "Here." Picking up the glass of water, she shoved both hands at Shannon. "Take these. Ash left orders."

She couldn't think straight. But one thing Jeri said rang as sharply as a bronze bell on a clear still afternoon. "How did I ruin your life?"

Jeri shrugged again, the movement both a mixture of defiance and defeat. "Doesn't matter now. But what does is Ash. He loved you, Shannon, and you broke his heart. He changed after you left—everything changed. He tried to put his life together, even married a sweet

girl, but she wasn't you. They were both miserable. Mary
Ann's just another person to add to your long list.''

Guilt was a heavy burden to bear and Shannon didn't
want to hear anymore. How was she going to make the
ones she loved realize that she was as much a victim as
they had been? Dean had to answer for the pain he'd
caused. If it took her the rest of her life, she'd see to it
that he paid.

Her head began to pound and her ankle throbbed.
There were pieces of the puzzle they didn't know. ''Jeri.
I can't think straight right now.'' The pills and glass were
wordlessly shoved at her again and she shook her head.
''Please . . .''

''Please what? Listen to lies? I know all about *you* and
Dean, and how you ruined his life, too. Mother said you
were trash and she was right. Here! Dammit, take these
so I can get out of here.''

The hatred in Jeri's voice shocked Shannon, yet even
in her drugged state she could also detect the hurt and
disillusionment there. She would not find any understanding from the younger woman now. Shannon took
the pills without a glance, popped them into her mouth
and gulped them down with the water. With sad, dull
eyes she watched Jeri turn and walk away. ''This is not
the end, Jeri. I'm back to stay. You'll have to listen to me
eventually.''

Jeri whipped around. ''What do you mean, you're
here to stay?''

Settling down on the pillows with a shaky sigh, Shannon realized she felt worse than she ever had in her entire life. ''Just what I said.'' She closed her eyes wearily.

''But what about Dean and . . . and . . . ?''

''That's over. Believe me, as far as I'm concerned he's
dead.'' A strangled sound from across the room forced

her lids open, but Jeri was gone, and only the empty room met her blurred gaze. Moisture welled in her eyes. She didn't know who the tears were for, and her confusion seemed to magnify everything, tipping the room out of kilter, as if the world were spinning around her, out of control. Then suddenly she was plunged into darkness.

The wind began to howl . . .

CHAPTER SIX

THE SPRING STORM that had swept through the high country dumping three inches of snow on the mountains blew itself out as it collided with the warmer air of the valley below and the town of Bartlet.

Ash maneuvered the truck through the melting slush on the streets, passing the courthouse square with its bronze statues of his ancestors, the glistening stone park benches and the old spreading live oaks, which wept with the dissolving snow.

A thousand questions needled him, making his expression fierce and preoccupied. He looked so harsh and uncommunicative that when he pulled up before the sheriff's office, got out and slammed the door, Sally Roland decided it best to refrain from speaking lest she get her head snapped off.

The taciturn face didn't stop her overly made-up eyes from following Ash, nor did it halt the fantasies that sprang up at the sight of such a gorgeous man. She hesitated outside the sheriff's office, torn between self-preservation and excitement. After all, she was a reporter for the *Bartlet Star*, and she smelled a story. Yet on second thought, after her recent encounter with Jeff, she decided it prudent to wait until later to approach Ash. With a disgusted sigh at her own cowardliness she pulled her coat collar closer and headed for the Cattlemen's Café, where she knew she could nose out some leads to these interesting current events.

The dispatcher looked up from the book she'd been lost in and absently pointed to the back office. "He's waiting for you, Ash." The paperback shielded half her face again as once more she became absorbed in the historical romance.

Without altering his stride, Ash nodded and headed for the nearest door in the small office. He pushed it open and came to a stop as his friend glanced up from a stack of files. "Bartlet couldn't be that riddled with criminals."

Tossing aside his pen, Jeff frowned at the pile of folders. "Red Tape, regulations and endless paper work. Sit down, Ash. We've got some real problems."

"I gathered that, from your urgent call this morning." Ash eyed the wooden chair across from the desk with distaste before he sat down.

Jeff leaned his elbows on the desk, scrubbed at his face then dropped his hands and studied Ash for a long moment before he spoke. "The district attorney came by a while ago."

"So? Hamilton's always sticking his 'honker' in your business."

Both men smiled, their mutual dislike for their childhood foe, Hamilton Watts, obvious from their tigerish grins.

"Ham got an anonymous phone call this morning, and he hot-footed it down here. By the way, I received the same call. A woman—and she took the precaution of disguising her voice. Ah, hell, Ash, there's no gentle way to say this. She accused Shannon of murdering Dean."

"What? That's crazy."

Jeff shook his head. "I know that, but Ham doesn't. I had to fill him in on the rescue and the fact that we didn't find Dean. He's got the bit between his teeth, friend, and he's not going to let go, not this time, not with the Bartlets and the Waynes involved. His political ambitions are well known and a case of murder involving the son of a French millionaire industrialist would be right up his alley. But what would be a real coup would be to tie you in—the son of a U.S. senator, one of the largest ranch owners in the state, besides Dean, and the onetime lover of the murder victim's wife. The newspapers would go wild and the publicity could launch his career."

Ash patted his coat, searching out each pocket. "Come on, Jeff, you're not going to believe this caller, are you? As for Hamilton, screw him." When Jeff didn't answer immediately, he looked up. "Jeff."

"What do you know about Shannon these past ten years?"

"Come on, man. You and I both know her well enough to know she's not capable of murder." He slipped his hand into the breast pocket of his shirt, then, not finding what he was after, he gave up and leaned back to stare at Jeff. "Just what the hell did the caller say?"

"That before they left the Rocking W, Shannon and Dean had one helluva fight."

"Not enough."

"She threatened to kill him. Dean's foreman and housekeeper verified that they both overheard her."

"I don't believe this," Ash exploded. "Give me a damn cigarette." He caught the pack pitched at him and reached in his pocket for the worn lighter he always carried. The flame flared and he squinted over the brief glare.

"She couldn't have killed him. Jeff, you know in the heat of an argument people say things like 'I wish you were dead' or they threaten to kill one another. That doesn't mean they're actually going to do it."

"Not even if it was in self-defense? We saw those bruises on her neck."

"I still say no." He felt as if a ton of rocks had settled in his gut. "Where the hell is Dean? Have you made any headway at all?" Ash surged to his feet, suddenly suffocating in the cramped confines of the office. He stuck the cigarette between his lips, pulled off his coat and threw it over the back of the chair. Smoke drifted in his eyes, making them water, and with a disgusted grunt he yanked the cigarette out of his mouth and crushed it in the overflowing ashtray. "Why the hell did you give me that? You know I quit."

"Calm down, pal. I've put an all points bulletin out on Dean. If he managed to get off the mountain and is heading for one of the surrounding towns, we'll hear soon enough."

"But you don't think he made it down, do you?"

Jeff shook out a cigarette, then put it back. He'd been smoking too much the last couple of days. "No. I don't think he made it, Ash. I think he's dead. How it happened is something we're going to have to find out—fast. The D.A. doesn't want Dean alive. He'd like nothing better than to be able to charge Shannon with murder, but he can't, not until he has a body. The weather's clear and the snow will be melting on the mountain. I have to go up there and find him, Ash. But before I do, I need to question Shannon. Is she up to it? Has she remembered anything?"

Ash nodded grimly. "She's well enough. As for remembering, I don't think you're going to have any luck
there until she's ready. Doc Henry feels it's psychologi-
cal and not physical. So it will depend on what, when
and how much she wants to remember." He picked up
his coat to leave, then stopped and turned back to Jeff.
"Over the past years you've heard the stories about
Shannon that filtered back here, haven't you?"

"Sure, who hasn't?"

"Where does that gossip get started? Who keeps it
going?"

"What's on your mind, Ash?"

"For ten years I've heard of Shannon's wildness, her
drinking and whoring around Europe, and that Dean,
no matter how hard he tried, couldn't control her. There
were even stories of her taking drugs and of being out of
control."

Jeff looked down at his desk and began to shuffle pa-
pers. "Yeah, I've heard. Doesn't mean I believe them,
though."

"Jeff, I found out yesterday from Doc Henry that
Shannon's violently allergic to alcohol."

Jeff's head snapped up, his gentle brown eyes narrowed in thought. He started to ask a question but Ash's
upraised hand stopped him.

"Wait. There's more. She also has a very low tolerance to drugs. Who started those damn stories? And if
those are lies, couldn't the rest be, too?"

"Rumors and their sources are hard to chase down,
Ash. But I have a good idea where in this town to start
looking."

"Chester," they said in unison.

Jeff reached for his coat, struggling into it as he walked to the door. "After I talk with Shannon, I'll find Chester and squeeze the truth out of him."

"Thanks, Jeff. The old coot wouldn't give me the time of day."

"He doesn't like me much, either. So I don't know how effective I'll be." A slow, sly grin etched itself across Jeff's scarred and weathered face. "But I'll tell you someone who can make the old man squeal like a stuck pig. Happy. Chester's afraid of Shannon's grandfather. Always has been as far back as I can remember. Haven't you ever noticed when Happy's around, Chester's not?"

"No. And I don't know whether he'll help or not. I called Happy this morning to tell him about Shannon and he was as noncommittal as ever. He's a tough, unforgiving old bird."

"No more so than you."

"What the hell is that supposed to mean?"

Jeff shrugged, his wide shoulders hunching under the coat like a bear beneath its fur. "You figure it out." His soft brown eyes hardened. "Hell no. I've kept quiet long enough. I'm telling you, what happened ten years ago should never have gone as far as it did. You were both young and there was entirely too much pride involved, yours, Happy's and Shannon's."

Ash opened his mouth then snapped it shut when he realized there was no way short of hitting Jeff to make him stop.

"You fell right into Dean's hands and he grabbed his advantage and ran—with Shannon."

A simmering anger turned Ash's eyes a deep glittering green. "You don't know it all."

"Don't I?"

"No!"

"I heard the rumors that Shannon was supposed to have been sleeping with Dean while the two of you were planning to be married. But I never once gave credence to that lie—you did, though."

Ash was shocked. "Who told you that?" His threatening tone and aggressive stance didn't intimidate Jeff in the least. He realized he was a hair's breadth from hitting his best friend and forced himself to relax. Ten years ago he would have punched Jeff, now he asked himself what difference it made. So many doubts were chipping away at what he'd long thought to be established fact, and he welcomed the chance to talk. "Jeri told you, right?"

"Doesn't matter," Jeff mumbled, sorry he'd ever brought up the subject.

Unexpectedly Ash grinned. "You two not getting along lately? Or is Paula interfering again?"

"Forget it, Ash." He clasped his friend's shoulder, wanting desperately to change the subject. "You've got enough problems without me adding to them." He opened the door, holding it back for Ash to go through. "I keep getting the feeling of a setup, Ash. But whose, and why?"

SOME UNSEEN FORCE pressed his foot heavily on the gas pedal. A chill crept up his spine, raising goose bumps along his forearms. The eerie sensation had nothing to do with the weather, and Ash had never laid claim to mystical powers. But he didn't question his instincts either; a man who lived so close to nature learned at an early age to trust premonitions.

Something was wrong, and the unknown force was pulling him home at a reckless speed.

The soggy landscape flashed by, a blur of colors. Yet to Ash the drive to the ranch seemed incredibly slow.

Hurry.

He glanced in the rearview mirror to assure himself that Jeff's car was following, then realized the distraction had almost made him miss the turnoff. The brakes grated and the tires fought to grip the wet pavement, but they lost their traction and the truck began to slide toward the water-filled ditch.

For a few heart-stopping seconds Ash wrestled with the wheel, cursing under his breath until he regained control and made the turn onto the ranch road.

Hurry.

As he rounded the bend in the road and caught sight of the ranch house, his mouth went dry. Doc Henry's old wreck was parked in front. The car itself didn't cause him alarm, but the angle of the car and the open, gaping door did.

Hurry.

Like Doc, Ash left his truck in the same manner, sprinted to the front door, shoved it wide and hit the stairs, taking them two and three at a time. His stomach knotted with fear as raised voices, one thick with tears, the other shrill with denial, clamored around him.

"What the hell's going on?" He reached the landing, took in the scene, and came to a stop. Shannon's bedroom door was shut and the heavy feeling in his gut changed to a pounding ache. "I asked what happened? Is Shannon worse?"

Jeri raised red swollen eyes to her stepbrother, then glanced past him as Jeff came up the stairs and halted on the landing. She burst into tears again. "It wasn't my fault. I swear I didn't know Mother had . . ."

A deep sob shattered Jeri's next words, and Paula gathered her close. "It was all a misunderstanding." She was pale herself and trembling.

"Goddammit, will someone tell me what's going on?" He laid his hand on the closed door, and just as he was about to push it open, Bridget squeezed through, shutting it behind her. "Bridget, will you tell me what's happened here?"

"Sure, and it's about time you showed up." Her clear blue eyes fixed on the two shaken women. "No, Ash, don't go in, Doc's with Shannon. Everything's under control now. The child had an overdose of her medicine."

The silence that followed Bridget's statement was palpable, the air electric with undercurrents he didn't understand. Jeff stepped forward. "Suicide?"

The housekeeper's angry glare hadn't left Paula and Jeri. "Lands, no!" she said in a tight voice, her lips puckering into a bud. "If I didn't know those two better, I'd have said they tried to kill Shannon."

Ash's hand stalled on the doorknob and his head whipped around to stare at the women huddled together. "Paula, explain. Now!" He watched his stepmother closely then frowned as she quickly lit a cigarette. They had both quit smoking at the same time. Something wasn't right. Paula was always immaculate, never a hair out of place, or heaven forbid, a chip in her nail polish. Today, though, she looked as if she was starting to fall apart.

She ran a trembling hand through her hair, stopping only when a hangnail snagged some strands. "I followed your orders and gave Shannon her medicine, then I decided to go riding and told Jeri if I wasn't back to be sure she got her second dose."

"Mother!" Jeri wailed. "You didn't tell me you'd already given her the medicine. You just told me to be sure she took it. I'm sure you didn't . . ."

"Yes, I did, Jeri."

"But, Mother." Her eyelashes batted up and down like a frantic butterfly trying to escape a net. "You didn't."

"Hush, Jeri," Paula shouted. "You just weren't listening." She looked at Ash with an expression of hopeless anger. "You know how absentminded she's been lately, with her head in the clouds, always daydreaming? She just wasn't paying attention, that's all."

Ash didn't know who or what to believe. He opened his mouth then snapped it shut as the door knob was yanked from his grasp.

Doc Henry stepped out, his smile reassuring the group. "She's fine. Maybe a little tired and wrung out. Her ankle's healing nicely and by late tomorrow or the next day, Shannon should be her old self." He set his black bag down and with the help of Bridget put on his coat. "I've taken the painkillers away. She won't be needing them anymore, and if she does, call me." As he buttoned his coat he glanced at Paula and Jeri. "You both were negligent and damn lucky Bridget checked on Shannon or it could have been worse. I gave her the medication more for the muscle cramps and spasms caused by the hypothermia than anything else. Dammit," he barked, his cursing so uncharacteristic that everyone jumped. "They were only to be taken *if* she needed them."

"May I see her now, Doc?" Ash asked.

"Is she up to answering a few questions, or should I wait until tomorrow, Doc?" Jeff put in quickly.

"Yes, to both of you. The medication I gave her to counteract the painkiller will give her some energy for a couple of hours, then she should rest naturally."

Before Ash pushed the door open, he glanced back at the two women huddled together. "Paula, I'll talk to you later." Then he turned to the man beside him. "Jeff, I don't want you to mention anything about the D.A.'s visit or the possibility of Dean's death. Let's take it nice and slow."

Shannon was sitting up in bed wearing one of his shirts, her hair brushed, her cheeks flushed and her eyes overbright. She reminded him of a fallen angel, with a halo of jet-black hair around her face. Her slanted amber eyes narrowed a fraction, and he immediately became suspicious. That particular characteristic usually meant she was up to something she wasn't supposed to be, but he quickly disregarded that thought; she wasn't well enough. Or maybe the look was just pure mischief. She'd always been good at that. Leery of the rush of emotions that washed over him, he watched, careful to keep his own expression neutral lest he show his concern and fall into a trap.

"Are you feeling better?" He couldn't take his eyes off her. She looked so desirable in the yellow flannel shirt, despite the multicolored bruises and scratches. He didn't even want to think of the naked body underneath.

Shannon caressed the collar of the shirt. Whatever Doc had given her made her feel wonderful.

"I've sent one of the ranch hands to the Rocking W to pick up some clothes for you."

Shannon nodded, still fingering the soft material of Ash's shirt. She was loath to give up anything that had been close to him.

"You're sure you're all right?"

He was nervous, she could tell. Something had changed. A warning went off in her head but she ignored it. Instead she decided to have a little fun and wipe the serious expression off his face. "I know you hate having me here, Ash." His sudden thunderous frown made her grin. "But to assign Paula and Jeri the duty of grim reaper is a little much. As I remember, you used to do your own dirty work."

"Dammit, Shannon. I had nothing to do with their stupidity." He stopped his tirade, realizing she was just trying to get a rise out of him. An answering grin cracked the stern, worried edges of his mouth.

Memories tumbled on top of one another as they became lost in each other's eyes.

Jeff felt more and more like a third wheel with each passing second. They'd actually forgotten his existence, which, considering his size, was quite a feat. He cleared his throat, then was forced to do it again, louder.

"Jeff. It's good to see you."

"Thank heaven," he mumbled. "I know you've had a rough time, but Doc said you'd be up to answering a few questions."

"Of course I can." She patted the side of the bed. "Sit down."

Jeff shot a sidelong look at Ash, then shook his head. He frowned at the only chair capable of holding his frame. It was overflowing with sheets and a blanket. Ash was no help; he just stood with his shoulder to the wall, watching Shannon like a cat watching an injured bird. Jeff pulled up a spindly-legged chair from the makeup table and sat down. "Have you had any luck remembering?"

"No." Shannon scowled. This wasn't what she'd expected or wanted.

"Would you tell me what you can remember?"

She felt odd, hollow, as she tried to think. She glanced down at her hands folded together and wasn't surprised to see they were trembling slightly. "The whole trip was a disaster. I should have known better," she mumbled. She touched her temples with her fingertips as if the pressure would help in some way. "Dean seemed possessed to get to Devil's Leap and pushed the animals beyond their endurance. At Willow Falls one of the pack horses went lame and he cut him loose and we went on."

"Devil's Leap. Is that the last camp area just before the timberline ends? Is that where you last camped?"

"Yes."

They waited.

Shannon stared at them, suddenly filled with an unknown terror that she frantically tried to camouflage with a weak smile.

"What happened there, Shannon?" Jeff asked, his deep voice pitched so low it was almost a whisper.

Ash pushed away from the spot where he'd been leaning and moved to stand at the foot of the bed.

"I'm sorry, Jeff, it's a blank. Nothing. I've tried."

"Calm down."

"I feel like such a fool. Why can't I remember anything?"

"Relax." Jeff reached out and covered her hand with his, squeezing it gently. "Go back to before you left the ranch. How were you and Dean getting along? Did you have a fight? Was Dean angry with you?"

Her shoulders moved, a gesture that needed no words at all. "Dean was always angry with me. Ash, what's this all about? Why is Jeff asking me these questions?"

The men shared a glance, then Ash said, "Dean hasn't turned up. We think he might still be on the mountain."

"Is that all?" Her voice was scornful, then she began to laugh. After a few seconds the laughter dwindled away as she saw their shocked expressions. "It's so typical of him to pull a stunt like this." They remained silent and her perplexed gaze shifted from one to the other. "Really," she said with a grin, "it's nothing to worry about."

"You mean he's alive?" Jeff asked.

"Of course."

"Where the hell is he then? He never returned to the ranch."

"Who said?"

"His foreman," Ash answered before Jeff could.

"Clyde Hanks? Clyde would do *anything* for Dean."

Jeff leaned back in the delicate chair and winced as it creaked ominously under his weight. "He's not lying this time, Shannon."

"Poppycock! Everyone lies and covers for Dean. You'd better take a closer look at Dean and Clyde's relationship."

"What are you saying?"

"My husband's tastes are very eclectic. He likes variety and excitement."

She'd stunned them speechless but refused to elaborate any further. Her personal life was none of Jeff's business. Ash was a different matter; she fully intended to tell him everything about the past ten years, but only when the time was right and when they were alone.

Jeff cleared his throat. Things were not going the way he'd expected. "Let's get back to Dean's disappearance, shall we? So, you're not worried then?"

"Heavens no." A chill set her heart pounding and fingers trembling. She clasped her hands tightly together. "Look, he's done this before. The last time it happened was three years ago." It was also the *last* time she went anywhere with him. "We were in Styria, Austria hunting Alpine ibex with a large party of his friends. Dean and I went off with separate groups. When I got back to camp around dark, I found out he'd come in earlier, then had one of the guides drive him back to town, where he caught a plane. I returned to Paris two days later and found Dean in the midst of one of his endless parties."

Ash exploded. "Do you mean to tell us he just left you?"

"Yes. Par for the course for Dean. He became bored easily." She wasn't about to tell them he had left that particular hunt with the wife of one of his so-called friends, in the hopes of embarrassing and humiliating her. She didn't even want to think of the husband's crude attempt to get even with Dean—by making her the victim.

Not comfortable with this line of questioning, Jeff changed tactics. "Did you and Dean have a fight before you started out on the hunt?"

"Yes."

"What about, Shannon?"

"I didn't want to go bighorn sheep hunting." She was hedging and realized both men knew it.

"Clyde said the two of you had a real shouting match. It was more than the hunt that you fought about, wasn't it?"

Shannon nodded and shifted her amber gaze to the man standing so still at the foot of the bed.

"What else did you fight about?"

She didn't answer immediately but continued to stare at Ash. A slight shrug of her shoulders was all he was going to get.

"Answer him, Shannon," Ash said.

"We are arguing about Ash. I told Dean I was going to divorce him and he accused me of leaving him for Ash."

"But you hadn't seen Ash in ten years."

Her mouth took on a mutinous twist, her expression stubborn as she continued to gaze at Ash. "I never made any attempt to hide my feeling for you over the years. Dean married me knowing how I felt. He said it didn't matter to him, but it always did."

"Jeez," Jeff whispered as he raked his fingers through his hair. He glanced over at Ash then back at Shannon. A deep pity for them settled over him. And he thought he had problems. Life hadn't been very fair to these two. But damn, he had a job to do. "Shannon..." He leaned forward, resting his elbows on his knees. "Do you remember how you came to be at the line shack?" His voice hardened, the next questions coming deliberately fast and clipped.

"No."

"Why were you wandering around in a snowstorm alone?"

"I don't know."

"Has Dean ever hit you?"

"Never," she breathed vehemently. "I'd have killed him if he had."

Ash stiffened and quickly interrupted. "That's just a figure of speech, Jeff. You know it as well as I do."

"How did you get those bruises on your neck?" he snapped.

"Jeff!"

"Shut up, Ash. She knows. Don't you Shannon?"

"No." Trembling fingers touched her neck. She suddenly felt empty and very fragile.

"Did Dean do that to you?"

"Yes—no. I don't know!" A shaft of pain shot through her head.

The wind began to howl in her ears . . . A splash of crimson seeped onto a white background . . .

Shannon's hands flew up, covering her face in an attempt to block out the pictures in her mind. "I wish I could tell you. Dammit, don't you think I want to know what happened to me?"

"Is Dean dead, Shannon?"

She dropped her hands and they lay still in her lap as she stared wide-eyed at Jeff. "No. I told you, he's just done one of his disappearing acts."

The wind screeched . . .

She was feeling odd, light as a feather on that tremendous wind.

"What's the matter, Shannon?" Ash raced around the corner of the bed as he watched all the color drain from her flushed face, leaving her skin a pasty white.

Jeff's thick arm shot out and stopped Ash. "Back off! Shannon, do you remember something? Shannon?"

She shook her head, her hair flying around her face then settling back in place as she stared at them through wide, blank eyes. "Nothing," she mumbled through stiff lips. Her mouth was dry but the dizzy feeling was passing.

"Don't lie, Shannon," Jeff commanded. "You remembered something. What!"

"Nothing, I tell you." Her voice was stronger but still lacking conviction. She had seen something and what she saw terrified her. She couldn't, *wouldn't* tell them.

Surely it was only a daytime nightmare, a reaction to the residue of medication or the aftereffects of the hypothermia. The picture had to be a figment of her imagination, but the terror was all too real.

By slow, sharp, painful degrees she was remembering. The crimson rose of her dreams was blood, bright and red. As though standing outside herself, she'd seen her hand covered with warm, fresh blood.

Somewhere in that mixed-up picture in her head she'd also seen herself frantically wiping the sticky stuff on the front of her brown suede sheepskin coat. Then, sickened by the sweet, tinny odor, she'd ripped the coat off and thrown it on the freezing ground.

"Shannon, don't lie to me," Jeff warned.

She felt a wave of fear roll over her, a fear not of the unknown but for herself. They were crowding her with their questions and their presence.

Shannon ducked her head, buying time to steady herself. She relaxed her white-knuckled grip on the sheets and took several shallow breaths. They must never know what she'd seen, not until she had remembered everything. "Please, I'm tired."

"Okay, that's enough, Jeff."

Ash's tone left little doubt that this time if Jeff didn't obey he would more than likely be thrown out of the house head first. Jeff threw up his hands and smiled. "I'm sorry if I've upset you, Shannon. Ash, may I see you for a moment?"

Outside the bedroom Jeff shook out a cigarette and offered one to Ash. He grinned at his friend's hesitation then watched as Ash stuffed his fingers into the tight pockets of his jeans. "This is really a mess and the only way to clear it up is for me to take a few of your men and go up to Devil's Leap. A day and a half up, a day and a half back. One way or the other, we should know in a couple of days what happened.''

Ash turned and walked down the stairs, wondering as he went why he was so uneasy about the situation. It was obvious to him that Shannon had remembered something, but what? And why wouldn't she tell them what it was? He'd known her far too long not to realize that she was terrified. But why?

CHAPTER SEVEN

JEFF SETTLED his Stetson firmly on his head and squinted at the sun as he rounded the front of his car. The day promised to be a warm one despite the wet ground. Hopefully spring in all its capriciousness had decided to settle in for good and his trip up the mountain would be an easy one.

"Sheriff. Jeffery!"

The voice automatically made him tense. His head snapped around and he had to force away a grimace of displeasure. Touching the tip of his hat, he said, "Mrs. Bartlet."

Paula stepped off the porch, her hand jerking up to shield her red, sensitive eyes from the sun. She patted the top of her head, found the sunglasses there and quickly pulled them into place. "How are you, Jeffery?"

"Fine, ma'am."

"Is it true the D.A. wants to file murder charges against Shannon?"

"Possibly." His mouth tightened, damning small towns and the way talk spread. But unlike most gossip, he knew where this story had originated. Hamilton Watts was laying the groundwork and setting the wheels in motion for his political career.

"Closemouthed as always?"

"There's nothing to tell. Speculation could be dangerous and destructive at this point."

"Jeff, this—" she swept a shaky hand around in a wide arc "—this is my home. Ash is my family. I'm worried, that's all."

"I understand." But he didn't, not really. Paula had never concerned herself about anyone unless it had a direct effect on her own well-being or Jeri's.

Exasperated, Paula stuffed her hands in the pockets of her apple-red leather bomber jacket. "I'm protective with those I love, maybe overly so."

He snorted rudely, making no attempt to hide his reaction to her statement.

"Just tell me, can the D.A. make charges against Shannon stick? Is there enough evidence?"

"There's no evidence, not until we find Dean's body."

What little color was left in her pale face drained completely away. She swayed, and Jeff grabbed her arm to steady her, but she quickly shook off his hand and asked, "Then you believe he's dead?"

"Maybe."

"You're going up the mountain, aren't you?"

"Yes, ma'am." He turned to leave, but Paula reached out and touched his arm, stopping him. An awkward silence as thick as honey spread between them; one Jeff refused to bridge. He waited, watching, careful to appear as calm as possible. The lady looked rattled, ready to shatter into a million pieces, and he wondered why.

"You don't like me very much, do you, Jeff?"

"No, ma'am. But then the feelings are mutual, aren't they?"

She waved away his question. "Because I've interfered between you and Jeri?"

"That's part of it, yes. Mainly it's the way you throw Jeri at anything in pants financially able to support you in the manner you'd prefer." Once he had started, it was like a small hole in a dam cracking little by little under the pressure. "You parade her around like a prize for your gain—never considering how she must feel or what she wants. You rule her life. And you've turned a beautiful, loving girl into an insecure, vacillating, vulnerable woman.

"When she defied you about going to Europe on another one of your manhunts, because you found out she was secretly seeing me, you decided to hurt her and me. Everything worked to your benefit, didn't it? When your friend Helen Pressman told you she saw me leaving Sally Roland's place at two in the morning, you told Jeri—convinced her I was there because we were having an affair. Even after you knew the truth, that I was at her house because her brother in New York had been killed in a car accident and they couldn't reach her, you lied. You twisted the events to suit your purposes. But the real tragedy, the one that makes me sick to my stomach, is the way you undermined her self-respect and confidence by telling her she's not woman enough to hold the interest of a man like me." He would have liked nothing more than to strangle the woman, but he took a deep breath and forced himself to calm down.

Paula's lips twisted in a parody of a smile. A light breeze ruffled her hair and she shivered, clutching her jacket closer. "At least you're honest. Jeff, I...I'm sorry for the trouble I've caused."

His mouth dropped open and if the wind had been any stronger, he thought, it would have knocked him over. For the first time in his life he was truly struck dumb. When he could regain the power of speech, he said, "Mrs. Bartlet, what are you up to?"

"You have every right to be suspicious." She smiled sadly up at him. "You'll take care of her, won't you?"

"Yes."

"She does love you, Jeff. She's just so very young in so many ways, and so mixed up right now. But you mustn't judge her too harshly. Everything she is, or has done, was for me. As you say, I pushed, lied, bullied and threatened her. Jeri needs you. And later," she said crisply, "she'll need you even more."

He watched her walk away, feeling as if he'd just stumbled through a field of land mines unscathed. Now what the hell was going on! He was too dumbfounded to figure out the Machiavellian tactics of that woman.

Instead of leaving, he set out to find Jeri, knowing she was more than likely in the foaling barn with the new arrivals. The sweet scent of fresh-spread hay and the fragrant odor of leather and oats wafted over him as he entered the shadowy barn. But as he advanced, the air was spoiled by animal droppings and soiled hay raked into piles waiting to be hauled off.

Jeri sensed his presence, knew he was standing in the open stall doorway before she heard him softly call her name. Her hands resumed their task of vigorously rubbing down the damp, spindly legged colt with a towel. "If you've come to tell me what a brainless twit I am, don't. I honestly don't remember Mother telling me she'd given Shannon her medication. It was an accident." She ducked her head over her work, refusing to meet his censorious stare. She was still deeply hurt and puzzled by her mother's actions that morning.

"I'm not here to fight with you, Jeri. I'm here because I'm tired of waiting. Ever since you returned from Europe you've been avoiding me. Why? Did Paula finally succeed in finding you a rich man?"

She let the impatient animal go to its mother, balled her hands into fists around the towel and rested them on her thighs.

"Look at me, Jeri."

"No." But she did, then wished she hadn't. There was so much sadness and confusion in his soft brown eyes she wanted to cry and scream out that it wasn't her fault, she would always love him. "Do you remember all the while I chased you, for months it seemed, and you were always telling me you weren't good enough for me?"

Jeff stood stiffly waiting for the final blow he knew was coming, yet when it did, it wasn't what he'd expected. "I remember."

"Well you were wrong. *I'm* not good enough for you."

"Come on, sweetheart. You don't know what you're saying."

"Yes I do. I don't think we should see each other anymore."

"Why?"

"It doesn't matter. It's over, Jeff."

"And if I won't accept that?"

"You'll have to, because I've made up my mind, and you know how hardheaded I can be."

He took a step toward her then stopped when she shied away, came to her feet and moved to the back of the stall, putting the foal and mare between them. "This has all come about since you've returned. What happened in Europe?"

"Nothing. Now if you'll please go, I have a lot of work to do."

"Just like that! After two years of loving you I'm to walk away as if nothing happened?"

"Go away."

For the first time since he'd come upon her he noticed how troubled she appeared. Even in the dimly lit barn he could make out the bruised look around her eyes, the vacant stare that came with pain. Her hands wouldn't be still, and she'd lost weight. There was a finality in her voice, a determination in her stance that was foreign to her nature. This decision of hers had been well thought out. She was serious, so serious in fact that he knew he wouldn't be able to change her mind; her verdict for their future had been given.

She watched him go, turn his broad back on her and without a word walk away. Jeri slid down the wall, landed on her knees, doubled over and began to sob. It was for the best, she kept mumbling to herself. For Jeff's sake. He would only hate her if he found out what she had done.

A hysterical laugh passed her lips and she slapped her hand over her mouth in case someone overheard and came to investigate. Hate was too kind a word for what he would feel toward her, and she couldn't bear to see him when her mother told him what had happened. And tell him she would, when she thought the time was right to wreak havoc, or to pull her daughter back in line with her wishes.

Jeri's shoulders shook and heaved with a pain that was tearing her apart. She searched for someone to blame other than herself and realized she didn't have to go very far for a name. Shannon. Her own problems could firmly be placed at Shannon's feet. Somehow, someway, she ought to be made to pay for all the heartache she'd caused in the Bartlet family. For as long as Jeri could remember, where there was trouble, there was Shannon.

ASH ROLLED OVER in bed and angrily kicked the twisted sheets from his legs. He felt as if his eyelids had been pinned to his forehead. The tranquility of darkness, the peace of the night gave him little comfort. Out of anger and frustration he had been pushing himself to the breaking point, and his men to near desertion.

Exhaustion weighed down his body, making his muscles twitch and ache. There had been times like this before when, late at night and for no reason, he would awaken in a sweat, sensing her nearness. Then reality would jolt him fully awake and he knew sleep would never return, so he would get up. But tonight was different. She *was* near, only a few steps away.

Staying in bed had suddenly become sheer torture. His mind wouldn't allow him to relax and fall back to sleep, and seeds of doubt began to germinate in a fertile field. He had to have some answers.

Swinging his legs over the side of the bed, Ash reached for his jeans. He rolled his shoulders to loosen the sore, knotted muscles in his back. Maybe a book from the study would help take his mind off the treadmill course it had been running. But even with his destination firmly in mind, his steps changed direction and he walked through the connecting bathroom and into Shannon's room.

A full moon shone through the sheer, lacy curtains, sapping away all the color and giving everything a surrealistic quality, like an old black and white photograph. He stopped just inside the door, letting his eyes adjust to the eerie illumination, when his breath caught in the back of his throat. She'd been as restless in her sleep as he had. The sheets were tangled and twisted around her, hiding little. His mouth went dry at the sight of her smooth flesh, and a heat seemed to sing through his veins.

It angered him beyond reason to admit that after all that had happened, he still wanted her. In some way her hold on him made him weak and he hated that. Would she let him touch her?

He cursed himself. Where was all that fine morality he'd preached so pompously not so long ago? Now here he was, wanting her so much he was willing to forget everything he'd promised himself he wouldn't do.

Wasn't the way she lay in such sweet abandon an invitation? Had she deliberately not worn his shirt to sleep in, knowing he would come in to check on her during the night? His muscles tensed. He closed his eyes. God, but he ached for her. But he couldn't—wouldn't go to her. Not now. It was too late for them.

First one slow step, then another and another, and he was beside the bed looking down at Shannon. She stirred restlessly and mumbled in her sleep. "What are you dreaming about, Daffy?" he whispered. "Me?" Reaching out, he touched the instep of her foot, her toes, then he lightly trailed his fingers up her calf, to her knee, then to her thigh. She was so warm and soft and wanton in sleep.

"Do you remember the first time we made love at the line shack? As hard as I try, I can never forget that day. You were scared and sexy and so brave." He caught hold of the crumpled sheet and eased it inch by slow inch away from her body until she lay bare to his starved gaze. Blood pounded in his ears at the sight of her nakedness. Even in the strange light that shrouded the room, her skin took on a luminous quality, like crushed pearls.

She must have sensed his presence because her eyes opened. She blinked, smiled softly then rolled over onto her back. "Ash."

He stared fascinated by the catlike movements as she stretched. She was so maddeningly sensuous. There was such an aching pleasure in just watching her. Never taking his eyes from hers, he clasped the top of his jeans zipper; tooth by tooth, metal struck metal, and the sound seemed loud even to his own ears.

The feel of her flesh took him into another world, where there could only be happiness, but that illusion soon passed and the reality of where he was brought back all the anger he tried so hard to hide. Ash entwined his fingers in the thick mass of her jet-black hair and tightened his grip. "Do you want me Shannon?"

She nodded.

"Say the words. I want to hear them from your lips."

"I want you. I've always wanted you—always loved you. Just you."

"Good, because I never want you to forget this. I want it to haunt your nights and torment your days. Maybe in the years to come there will be brief times of peace, but only short periods, I hope. Something here—" he touched her bare breast just above her heart "—will never let you forget. The memory will always be there." His hand began to caress the mound of firm flesh, teasing her rosy nipple to a pert bud.

She enfolded him in her arms and for what seemed an eon he lay there, feeling her against him, sensing her needs, her love, and that enraged him. He wasn't coming to her as the young lover of years ago, but a grown man with a passionate appetite edged with hostility. His bad years far outweighed the good, and in his mind he wanted nothing but retribution.

He lowered his mouth to hers, and too many years of being alone poured into the first meeting of their lips. He took possession of her, not in gentleness, yet there was no brutality in his touch, either. His hands were both invader and owner as they moved over her body.

"Do you ever dream about us like this, Shannon?"

"Every night," she whispered. "I . . ."

He didn't want her to talk anymore, afraid of her power over him, her lies—her truths. His mouth cut off her next words as his fingers sought out all the hidden places she had once loved to be touched. But she didn't need words. He thought he could almost hear what her eyes were saying. She was as intoxicating as a fine wine, but then, he told himself, she always had been.

Her wet heat surrounded and engulfed him like a custom-made glove. She took him out of himself, making him forget his purpose. Lost! He was lost in her, lost to himself. His eyes shining like emeralds, his mouth tense, he was poised above her, his entire being braced for the moment when he would make her scream his name.

Suddenly everything changed.

He shared her excitement, the beat of her heart, her very breath. It was a moment of surrender for them both, a release after years of holding back too many emotions. They were children of the land, of nature, and their lifelong commitment to each other had been fated by someone greater than they. Time and distance had not changed that. They were one once again.

The pure perfection of their joining, the sound of his name on her lips was too much. Ash fought for control. He jerked away—and knocked his head back against the door frame.

He'd been dreaming, suspended in a world of his own making.

Sweat made a fine sheen on his bare skin as he stood there alone, fighting to regain some modicum of control. *He'd been dreaming.* He'd been making love to Shannon, but only in his head. His legs quivered with tension and his hands, when he held them out in front of him, shook. Fool! Nothing could have been that perfect . . . not even Shannon.

MORNING WAS A WELCOME SIGHT to Shannon. She opened her eyes, disoriented at first as she tried to figure out where she was. Her roaming gaze picked out the unfamiliar in the familiar room and she smiled. Her smile grew as she spotted the four Louis Vuitton suitcases piled in the middle of the braided rug. At last she was going to be able to get dressed.

Whether or not it was true that clothes made the man or woman, once she was dressed she felt like a million— better in fact than she had in weeks. Her hair was brushed into a shining cloud around her shoulders, her makeup carefully applied, expertly hiding the bruises and scratches, which had already begun to fade.

She stepped back from the full-length mirror in the bathroom and painstakingly inspected herself, her guarded gaze careful not to stare at her neck. The burnt-orange wool gabardine slacks and matching sweater gave her a much needed lift. The last touch, laboriously tied while she deliberately ignored the rainbow discolorations of her neck, was a bright yellow and orange scarf.

The only good to come from her marriage to Dean was his grandmother, Lilith, a wise old dragon with impeccable manners and an undisputed taste and style. Her knowledge of fashion, Persian, Italian and even the bourgeois American, was astounding, and her comments could be hilariously caustic. Finding her granddaughter-in-law much like herself in her younger days, Lilith had been willing to teach the urchin from Montana a few tricks of the trade. One day, Shannon kept telling Lilith, she was going to leave Dean. But Lilith could talk her into almost anything, and if she couldn't persuade her to stay with Dean with one tactic, then she wasn't above using another. A little bribery wasn't against the woman's scruples if it got her what she wanted.

Finally satisfied with her efforts, Shannon turned from her reflection and hobbled to the door, telling herself that shoes were her only concern at the moment.

A noise from the bedroom froze her hand on the knob for a second. Her breath hung in her throat as she sent up a silent prayer that her intruder be Ash. Her heart pounding, she quietly eased open the door, only to stop and draw a breath in disappointment.

"Well now, you shouldn't look so glum. I know I'm not who you hoped for but I'll have to do."

"Good morning, Bridget."

"And a fine good morning to you."

Shannon hopped over to the overstuffed chair and flopped down. "Where's Ash?"

"Himself rattled his bones out of here around dawn, muttering something about some lost cattle." Clear blue eyes, far too knowing, gave Shannon a steady glance before shifting downward. "Here now, should you be up and about?"

"I'm fine. Besides, it's time."

Bridget, now thoughtful, nodded. She took Shannon's chin in her hand and stared into her eyes. "Yes, you'll do. And you're right, it is time to take the bull by its horns and settle this mess once and for all. But wait a minute." She disappeared through the bathroom door and into Ash's room, returning with a silver-handled cane, which she handed over to Shannon. "You'll need the support, child, because it's the only help you're likely to get."

Shannon looked down at the ornate lion's head handle, then glanced back at Bridget. The senator's? It wasn't a question of previous ownership but one of permission.

"He'd be proud for you to take on his son with it. And a few whacks across that lad's backside wouldn't go amiss, either. I'll tell you, Shannon, he's as touchy as a bear just out of hibernation." Turning to leave, she added, "I'll bet Ash Bartlet hasn't slept more than a few winks since you showed up."

"Oh, dear."

"You remember, do you, what he's like when he's missed his beauty sleep?"

Shannon grinned and nodded.

"Good, then you know what to expect."

The door closed and Shannon touched the tip of the cane to her bandaged foot. She poked and thumped and wiggled her toes till her ankle began to throb a little. She hated meeting Ash with any disadvantage, but meet him she would, and this time there would be no walking away from the truth. He might never want her again, but he was going to listen to her whether he liked it or not. There were bits of the puzzle from the past that needed to be filled in, and only Ash and her grandfather could do that.

She was back.

To stay.

CHAPTER EIGHT

WITH A GREAT FEELING of relief and homecoming, Shannon wandered from room to room. The house hadn't changed. Oh, there was new upholstering in spring florals; different, rather elegant drapes that framed the sunny floor-to-ceiling windows; furniture, antiques mostly, transferred to other parts of the house and rearranged with newly acquired pieces. But the place hadn't really changed.

Shannon was a little amused as she moved through the house, realizing that in her absence she'd given Ash's home human characteristics, a personality. Glancing about, she now knew she hadn't been wrong. There was a heritage of four generations here—life, laughter, love, sadness and death—that had bequeathed the house with a heart, breath and soul.

She let her fingers glide over the cold surface of a marble-top table as she skirted the edges of an Aubusson rug in soft muted shades. The Bartlet women's collection of Dresden dolls adorned a glass, bow-front curio cabinet. A Paul Theodor van Brussel painting of flowers and fruit, signed and dated, hung on the far wall of the living room. And Anna Vaughn Bartlet's treasure, brought overland in the 1830s—a Hudson River pine fireplace mantel that held eighteenth century Lumeville lions, the bounty of one of her pirate ancestors.

She saved the study—or the senator's room, as she had called it all her life—for last, because if the house truly had a heart, it beat most strongly there.

The heavy carved door opened smoothly beneath her touch, and as it swung wide she heard the tiny telltale squeak that had been there for as long as she could remember. Some things were just meant to be, in spite of the attempts of others to prevent them. Her gaze was immediately drawn, as it had always been, to the French painting of a Sudanese warrior, the savage face so fascinating in its stillness, the skin so black it shone like polished ebony. The wickedly curved sword mounted above only added to the brutality of the painting. A pair of terra-cotta Moorish busts still rested on the Egyptian ivory inlay table. In one way or another, whether by their wandering nature or their profession of politics, the Bartlets had always been world travelers, bringing back with them some memento of their trips.

Shannon's eyes closed as she inhaled part of her past: this was her second home and she had spent so much of her time in this very room. The fragrance of the senator's cigars still inhabited the room as if he had only just left.

For a moment she was a child again, lying in front of the television with Ash and Dean on either side, a handful of popcorn suspended between the bowl and her mouth. They were hypnotized by a show on prehistoric animals and monsters that stalked through an eerie, misty land. That particular night had resulted in severe punishment for the three of them the following day. Ash had been the first to notice the manner in which the animal heads mounted on the walls seemed to be staring down at them with rather hungry expressions. She guessed she was the one who had come up with the idea that if the animals couldn't see them, they wouldn't come to life and eat them. The next few hours had been spent with her water colors painting the glassy eyes of every animal black. Of course, under the stern supervision of Bridget and the senator, the three of them spent days meticulously cleaning the paint away with Q-tips.

She was a young teenager, secreted away in her favorite overstuffed chair, with Ash and Dean hanging over the back as she read *Lady Chatterley's Lover* out loud, stopping only to gaze up disgustedly when the boys either turned beet red and made strange noises or gave a husky nervous laugh at the parts she didn't understand. So many memories.

She was a young woman, boldly facing her grandfather and the senator as Ash asked Happy first, then his father, for permission to marry her. The two old men had nearly cracked up laughing, but not before they had given Ash and her a hard time first. So many wonderful memories.

Shannon inhaled deeply once more then opened her eyes as she took careful steps farther into the room. Men! What was it in their nature that made them hang their trophies on the wall like some medal of bravery? Yet it had always been so, and she found it more barbaric than the killing itself. She loved the thrill of a hunt as much as any of them, enjoyed the challenge of tracking something wild and primitive, but long ago she'd ceased taking the fatal shot, preferring to let the creature go free. Freedom had become a precious commodity lately, something sought after and guarded jealously. She never intended to let herself be caged again.

Her ankle began to throb and she shifted her weight to the cane, still lost in her inspection of the room. When she spotted her favorite mounted animal head, she forgot the nagging pain and hobbled her way across the room. Some inept taxidermist or a man with a strange sense of humor had managed to give the vicious-looking Bengal Tiger the wrong glass eyes. They were soft, almost dewy with innocence, in direct conflict with the frozen snarl and lethal teeth. Then there was the African Lion, the king of beasts, with his thick royal mane and the silly grin that always made her laugh.

A door behind her opened then slammed shut.

"What are you doing in here?"

Shannon turned too quickly. She sucked in a breath of air then scowled at the pain that shot through her foot. Carefully edging her way to the coffee-colored leather couch, she sat down gingerly. "Hello, Jeri." She had expected the younger woman to bolt after their previous encounter.

Instead, Jeri stomped across the room and flopped down in a matching chair across from her. She propped her boots on the oak table and glared at Shannon through red swollen eyes. "I'm sorry about the mix-up with your medicine yesterday. It wasn't intentional."

"I never thought it was." Shannon grinned encouragingly, saying a silent prayer that she was going to be able to get through to at least one person in the Bartlet family. "What could you possibly gain from my demise?" She received only a glare for her efforts. With a sigh she said, "Jeri, can't we discuss the past like two grown women?"

"No." Jeri started to get up, then sat back down with a bump. "Yes."

"What's the matter, Jeri? It's not just me or the incident of the medicine, is it? You used to come to me with all your problems."

"There's nothing wrong with me," she said belligerently. "Besides, we should talk about when you plan to leave this house."

"That's very important to you, that I leave here, isn't it?"

"Yes."

Her jaw ached from clenching her teeth. "Fine, I hope to be gone in a few days. But that won't be the end of the problem. I told you earlier I wasn't leaving Bartlet and I meant it."

"Why, for heaven's sake, would you want to stay where you're not wanted?" She did get up to leave this time.

Shannon watched with angry eyes. "Sit down!" she snapped, and Jeri sat. "What happened between Ash and me is between the two of us. It's not for you to question or judge me. But the way you feel is between us, and I care enough to want to straighten it out. Jeri, I never did anything in my life to hurt you. I love you. You were always the younger sister I would never have but yearned for." Jeri burst into tears and Shannon felt helpless but decided to let her cry. Sometimes tears were as cleansing as a fresh spring rain.

Jeri struggled for control and wiped her wet cheeks with the sleeve of her blouse. "You don't know the meaning of the word *love*," she spat.

"Don't I?" Shannon's voice was soft, each syllable precise.

If Jeri had been sensitive to Shannon's intonation, she would have remembered that tone and realized she was treading on dangerous ground.

Shannon leaned back against the thick leather cushions. "What gives you the idea that I don't know anything about love?"

"It's obvious, isn't it, after what you did to the people you *supposedly* loved?"

Amber eyes, suddenly as cunning as any feline predator, narrowed on her prey. "And just what did those same people, those who *supposedly* loved me, do?"

"I . . . I don't know what you mean. You're trying to confuse me."

"No, Jeri. I'm attempting to make you see both sides of your carefully constructed story. For heaven's sake, stop acting so self-righteous. Everyone turned away from me ten years ago. Granted you were only fourteen, but damn well old enough to realize what had happened. But worse yet, my so-called loved ones completely deserted me when I needed love and understanding the most. Do you think I enjoyed being cut off from my home and life here? I felt like a leper without the disease."

"But you never came home. Nor did you ever call any of us at the ranch."

"Didn't I? Are you so sure? What if I told you my attempts . . ." She broke off with a wave of her hand. "Never mind. Jeri, do you really remember me as being so heartless? I always took up your cause when your mother was on your back. I taught you how to ride when Ash lost patience and quit." She moved forward, speaking quickly as she noticed Jeri's belligerent expression waver slightly. "I patched you up when you skinned your knees and I dried your tears." Leaning back with a soft smile, she lowered her voice, making Jeri come to her. Then, suddenly, she bent forward over the knee-high coffee table so her face was close to Jeri's. "How many times when Ash and Dean complained and yelled did I get my way and you were able to come to the movies with us? Or the café? Or to the local dances? Does that sound like the actions of a self-serving bitch?''

"No...I..." Jeri jumped to her feet and began to pace the space between the couch and the table. She stopped and spun around. "You were more a mother to me than my own. She was always leaving me here so she could go with the senator. You were always there for me. Goddammit, I worshiped you. I thought you hung the moon and the sun and could do no wrong."

"Then you found out I was human?"

"I wanted to be just like you, despite Mother's warnings. It was the first of many times I defied her. I wanted to act like you, talk like you, be funny, make people laugh like you...make everyone love me like they loved you. I loved you, damn you, and you left."

"Ahh, Jeri. You make me sound like some wise old woman. I was only seventeen and a young seventeen besides. So your idol has feet of clay. Your little girl dreams were shattered. I'm very sorry. But what about me! What about my dreams and life? You stayed here with the ones you love and who loved you. I didn't get that privilege. What about me?"

Jeri ignored the question and walked back to stand in front of Shannon. "Everything changed after you ran away and it was never the same again. Ash disappeared for weeks. Finally your grandfather had to go to Missoula and bring him home. He'd been drinking and was in terrible shape."

Shannon's eyes squeezed together for a moment. The pain of Jeri's disclosure almost took her breath away. At least now she knew part of the reason why he had never come after her. But Ash hadn't been a heavy drinker, so there was more to his long absence from the ranch. She wondered just what condition Happy had found him in.

She opened her eyes and took her hurt out on the wrong person.

"Grow up, Jeri," she snapped. "Nothing ever stays the same. Surely you know that by now. And if you don't you'd better come out of your dream world. I'm sorry, more than I can say, about the anguish I seem to have caused, but I haven't been left unscathed, either. There's a well of bitterness I have yet to overcome. If you've ever been in love, truly in love, you should know people hurt each other without meaning to. We can't—" She didn't get to finish, as Jeri burst into tears and rushed from the room.

If she had learned anything from her marriage to Dean, she'd learned to be brutally honest. She was willing to take most of the blame for the mistakes in her life, but there were some things she absolutely refused to take responsibility for. She was wrung out. If trying to convince Jeri she deserved another chance proved to be so hard, what were her chances with Ash? She almost dreaded the ordeal. Shannon laid her head back on the couch and mentally shrugged. But it was a start anyway, no matter the outcome. Little by little she would wear these people down until they were willing to at least see her side to this fiasco. This time she wasn't giving up, too much was at stake.

A cool breeze fluttered the edges of the curtains and she turned her head, gazing out the window toward the buildings beyond. The sun played tricks before her eyes, sending a false rainbow of colors dancing across the ground like so many fireflies.

The wind began to howl...

Suddenly she was cold, colder than she had ever been in her life, and colder still as the wind of her dreams

seemed to wrap harsh words around her like a smothering blanket.

*"Do you think Ash will want you if you leave me? It's
taken me ten years, but I've fixed it so he never will."*

Shannon tore her eyes away from the window and
buried her face in her hands. She was suffocating and
had to get out of the room. Surging to her feet, she
grabbed the edge of the couch and her cane as a fierce
shaft of pain traveled up her leg, but it didn't stop her
and she continued to hobble out of the room. She
needed to get outside and let the sun warm her bones and
the clean Montana air wash away the residue of her
fears.

The kitchen smelled of apples and cinnamon. "Bridget, are there some rubber boots around here that will fit
me? I'm sure the ground out around the barn is still
muddy."

"Lands, yes. Look in the mudroom. There's enough
galoshes to shoe an army, any size too." She turned away
from a big black cast-iron pot, laid the wooden spoon
down and wiped her hands on her apron. "But what
about your ankle?"

"I'll make out."

Bridget grinned. "That you will." Then she turned
back to the stove and allowed Shannon to help herself.

It took a few experimental steps before she got the
hang of having the oversized rubber boots on, especially since she had to stuff the one on her sore ankle
with a few extra socks she found on top of the dryer. As
she was on the way out the back door her gaze fell on the
wall telephone. Before she could change her mind, she
reached up, snatched the receiver down and dialed her
home. Her heart suddenly felt like an overworked pump,
making the blood pound in her ear as she counted each

endless lonely ring, hoping that her grandfather wouldn't answer, then praying fervently he would.

After the sixth ring, just as she was about to hang up, a gruff voice growled, "Hello." She didn't know what she expected, a frail quiver that would prove he had suffered as much as she. But the sound of his voice, healthy, unchanged, both angered and tore her apart. She couldn't say anything; her lips moved, but nothing came out. Finally, ashamed and disgusted, she quietly hung up.

A SWEET BREATH of air caressed her face and she raised it to the sun as prehistoric man must have done when he crawled out of his dark cave. At least that's the way she felt, as if the past was a black cavern and she was finally at the end of the long tunnel, ready to step once more into the light.

Her walk to the barn would have been easier, she chuckled to herself, if she had had a skateboard to rest her injured foot on. She could just see Ash's face as she came gliding in. She hop-stepped her way through the door then stopped, letting her eyes become accustomed to the gloom. After a few minutes, tuned in to the noises going on around her, she managed to separate the low-pitched male voices from the stomping, snorting, chomping and thumping of the horses, and she followed the human sounds. She slowed her uneven steps now and then to admire the occupants of the stalls as she passed.

The horses' whinnies alerted the two boys that they were no longer alone and were about to be caught goofing off. Without looking up they set their rakes to work on the pile of dirty hay they were cleaning from the empty stall.

Shannon's attention turned from the boys to the beautiful chestnut mare tied to a nearby post. When the animal stamped nervously then snorted for attention, Shannon's eyes narrowed. "What's her name?" She glanced over, recognizing the young man who had brought coffee to the tent after her rescue. "Bob, isn't it?"

"Right. And this—" he poked the boy next to him in the ribs with a sharp elbow "—this is my brother, Cal."

"Hi." Unlike his brother, who had a bold way of gazing at Shannon, he ducked his head and studied the ground between his feet.

"Cal . . ."

His head popped up like a slice of bread from a toaster, his cheeks red.

"What's her name?" Shannon asked.

"Daffy," he told her. "Sort of a weird name for a pretty thing like that, but the boss named her." His expression spoke volumes about the boss's choice.

If someone had torn out her heart, it wouldn't have affected her as much as hearing the name of the horse. That Ash would give the animal her nickname—maybe there was more of a chance for them than she thought. Her fingers shook as she ran them over the horse's warm slick chestnut coat. With sure, knowledgeable hands, she felt along the fragile-looking front leg. A quick turn put her sideways to Daffy, her shoulder pressing against the animal. "Here, hold this." She handed Bob her cane. "Cal, grip my shoulder and keep me steady."

"Mrs. Wayne—I don't think . . . Mrs. Wayne, what are you doing?"

"Shannon, please." She lifted the horse's hoof, studied the frog and nail, then probed the muscles along the long fine leg. "Mrs. Wayne makes me sound like an old woman. You need to wrap this leg and you'd better get someone to trim this right front hoof back some." She released the horse's leg and leaned away, using Cal's forearm to hop over to an open stall gate. "You might tell Ash or Tom that a lighter shoe with a reinforced toe plate would solve the problem with her limping."

Bob and Cal stared at her for a long moment. It was Bob who finally broke the silence, his awe making his voice squeak. "Happy—Mr. Reed—uh, your grandfather..."

"I know who he is, go on."

Bob reddened.

Cal grinned.

"Yeah, well your grandfather said the very same thing. How come you know what's wrong with her, too?"

She smiled, enjoying their loss of cool and the open admiration. "Runs in the family, I guess." From the half-open stall door across from her, a magnificent black horse with intelligent eyes arched its head out toward her. A soft breath whispered over her cheek. Mesmerized, Shannon took a step forward, only to have her way blocked by Bob and Cal. A little nonplussed at their sudden protectiveness, she asked, "And who is this beauty?"

"That's The Shadow. The boss's uncle in Kentucky shipped him up here for your grandfather to work with, but Mr. Reed didn't have the space to board him, so Ash is letting him stay here."

"I see." Actually, she saw more than they wanted her to. They'd obviously heard about her checkered past and were protecting The Shadow from her. She got a firm grip on her cane and began walking away, then stopped, turned and gave the two rather shamefaced boys a glacial stare. "One dead horse does not a horse killer make."

She left them, her anger making her reckless in her movements. When her ankle protested, and the tip of the cane persisted in getting stuck in the soft wet ground, she slowed down, realizing she had come farther than she'd originally planned. Interest in the large greenhouse off to one side of the barn and the impressive arrangement of stock pens to her left overrode caution, however. Carefully testing the muddy ground, she pushed open the first gate she came to.

She hobbled around slowly, studying the cattle behind the fence, moving from enclosure to enclosure, dutifully closing each gate securely behind her as she made her way through the maze of walkways between the pens. Finally coming to a wide open, empty arena, she rested her back against the wood rail, lifted her sore ankle and stared off dreamily to the snowcapped mountain peaks.

It was the sound of Ash's voice yelling her name that startled her out of her daydream. She straightened away from the fence post, spotted him running toward the arena and knew something was terribly wrong. As if in slow motion she heard a snort and grunt behind her and spun around. Through the yawning gate trotted the biggest, blackest, meanest looking bull she had ever seen.

Animal and human seemed to spot each other at the same instant. She felt a sick chill ripple her insides as angry, fathomless black eyes met frightened amber ones. Shannon couldn't decide who was the most surprised. But she didn't wait around to find out what his reaction was going to be. With the agility of a cat and total disregard for her injury, she dropped the cane, grabbed the top railing of the fence and vaulted over, landing on the other side with enough force to knock the breath out of her.

When she opened her eyes she found herself looking up into three sets of worried gazes. Bob and Cal had reached her at the same time as Ash, and it was into Ash's angry glare that she smiled. "Hi. I was looking for you."

Her words and the fact that she was unhurt set Ash off. He bellowed down at her. "Have you forgotten the cardinal rule of ranch life about never leaving a gate open?"

"I didn't." She could feel the wetness from the ground beginning to soak through her clothes and she squirmed.

Ash wasn't in the mood to listen. He glanced up at the two boys and bellowed with more force than anger, "Why did you let her wander around here alone?"

"Would someone help me up?"

"And *where* the bloody hell is Paula?"

"I'd like to get up now."

"I found her horse left standing, lathered and winded by the corner of the barn."

Within the circle of the men's legs, Shannon raised herself up on her elbows. She was about to climb to her knees when another pair of legs joined them. She gazed up at Paula, feeling an absolute fool, then, realizing she wasn't going to get any help just yet, rested back on her arms to wait.

Paula squatted down beside Shannon. "Are you hurt?"

"No, but I'd like to get up."

Ash interrupted. "What do you mean leaving your horse in that condition?"

Paula stood and faced Ash without offering to help Shannon. "It was only for a few minutes, Ash. I planned to walk him, but if you must know I needed to go to the washroom."

Shannon tugged on Ash's jeans and held out her hand. "If you don't mind, it's getting cold down here."

"Well for God's sake, why didn't you say so?"

This was not going to be one of her better days. "I've tried about three times."

Ash took hold of her hand and pulled her to her feet. Then remembering her ankle, he shifted his hold under her arms. His fingers sunk into caked mud. With Shannon protesting, he scooped her into his arms. "You're a mess."

She stopped objecting to his rough treatment the moment she was in his arms. After all, no matter the circumstances, this was where she had longed to be. Wrapping her arms around his neck, she smiled sweetly. "Am I a jinx or is this place proving to be a little too dangerous for me?" Ash eyed her stonily. "I didn't leave the gate open." He snorted, not unlike the bull, and her smile grew. Ash was uncomfortable and nervous with her so close. She adjusted her hold to the sway of his walk. "Is that beast as furious as he looks?"

"He's a breeder, Shannon, and stays ready about ninety percent of the time. He's never hurt anyone, but when we have him penned for mounting, people tend to do the intelligent thing and stay clear."

She wanted to touch him, and without thinking she began to play with the hair at the back of his head. "He's a magnificent animal." Her gaze had wandered from the side of his clenched jaw to the nape of his neck. She remembered one of his favorite erotic spots and wished she had the temerity to kiss the soft skin just below his shirt collar. She closed her eyes on the delicious thoughts, then was jolted back to reality when they reached the back door of the ranch house and Ash's hold loosened as he started to set her down.

Shannon tightened her grip around his neck, making Ash turn his head. With their faces only inches apart, she asked, "Are you ever going to talk to me?"

"What could we possibly have to say?" He tried to set her down, but her arms only clamped tighter around his neck. "You're going to strangle me."

"Good! Ash, you know as well as I do that we have to talk about the past to put it to rest. I'm tired of the pain and I think you are, too."

He wanted to march her into the house, up the stairs and into the bedroom, but he didn't want to hear what she had to say. He'd played the wronged man to perfection and with an arrogance that was beginning to wear thin. He wore his wounded pride like a medal, a badge of courage. He was the victim after all. For the past few days it had been easier to be an emotional coward than to admit his pride had been his downfall. She was right, it was way past the time to talk.

"Let go, Shannon, you need to get cleaned up."

"A little Montana mud and manure won't hurt me."

He smiled. "But you smell."

"And you're evading the issue." She let go of her hold on him and was set on her feet.

"I guess I am and maybe I've fought it as long as I can. You win, Shannon. We'll have that talk tonight, but don't expect much."

"I've learned never to expect anything, Ash." He opened the door and motioned for her to go on in. She knew he was watching her struggle but didn't offer to help. "I dropped your father's cane back in the pen. Will you get it for me?" When only silence met her request, she held on to the wall and turned her head to find him staring at her, his expression pensive and troubled. "What's the matter, Ash?"

"Do you love him?"

"No!"

"Did you ever?"

"I hate him. My feelings have never changed from the moment Dean took me away from here till now."

Ash's grip on the door tightened, his fingers white to the bone. "Then why did you stay with him?"

She turned away so he couldn't see the wound his question had opened up. "Because you didn't want me back, because you didn't love me."

Ash watched her go, wondering for the millionth time in the last few hours if he could have been so wrong about what had happened. His own shortcomings were hard to face, but one major question kept nagging him lately. Why hadn't he gone after her ten years ago?

CHAPTER NINE

SHE FELT LIKE A CRANE wobbling on one leg. Worse, she resembled a peg-legged pirate when she tried to walk. Still, the prospect of making an ass of herself and falling flat on her face didn't deter her.

After so many years, Shannon wanted Ash to see her poised and elegant, not the ragamuffin she'd usually been. She wanted to appear sophisticated, polished, completely different from the way he remembered her. But how, she wondered, could she manage it with a high heel on one foot and a fuzzy pink slipper on the other? Even her slow hobble had to be reduced to a snail's pace, but worse was the drunken sideways lurch she was forced to take with each step.

She called herself all kinds of a fool as she perched on the end of the couch, waiting for the others to join her in the library for pre-dinner drinks. With a nervous hand she smoothed out the folds of the black wool jersey dress, then pulled at the high mandarin collar of the matching bolero jacket. The collar hid her neck, and her carefully applied makeup covered her bruised and scratched face enough that she felt comfortable.

When she heard the rumble of Ash's voice she picked up the cane that had suddenly appeared in her room while she was taking a bath and folded both hands over the silver head, poised and waiting like any well-bred lady. As his footsteps came closer she glanced down for a quick once-over, saw her pink slipper sticking out like a sore thumb and hastily wrapped it behind her other leg.

She was so busy arranging herself she missed Ash's sudden halt and the way his hungry gaze devoured her until he got command of his wayward senses.

"You look nice."

A first compliment. Shannon looked up and smiled, but the smile seemed to freeze at the corners, making her mouth feel stiff and unnatural. There was a stinging sensation behind her eyes as she gazed at him. For as long as she could remember there had always been a rule in the Bartlet household. No one showed up in jeans and boots at the evening meal. It was a special time of day and everyone adhered to the practice.

Ash was dressed in a navy-blue blazer with a pale blue-and-white-striped shirt, and his rugged good looks brought a painful lump to her throat. As he stepped into the room she noticed the way his dark, front-pleated slacks managed to show off an enticingly firm behind. The fabric seemed to caress his hard muscled thighs as he walked. She tore her eyes away before he could notice the intensity of her gaze. Was it so wrong to want him so badly?

Ash moved behind the oak bar tucked in the corner of the room and with a heavy hand poured himself a drink. "Can you drink wine?"

"Afraid not. But I would like some soda with a twist of lime, if you have it."

He nodded, watching her out of the corner of his eye as he poured her drink.

The silence was suddenly strained and she became uncomfortable. She could feel him staring at her and was puzzled as to why it made her so nervous. She'd never been edgy in his company before. With an awkward movement she lurched to her feet and hobbled to the large portrait of his father. Senator Bartlet had died four years ago in a light airplane crash along with two of his constituents. They had left Bartlet and as they banked over the mountains their engine failed.

As if he'd read her thoughts, Ash said, "These mountains and their air drafts and currents are treacherous for small planes. First Dean's mother and some of her friends, then years later Dad. Thank heavens Happy's not fond of flying."

"I'm sorry about the senator. I know you must miss him."

He was beside her as she stood gazing up at the almost life-size oil painting. "I do. But he lived a rich full life." The evening sun coming from the open window caught the highlights in her hair and made it shine as if it were sprinkled with diamond dust. He caught a whiff of her perfume and the curved edges of his nostrils flared like a stallion scenting its mate. "Here," he said gruffly, handing her her drink and stepping back a pace, out of range of the heady excitement that seemed to emanate from her. "Thank you for the wreath you sent for his funeral. You should have signed it."

Shannon took the cold glass from him, and at his words her head shot up. "How did you know it was from me?"

One dark blond eyebrow rose like a question mark. "Who else would have sent a spray of gardenias? If I remember right, you and Dad were very fond of them and very few people knew of his passion for that particular flower."

She ducked her head to take a sip of the soda, not because she was thirsty, but to hide the fresh gleam of moisture in her eyes. "I'm sorry I couldn't be here."

Ash nodded and took her drink from her as she tried to walk, use the cane, and hold the glass at the same time. "Sit down. You're not going to last more than a few minutes with that ankle and that ridiculous high heel." He set down both their glasses and took hold of her arm, helping her to the couch. Once she was settled, he sat down opposite her.

They stared at each other.

"I was surprised to learn that Paula is living at the ranch. She never particularly liked it here unless the senator was here with guests." She was making small talk and he knew it and was seemingly amused by her efforts.

"After Dad's death, Paula sold the Washington brownstone and ran through the money like it was water. She's had to move back and live off the investments Dad made for her and the allowance I give her."

"I bet she hates that." Shannon smiled, knowing how Paula had always been obsessed by money.

"And me probably."

"Jeri and I had a talk earlier. She's very unhappy, Ash. Why?" She sat on the edge of the couch, her fingers gripping the head of the cane. She was as tense as a tightly strung violin string, waiting to see if he was willing to talk.

Like a hunter watching his prey, he stared at her, trying to analyze her every move as if by his close scrutiny he could figure her out. But the woman sitting across from him wasn't the girl that had left him. No longer could he read the nuances of her beautiful face the way he once had been able to do. She hid behind a calm expression, her amber eyes direct and surprisingly honest. How, after all that had happened, could she look at him with such frank openness?

He realized she was waiting for an answer to her question. "Jeri and Jeff have been in love for a couple of years now. All that time slipping around behind Paula's back has obviously taken its toll. Jeff gave her an ultimatum before she and Paula went to Europe a month ago. When they came back she was to tell her mother about them or else. As far as I know, Jeri hasn't done it yet. When she came back from her trip she'd changed. Both she and Paula seem edgy and quick to get on each other's nerves."

"You haven't tried to help or find out what's the matter?"

Ash lifted his drink to his lips then hesitated. "I learned a long time ago not to interfere in other people's lives. They're grown women capable of making their own decisions."

"That's rather hard and unfeeling, Ash."

He nodded. "It saves a lot of grief, though."

"Is that why you never tried to contact me? Did you decide it would save you a lot of suffering just to forget about me?"

"I wish I could have forgotten you." He took a gulp of his drink.

She felt her facial muscles freeze as she tried to hold on to her neutral expression. "But you couldn't?" The excitement pounding in her ears grew louder as she waited for his answer.

"No."

"Is this going to be a one-sided conversation? Do I have to drag out every one of your words. Dammit, Ash, I'm trying."

"That's what I don't understand, Shannon. Just *what* are you trying to do? What are you hoping to accomplish?"

He wasn't going to give her an inch.

"Oh, Ash. We have to talk about the past for either of us to go on with the future. Surely you can understand that?" She leaned forward eagerly when he didn't dispute her, but her next words were cut off as Paula and Jeri walked in. Disappointment marred Shannon's welcoming smile.

Ash rose and moved to the bar. "The usual, Paula?"

"Make it a double martini, please."

"Jeri?"

Jeri glanced from Ash to Shannon then back to her stepbrother. "Nothing for me, thanks." She perched on the arm of the couch beside her mother and stared down at her swinging foot. "How are you feeling, Shannon?"

"Much better."

"How about you, Paula?" Ash asked. "Are you all right?"

"I'm fine. Just a little tired."

In truth, he thought she looked like hell. Jeri didn't look much better, with dark shadows under her puffy, red-rimmed eyes. There was a gauntness to her face, as if the skin was stretched too tightly across her usually round cheeks, and her complexion was too pale. She must have felt him staring at her, because she glanced up, then away. "Are you on another one of your crazy crash diets, Jeri?" She didn't answer him, only shook her head, refusing to meet his steady gaze. Women! All three of them looked like something the cat had dragged in and dumped.

Ash rejoined them and stood over Paula, holding her drink out to her, but before handing it to her he said, "You know the rules around here about mistreating my horses. If you ever ride one into the ground like you did today, you can just stay the hell away from them."

Paula accepted the frosty, delicate-stemmed glass and slid a malicious glance at Shannon. "I'm sorry. She was determined to have her head and got away from me. It wasn't deliberate. Spirited horses do that sometimes, don't they, Shannon?"

Shannon stared at her stonily, watching as the other woman eyed her dress.

"That's a Chanel, isn't it?" She didn't give Shannon time to answer. "It must be nice to be married to a rich man who can afford to buy you designer clothes. But where are all those fabulous jewels Dean bought for you?"

The light frown that was beginning to crinkle Shannon's brow made a deeper furrow. "You must be having delusions, Paula. I don't have any jewels." She held out her bare hands. "Not even a wedding band."

Ash watched them closely, wondering what the hell was going on. They were like cats with their backs arched and claws unsheathed, waiting for the other to pounce.

Paula took a tiny sip of her drink, eyeing Shannon over the fragile rim of the crystal glass. "I find that hard to believe."

"Do you? Why?" She knew Paula had always disliked her, when she took the time to think about her at all, but the hate that now radiated from the older woman was more than puzzling, it was scary.

"Well, dear, with the opportunities that Dean's money afforded, surely you must have taken advantage of such a windfall and socked away a nice little nest egg before he left you."

"Wait just a minute. Let's get something straight. I left Dean." She stopped herself and inhaled quickly to calm down. "And just where did you hear that ludicrous story anyway?"

Paula shifted, then got up and began to walk toward the door. "I believe dinner is ready."

"Paula, you didn't answer Shannon," Ash pointed out abruptly. "Where did you hear that Dean left her?"

"Why, it was all over Paris when we were there. Wasn't it, Jeri?"

"Mother, please!"

"Wasn't it, Jeri?" She gave her daughter a hard, merciless look before she turned around and began walking away again.

"Yes, mother."

As she reached the door Paula glanced back over her shoulder and smiled sweetly. "As always, you were the talk of Paris."

Bewildered, Shannon stared after Paula then glanced at Ash to see his reaction to his stepmother's lies, but his expression told her little. She slowly stood, using the cane to get her balance. Something strange was going on here, but she couldn't put her finger on what it was.

Ash took a firm grip on her arm. "Don't mind Paula, it's sour grapes more than likely."

"No, I think it's much more than that. She hates me, Ash. Why? I never did anything to her."

He shrugged, then stopped their slow, ponderous process to the door. "Take off that damn high heel and that silly slipper before you fall and kill yourself."

He was so close she could feel the heat from his body. A wave of emotions washed over her all at once and she could only gaze up at him for a second, lost in another time when life was full of love.

Ash shook his head, squatted down and pulled off the offending shoes.

She could only smile stupidly at the back of his head.

DINNER WAS A DISASTER.

As soon as she could politely excuse herself, Shannon retreated to the library, knowing Ash would soon follow. This was his sanctuary after all, and she wasn't through with him yet. Closemouthed and reluctant to broach the past he might be, but she couldn't leave his home without some hope of forgiveness. And leave she must, as soon as possible. For the first time in her life, she didn't feel safe here.

There was no reasonable explanation for her fears, yet some inner voice kept nagging at the back of her mind that she needed to be wary, on guard. The tension in the house was more than just emotional strain, and she felt herself physically threatened.

But why, and by whom? Granted, after ten years people's attitudes toward her had changed. Jeri obviously despised her. And Paula.... Shannon couldn't figure out why her instincts screamed warnings of danger every time the woman looked at her.

And Ash?

Surely he didn't hate her so much that he would want to harm her?

A light shiver ran over her skin and she shuddered. She rubbed her arms briskly to ward off the chill her disturbing thoughts had caused and leaned back into the comforting softness of the glove-leather couch.

Maybe it was all her imagination. Enough had happened to her lately to warrant the suspicions. Perhaps

Dean had warped her mind and destroyed any trust she had left for the human race; he'd certainly tried hard enough.

Thoughts of her husband sent another chill up her spine. Why had he been so insistent, almost to the point of physical violence, that she come to Montana with him, then leave, knowing she intended to divorce him, knowing how she felt about Ash? Who could figure Dean out? He'd left her stranded before then shown up with no explanations. Then again, she'd never asked for any, either. Not for a minute did she believe he was dead. No, she wouldn't allow herself to even think along those lines again. Dean would turn up, eventually.

When the sound of the library door opening reached her, she stiffened, her head whipping around in dread.

"You can wipe that harried expression off your face, it's only me." Bridget tapped the door shut with her foot and carried the heavy laden tray, loaded with a big cof-feepot, plates with huge slices of pie and two coffee cups, to the desk and set it down. She saw Shannon eyeing the pie and grinned. "You hardly touched your dinner. I figured even with all that fancy French food you're used to you still might be partial to my coconut cream pie."

"You're right, and there's not a chef in the world that can match yours."

"Go on now," Bridget said gruffly, but beamed at the praise. "Himself left orders that the two of you were not to be disturbed." She winked, her bright blue eyes twin-kling like diamonds. "Put a kink in the tail of two busybodies, I can tell you." She walked over to Shan-non, giving her a hard searching look, then nodded her approval and patted her shoulder tenderly. "You get that boy straightened out."

"I'll try." The affection shown her brought a lump to Shannon's throat. "But he seems dead set against anything I might have to say."

"Pooh. Just bat those long eyelashes at him a few times. Men are fools."

"Not Ash."

Bridget snorted. "Pigheaded just like his daddy and stubborn as a mule. He'll listen. But if he gives you any trouble you just call Bridget. I'll hog-tie the lad to a chair so he'll have to hear you out. I've done it before—when he was a youngster, mind you, and I needed to get something through that thick head of his. He'll listen or I'll know the reason why."

They were both laughing at the prospect of tying Ash to a chair. Shannon even considered including it among her other options when he strolled in.

Ash missed a step at the sound of Shannon's unrestrained laughter. She had a delicious laugh, low and throaty, and he'd forgotten how it affected him. His jaw hardened and his eyes changed hue, darkening to a deep forest green. "Thank you for the coffee, Bridget. Good evening."

"Don't you get high-handed with me. I used to change your dirty diapers and spank your bare bottom, young man."

The door slammed on his housekeeper's last words, leaving Ash to stare after her. He shrugged, knowing defeat when he faced it, and walked over to the desk. He poured coffee into two cups, then picked up Shannon's to take to her.

She didn't really want the coffee but knew it would at least bring him close to her. She wasn't surprised when he handed the cup to her then retreated behind the desk to sit down. Sighing inwardly, she wondered why he had

to make it so hard for her. But she wasn't going to give
him time to build up his defenses any more than he'd al
ready done. She'd carried a load of guilt on her shoul
ders long enough. It was time to jump right in.

"There's something I must do first off, Ash, and
that's to apologize for Ashland's Fire. You must know
I loved that horse and would never have hurt him for the
world?" She waited, praying he was now ready to talk
about the past.

"What possessed you to ride him?"

"Dean." It was the simple truth, and though ashamed
of her confession, she locked gazes with him. "He dared
me."

"Oh, hell, Shannon."

"Come on, Ash, don't give me that holier-than-thou
look."

"But a goddamn dare. You ran that animal into the
ground on a *dare*. You killed him on a thoughtless
whim?"

The disgust on his face brought her to her feet. She
hobbled to the desk, planted her palms on the cool
smooth wood and leaned forward. "Thoughtless, yes.
A whim? Never! A dare, Ash. You remember how I
was? How we all were? No challenge too great, no fear
impossible. Bravery in the face of death—or adults.
Never back down. One for all—all for one. Three rebels
to the end. That was *our* motto, yours, mine and Dean's.
Surely you haven't forgotten? They were your words,
you came up with them and made us memorize them.
You were always daring me to do stupid and even dan
gerous things too. We were just kids, for heaven's sake.
Dammit, you took delight in daring me because you
knew I'd do it. Why should Dean be any different? He

wanted to be you. He wanted everything you had. He wanted me—and you let him take me.''

Ash shoved the chair back and surged to his feet. ''You left with him.''

Now she was getting somewhere. ''But not until you turned your back on me. You, my grandfather—everyone. You called me names that day I'll never forget.'' She still heard them in her dreams. They had haunted her. ''I didn't leave with Dean. He took me away. There's a big difference.''

''You're splitting hairs.''

''The hell I am.''

''What happened that day?''

''I never, ever loved Dean, Ash.''

A muscle knotted along his jaw and he sat back down, trying to calm the sudden urge to reach out and throttle her. ''I don't want to hear about your life with Dean, not yet. I want to know what happened the day I had to shoot Ashland's Fire because you rode him into the ground and he broke two legs. How did it happen?''

Shannon sagged against the desk for a moment then positioned herself on the edge. The pain of her memories made her close her eyes. This time she wasn't going to be able to push them away. She was going to have to face Ash with her own guilt.

He was watching, waiting.

Her eyes opened and she braced herself. Was he willing to hear and accept the truth of her words? Would he be unable to understand and forgive? How could she tell him what had happened when she still wasn't sure herself?

She had been so happy that day ten years ago. She and Ash were to be married. The only thing that had marred her morning was learning that Dean had come back from France earlier than he was supposed to. She knew there was going to be trouble when he found out that she was in love with Ash. He'd made it clear when he realized Ash was in love with her that he wanted her, too.

There had been a horrible scene before he left to join his father in Paris, one she'd never told Ash about. She was sure if he'd known he would have killed Dean. She had been down by the creek when Dean had found her and almost raped her. If it hadn't been for a handy rock that she applied to the side of his head she never would have been able to stop him. But she'd managed to get away. The next day he was gone.

But he was back, contrite when he realized she was nervous in his company. He'd made her believe he was happy for her and Ash. Deep down she'd known he wasn't.

She should have heeded her instincts.

"Why didn't you tell me he'd attacked you?"

Shannon lifted her head, stunned by his question. She hadn't realized she'd been speaking her thoughts out loud. "There had already been enough arguments and fights between the two of you. We were supposed to be friends—blood brothers, remember? What good would it have done? The only thing he hurt was my pride, and scared me a little."

Ash tried to control the slight tremble of rage that shook his hands by making a fist around the coffee cup. When he realized the delicate porcelain was in danger of breaking, he loosened his grip. "Go on. He dared you to ride Ashland's Fire?"

There was no compassion in his unrelenting stare, no understanding, only bitterness. "He'd ridden over to the Bar B on Dictator and challenged me to a race on Ashland's Fire." She shook her head. "Ash, I don't know what happened. One moment I was in the lead, laughing back at him, then suddenly he was beside me." Never as long as she lived would she be able to explain the expression on Dean's face, the utter joy.

"He was yelling at me, but I couldn't hear his words, the wind kept snatching them away. Then Ashland's Fire was bucking, making wild screeching, snorting noises and was totally out of control. The next thing I was airborne. I must have been knocked crazy for a moment because when I got my breath back and realized I was okay, I heard that horrible screaming. As God is my witness, Ash, I never meant anything to happen to Ashland's Fire. I loved that horse and knew what hopes you and your uncle had for him."

She sat waiting for a sigh, contempt, understanding, anything. With each passing, silent second she waited, thinking she would scream. If only he'd just look at her and see the truth in her eyes. "Say something, anything."

"Why did you leave?" He raised his gaze to hers. "Why didn't you ever try to come home or contact your grandfather or me? Why the hell did you marry him if you didn't love him?"

"Why didn't you come after me?" she shot back, asking the one question that had always plagued her through the years.

Ash pushed the desk chair back. What surprised him was that her question was the very one he dreaded most of all. Jeff had pointed out to him that they'd *all* blown everything out of proportion over the years and he was right, he could see it now. He'd let his pride get in the way and deserved part of the blame. He, her grandfather—everyone had been too quick to judge Shannon. Pride was a lonely companion, and a poor substitute for love. His shame ran like a deep current, cold and unending. "I want to hear why you stayed with him when you so obviously didn't want to."

Shannon scooted around a little closer to where he sat, smiling to herself when she saw him move a fraction of an inch away. She doubted he was even conscious of the withdrawal, but it gave her hope that her nearness disturbed him.

"Think, Ash. I was hurt, confused and scared—and worse yet, alone. Everyone had turned against me. In the midst of everything else that was going on right before you shot Ashland's Fire, Happy told me I wasn't his blood kin if I could so thoughtlessly do what I'd done. In all my life and all the trouble I'd gotten into, I'd never seen him so angry. He told me to get out of his sight and his house. Then you started in on me."

Ash watched as she fanned shaky fingers through her hair. The lamplight caught the jet-black strands, absorbing the light and making them sparkle like rain drops captured by the sun. The pull of her dress across her breasts emphasized their firm fullness, and the taut nipples were visible through the supple material. One shapely leg in sheer black silk swung entirely too close to his hand.

"I was numb with hurt, and before I realized what was happening Dean dragged me back to Happy's, packed some clothes and found my passport." She noticed the way he was staring at her and stumbled over her next words. "The—the next thing I knew I was on an airplane heading for Paris without any financial means of returning home."

"You could have called or written." Her toenails were painted a seductive shade of pink.

Shannon leaned forward, revealing a deep cleavage. "I have my share of pride too, Ash. I was waiting for you to either call me or come get me. When weeks went by without any word from you or Happy, I swallowed my pride and wrote to both of you."

He tore his gaze from her breast and cursed himself as a weak fool. Anger laced his voice as he pushed a little farther away from her. "Wait a damn moment. I was told you married Dean within a few days after you got to Paris. And if you'd written, as you now say you did, why didn't I get your letters?"

Shannon inched a little closer. "I'm not a liar. I wrote to you and Happy. I don't know your sources, but I'd been in Paris five months before I married Dean. I was waiting for you, damn you. Where were you?"

"I never received your letters." He was shouting at her and fought to regain some semblance of his earlier composure.

"I know."

Damn her. He felt the quickening of his senses, his anger fading.

"Just hear me out, Ash. Please."

He wanted her, but he didn't want to love her. Loving Shannon was too painful. The glow in her amber eyes made him realize she knew she was getting to him, and that inflamed his anger.

"Every day for weeks I wrote you and Happy." She remembered the pain of those endless hours, waiting for word that never came. Dean and his grandmother, Lilith, were putting the pressure on me to marry since I'd heard nothing from home. Dean was her only grandchild and Lilith spoiled him rotten. She was his mentor and a worthy opponent. After months of being hounded day and night and never a word from you, I simply gave up.''

Shannon sat up, suddenly feeling guilty at using his hunger for her as a weapon. ''Ash, it wasn't until after Dean and I were married that I found all the letters he and his grandmother were supposed to be mailing for me.'' She couldn't tell him, not yet, that that was the day her contempt for Dean had turned to hate and she deliberately made his life the living hell he'd made hers. ''At that point I didn't care if I had to walk the streets to get money to come home. I was going to divorce him. Lilith was appalled at the thought of another divorce in her family and probably a little ashamed when she realized how she'd been used by Dean.

''She convinced me that going home wasn't the answer. I guess you could say I let her bribe me. After all, I had no place to go. Dean had made it clear if I tried to leave him he would fight it and cause such a scandal that I would never be able to face anyone in the whole state of Montana. Lilith and I made a pact, a deal. She knew how much I wanted to be a veterinarian, and if I stuck with Dean, she agreed to finance my education.''

''You stayed for money?''

His bitter, incredulous tone made her wince inwardly, but that was exactly what she'd done. Yet how could she ever explain or make him understand how alone and miserable she'd been? The offer to make something of herself, to regain her self-esteem, to eventually be free of Dean was too tempting to pass up. ''For money? No! For my independence, yes. Ash, I never took anything from Dean if I could help it. Lilith bought my clothes, paid for my education and gave me pocket money until I got a part-time job with a local vet while I went to school.''

She reached out and gently cupped his cheek. When he didn't move away from her touch, her thumb caressed the corner of his mouth. "Was my sin so great? We were so young, Ash. The land and our families had protected us from the evils of the world. We were so full of false pride. Haven't we hurt each other enough?" She slipped off the edge of the desk, her hand never leaving his face, and as she moved toward him, he rose to his feet.

Mesmerized by the smoky lights in her eyes, the shadows of promise that made them sparkle and her lips so close, so vulnerable, he felt weak with wanting her. Without realizing what he was doing, his mouth clamped down on hers like a drowning man seeking the sustenance of life. His arms went around her and he jerked her to him roughly.

She was home at last.

Ten years of loneliness—ten years of loving him—were transmitted in that one kiss. She let his anger abate, absorbing it with tenderness until his lips softened and he let passion consume them. She was free and wild with love. When she felt him pull away she wanted to cry at the loss. "Say you forgive me," she whispered against his lips. "There was never a day that passed that I didn't remember you. Never a night that I didn't think of you and wish I was in your arms."

Ash's fingers tangled in her hair, tightening until they nearly brought tears to her eyes, then slowly he pulled her head back so he could peer down into her overbright eyes. "Never did a night go by that I didn't visualize you with him," he said, his voice gruff with pain and jealousy. "In his arms, kissing his mouth, lying beside him in sleep. Were your dreams peaceful, Shannon? Did you take him to heaven as you did me?"

"Oh, Ash. No! Listen to me. Please never think..."
She tried to tighten her arms around him. "Don't do this
to us. I love you...I want you."

"No."

He pushed her away so fast that she had to grab the
edges of the desk to keep from falling.

"I've done many things over the past ten years that
I'm not particularly proud of. But this, Shannon?" He
shook his head and moved farther away from her.
"You're a married woman and I won't have this on my
conscience. I've listened to your explanations, I believe
you, but I don't want you, not this way." He wanted her
so badly he hurt.

"You believe me, but do you forgive me?"

He knew she'd misread his silence when she flinched.
But he needed time to think, to be alone with his own
guilt before he admitted it to her. He could see by her
angry expression that he wasn't likely to get the chance.
Sooner or later she would ask the one question he'd been
afraid of, dreaded from the moment she returned. Then
he would have to face his own shame.

"I asked you a couple of times earlier and you never
answered me. Why didn't you come after me? Where
were you, Ash, when I needed you? What else could
possibly have happened to make you turn your back on
me?"

A muscle worked spasmodically in his cheek. "I was
told you were sleeping with Dean."

The breath she sucked in almost strangled her, and it
took a second before she could regain her voice. "Who
told you?"

"Dean."

"After all that had happened between us in our
childhood, all the lies he told, the maneuvering he did to

get his way, you believed him? Knowing that he wanted everything you had, including me, you believed him?"

"Yes."

As if the hand attached to her arm belonged to someone else, she watched it swing up and slap Ash across the face. "How could you ever believe that of me? Anything else I might have been able to accept, but not that, never that."

She left him there with her hand print on his cheek and her heart feeling as if it were shattered into a million pieces.

Ash's eyes followed her awkward steps until the library door slammed shut. He rose, walked to the bar, poured himself a double bourbon with a steady hand then gulped it down. He wished he had it all to do over again. He would have lied to save her the pain he saw in her eyes. Damn the arrogance and insecurities of youth. She'd asked for his forgiveness.

Now it was his turn to beg.

CHAPTER TEN

SHE'D FORGOTTEN how beautiful a Montana night sky could be. The half moon seemed suspended on a background of black velvet like a brilliant sliced jewel surrounded by twinkling diamonds. Stars so close she felt she could reach out and snatch one from the sky.

She yawned and shivered. There would be no rest tonight, no peace in the one safe haven she'd made for herself. Not after what Ash had revealed.

She'd stumbled up the stairs, the pain of his accusation so devastating she couldn't even cry. Once behind her closed door she'd torn off her clothes, heedless of the ripping sounds that followed when the zipper refused to obey her frantic tugs. The terry robe was an old friend and she slipped into it with a sigh, then shoved the clawfoot wing chair in front of the open window.

Sleep was a dreaded enemy now. A monster that would rear its ugly head and laugh at her and all her dreams.

A light breeze carrying the chill of the snowcapped mountains ruffled the edge of the lacy curtains and she folded the robe closer to her body. A heart could be broken after all. It was ironic. All those miserable years she'd thought Ash was her only salvation. He had been her hope, a lifeline that made getting through each day and night possible. And to think he should turn out to be the destructive force that would finally crush her spirit.

If tears would come she would cry but the blow had been too well placed and she felt no emotion at all. She was dead inside, as surely as if Ash had taken a knife and carved out her heart.

A door opened behind her.

"Ash, I think it's time I left here. Tomorrow I'm going to see my grandfather and if he doesn't want me to stay there with him, I'll check into a hotel until I decide what I want to do."

"Shannon."

She waited.

"I'll drive you over to Happy's after I take care of some business in town."

She felt his presence looming behind her, sensed his hesitation and closed her eyes, praying he wouldn't walk away from her.

"Earlier you asked me if your sin was so great. Was mine?" Deep down he knew it was. He'd used it to avoid facing his own guilt and shame.

The lump that had lodged in her throat with an unbearable ache eased a little. "I'm sorry I slapped you."

"Don't be." His fingers dug into the back of the chair. "You had every right, and God knows I deserved it." A gusty breeze ruffled the curtains, making the only sound in the quiet room seem louder. "Was it so great, Shannon, that you can't forgive me?"

"I honestly don't know."

Ash moved around from behind the chair and sat down on the window seat facing her. The moonlight caught the blond head and turned his hair the color of molten gold. He leaned forward, placing his elbows on his knees, his hands dangling limply between his legs.

"How could you believe that of me after the way we loved each other? How could you ever think I'd let Dean touch me? I need to understand why, Ash."

"I know you do, and I'll try to explain as best as I can." He lowered his head and ran his fingers through his hair before he looked up at her. "Insecurity. Or maybe I was just plain scared and it was a way out."

"You didn't love me?"

"Of course I did, never doubt that. But Shannon, as you reminded me several times, we were young. The ranch was falling apart; we'd just lost a hundred head of cattle to disease and an exceptionally long, hard winter. All our hopes were built on winning the prize money from racing Ashland's Fire. Dad had suffered his first heart attack. The bills were staggering with no end in sight, and suddenly I was going to be a husband. I'll admit the prospect gave me nightmares. What if you got pregnant? What if I lost the land? I could support myself, but not a family."

"I didn't know the pressures you were under, Ash, you never told me. We never had any secrets from each other, at least that's what I thought. Obviously I was wrong. Why didn't you talk to me? We could have postponed the wedding. Why?" she asked, anguish the first emotion she'd shown since he entered the room.

"Stupid, misguided pride. I am a man after all." There was a wealth of sarcasm in his tone, but it was directed at himself. "And a Bartlet to boot, don't forget."

Shannon offered him a sad smile. "We're a real pair, aren't we?" She wanted desperately to ask him if he still loved her. The question hovered on her lips, then died unspoken. Better to wait than face an unwelcome answer.

Ash reached out, picked up her cold hands, which were lying clenched in her lap, and closed his fingers around hers. "Over the years I've let jealousy corrode my judgment. The thought of you and Dean together—that's hard to accept, Shannon." He absently began to rub the chill from her hands. "I've had to fortify myself with booze to ask. Can you understand that it's not morbid curiosity? I have to know."

She stilled his hands then quickly released them and tucked her own around her ribcage. "It's not what you think. Somehow I wish it was. For years I blamed myself for what Dean had become, but there was nothing I could do to help him. Then I realized it wasn't me, Dean was the most self-destructive human being I've ever met."

Ash's back was to the moonlight, throwing his face into shadows so she couldn't see his expression, yet she felt his confusion. She knew she wasn't making much sense. "Do you remember when we were young and the weather kept us housebound for days? Happy would pick up Dean and bring us here so we could lie before the fire and tell stories?"

"I remember," he said softly, the memories sweet in his mind.

"Do you recall how we would spend hours spinning tales of what we would do, what we'd make of our lives?"

"Yes."

"I'm going to tell you a story that has nothing to do with me, though it's about Dean and myself. The Shannon you knew, the girl you remember, is not the girl in the story. She died in an airplane on her way to France ten years ago, and only came back to life when she saw you."

Ash sucked in a breath, wanting to deny what she was saying. But deep down he knew it was true.

"You're not going to like that girl much, neither do I. Yet I think you'll understand why I did what I had to do."

She was quiet for so long Ash thought she'd changed her mind and wasn't going to tell him after all. He was just about to ask her why she had stopped when she began to speak again.

"When I finally came to the realization that I was actually alone, with nowhere to go, no family to turn to but Dean and his grandmother, I was devastated. Dean left me alone, and Lilith mothered me. They took care of me, Ash. And when Dean started pressuring me to marry him, I wouldn't hear of it. It wasn't fair to him after all. Then he enlisted his grandmother's help. I felt guilty and ashamed. They only wanted what was best for me. At least that's what they repeatedly reminded me day and night for weeks. I gave up.

"But, Ash, I never deceived either of them. They both knew I didn't love Dean. Lilith said plenty of her ancestors' marriages were based on friendship in the beginning. If it was good enough for her family, it was good enough for us. I was very emphatic in telling Dean that I would never love him, that I'd always love you and my feelings would never change. He accepted that, said he only wanted to take care of me."

She gave a sad laugh, so full of mockery that Ash winced. "Fool that I was, I believed him. I guess as outdated as the term is, we were to have a marriage of convenience—without conjugal privileges. Those were my terms."

Ash knew how much Dean must have hated to agree to that.

"Again, Dean agreed eagerly."

"But he didn't keep his part of the agreement?" Ash asked, his body tense with jealousy and something more primitive.

"For a while he did. He stayed away from me. Oh, he wasn't celibate by any means. There were many women during those first months. Lilith took me under her wing. She was ecstatic at the prospect of transforming me into a true Duval-Wayne. She bought my clothes, taught me manners—how to dress and comport myself in French society. She took a motherly interest in me, one I'd never had before. She insisted I take an extensive course in French, learn to tell an authentic antique from a fake and appreciate art and fine French cuisine. For a while I was happy.

"Then Dean started pushing really hard for our marriage to be a real one. He wanted me. Suddenly, just when I was beginning to accept my new life, things began to change. He even persuaded Lilith to join him in his campaign. God, they made me feel so damn guilty, reminding me in such sneaky ways that they were the only family I had, that they were the only ones who loved me now. You know how Dean was when he wanted something he couldn't have? Well, he must have inherited his strength from Lilith because she was just as determined. She wanted great-grandchildren to carry on the Wayne tradition and business."

She knew Ash dreaded hearing what was to come next, but not as much as she dreaded the telling. There were some things she would never be able to talk about, not with him or anyone else. Incidents so horrible they were best left buried deep in her mind. Reaching out, she took hold of his hands once more, but this time it was to draw strength from his touch.

"I gave in—or gave up, if you like. That night was an utter disaster." The statement was totally inadequate, yet she could never put into words the feeling of revulsion at having Dean's mouth and hands on her. He knew it, too, and at first took a fiendish delight at her resistance. Then his cold passion had turned to anger and he took her despite her pleas and resistance.

Ash watched and waited, feeling helpless, knowing what Dean had been like with earlier conquests. He was sure the man's attitude toward women hadn't changed just because it was Shannon.

"The next morning, trying to forget what had happened and to keep busy, I went on a cleaning spree. It was ridiculous since Lilith had maids, but it was a mindless chore, and it kept me from considering bounding over the railing of the nearest bridge." Shannon glanced up, wishing she could see Ash's eyes so she'd have some idea of his thoughts and feelings. But the bright glow of the half moon made him a silhouette, a dark unmoving shadow.

"That was when I found the letters. All the ones I had written to you and Happy were stuffed into an old box at the back of his clothes closet. Something snapped inside me, Ash. The apathy I'd felt until then turned to hate. I told him in no uncertain terms that if he ever touched me again, I'd kill him."

Ash flinched.

She wished he would say something, anything. "I did and said things I'm not proud of, Ash. But hate is such a blinding emotion."

"Dammit, you should have come home."

"To what? My lover and ex-fiancé who didn't want me? A grandfather who despised me?" She yanked her hands from his grip, determined to go on. "We limped along for a year until I couldn't stand it anymore. Dean started to flaunt his women openly. I guess somewhere in his warped mind he thought he was going to make me jealous.'' She leaned her head back and closed her eyes, knowing the next part was going to be the hardest to tell.

"One night Dean came home early. He was jubilant over something, Ash. Smug and secretive. All through dinner he taunted me, reminding me what the Waynes had done for me...what I owed them. He was happy and I couldn't stand it when I was so miserable. So I told him I was going to file for a divorce.'' Her eyes opened and she stared over Ash's shoulder, off into the darkness that matched her thoughts.

"He laughed at me. Laughed! Vicious, ugly laughter. Mad laughter. I think he was a little crazy that night until he told me the reason. You had married. He was drunk with his revenge. For the first time in my life I was actually afraid of him that night. He was so wild, out of control.''

Something in her tone changed and Ash, alert to her every word, her every move, tensed. "What else happened?''

Shannon shifted her gaze to his shadowed face and smiled, a turn of her lips that was totally devoid of anything resembling humor. "I had the last laugh, Ash.''

Her voice trailed off and he had to gently prod her to continue. "What happened, Shannon? Tell it all now, and we'll never speak of it again.''

"He tried to rape me, but, Ash, he couldn't do anything. I'd emasculated him. At least that's what he accused me of doing. He could perform for his women, but not his wife. It was my revenge, you see. I never let him forget I was yours. No matter what he did or said to me, I always wanted you instead of him. He never was good at competing with you, was he?"

"No."

"Still he wouldn't let me go. He couldn't have me, but then neither could you. Even if I could have divorced him, where would I have gone? Lilith and I made our bargain. I was safe from Dean and wanted to make something of myself, be independent."

"Did he ever try to touch you after that?"

"Yes, but his physical incompetence toward me hadn't changed, and I never let him forget it either, not after some of the things he did. So you see, I did have the last laugh."

He saw far more than she wanted him to. His life had been a bed of roses compared to hers.

Ash's silence grated on her nerves. She wished he would say something. "I told you it's not a pretty story and I'm not very proud of what I did. He grew worse over the years. His drinking, drugs, women—men. No decadent act was too great. He flaunted all his perverted activities, but I didn't care, and that was something he couldn't endure so he constantly tried to best his deviousness. It was a vicious circle but he seemed to thrive on it.

"Lilith was the only one to suffer when she finally came to realize what Dean had become. She didn't blame me, though heaven only knows she had every reason to. She was afraid for me, kept warning me that Dean was too quiet, that he was planning something terrible. Then she really shocked me when she heard about the trip to Montana and that Dean was pushing for me to come with him. She advised me to come, leave him and get a divorce. She assured me she would see to it that Dean let me go and would never bother me again."

"And was this Lilith right? Was Dean planning something? Were you afraid of him? Did he try to hurt you up on the mountain?"

A coldness stole over her, a creeping chill that started from within. "I wish I knew, Ash. I have..." She stopped, loath to put into words what she'd seen.

"You do remember, don't you?"

"Not really, just fragments that don't make sense or mean anything." She couldn't tell him the unreasonable fear those few memories caused, not until she was sure what they meant.

Ash stood, a rising shadow that seemed to loom over her. Inwardly she cringed, thinking he was going to leave her.

Instead Ash clasped her arms, hauled her up, then sat down and pulled her onto his lap. "I need to hold you. Just for a while."

Shannon snuggled closer, reveling in his warmth, his hard body and the scent of his after-shave. Her eyes were bright with relief and love. "I wish we could just forget the past as if it never happened."

"That won't solve the problem." And if Dean was dead, he thought, their problems were just beginning.

Lifting her head from the crook of his neck, Shannon studied his face, trying to glean some hope from his expression, but as usual, Ash kept his feelings to himself. There had been a time when she had had the ability to read his very thoughts because of their closeness. Now she was at a loss as to what to think. "Is there any hope for us, Ash?"

He touched her hair, letting his fingers slide through the thick silken strands. "Everything will work out." He nudged her head back to his shoulder.

It wasn't the answer she wanted to hear, but it was better than his previous silence.

"I swear to you, Dean will never have the chance to hurt you again."

For now, that was enough. She relaxed and closed her eyes as exhaustion claimed her. "What about forgiveness, Ash?" she mumbled sleepily.

"We both have to do a lot of that, don't we?"

"Yes."

He held her in his arms, listening to her slow, even breathing and realized she'd dropped off to sleep. If only he hadn't wallowed in his own self-pity and pride and had gone after her all those years ago then none of this would have happened. Her life wouldn't have been a living hell. He gazed out the window, his turbulent thoughts blinding him to the calm beauty of the night. He'd always loved this woman, even when he hated her most.

What amazed and humbled him was the fact that after all that had happened to her, she had never stopped loving him. And if now he was quiet, wary and noncommittal, it was because of the happenings of the past few days. Not knowing about Dean was slow torture. Now, for both their sakes, he was going to have to be strong when he wanted to give in. He had to wait until Jeff brought news, then he would know what he had to do.

Ash pressed his lips against the top of Shannon's head and waited for the dawn of a new day. Content to hold her close to his heart, he shut his eyes as a thousand little memories from their childhood together played through his mind. A gentle smile curved his mouth. As hard as he tried he could never really tell her how much she meant to him. How could he ever find the right words, the words she needed to hear from him?

THE MORNING SUN peeked over the horizon, chasing away the darkness with its delicate pink fingers of light.

Shannon stirred.

A cold wind howled in her ears...

She shifted in Ash's arms.

A red rose wept drops of bright blood...

She moaned, her head moving against Ash's shoulder as if to silently deny the nightmare access to her beautiful dream. She mumbled, "I'll kill you."

Ash, wide awake, alert to what she'd just said, stiffened and waited for more.

"I'll kill you before I'll let Ash have you..."

She couldn't breathe and began to struggle against the arms that held her too tightly, fighting for every breath.

"Easy." Ash increased his hold around her shoulders. "Wake up, Shannon. You're only dreaming."

Amber eyes, glazed and wide with terror, popped open. "Only a dream?"

"Yes." He watched her closely, the words she'd mumbled in her panic burning him like a raw wound. Then her eyes cleared, and he knew she didn't remember anything, or if she did, she didn't want him to know. "A bad dream?" She nodded, tearing her gaze away from his. "Do you remember what it was about?"

Her skin was pale, but the tone of his question made any remaining color drain slowly away. Did he know? Could he suspect? "No."

He knew she wasn't being totally honest with him, and his disappointment ran deep at the realization that she didn't trust him enough yet. But who could blame her, he asked himself, with the life she'd had to lead.

Shannon sat up and stretched, making Ash catch his breath as her robe gaped open, revealing warm, smooth, pink flesh.

"I bet every muscle in your body is cramped from holding me." She scooted off his lap and stood in front of him. "Why didn't you wake me up?"

She seemed nervous, fidgety, as if she was afraid he would pursue the subject of her bad dreams. Ash forced a smile, but his eyes were watchful. "I enjoyed holding you."

She'd taken a few steps away from the window, stopped, and stared at him for a long second. That was the first encouraging thing he had said to her. Then she returned his smile. "I enjoyed it, too." Why couldn't she think of something romantic and clever to say? Her smile overflowed with happiness.

Ash rose awkwardly, shaking his numb feet and laughing when the fingers of his left hand wouldn't move properly.

She wanted to go to him and hug him and bask in his laughter. It had been a million years since she'd heard anything so welcoming and wonderful; she didn't want him to leave her. But Ash was already walking toward his room when he shattered her happiness.

"I'll be back around noon to take you to your grandfather's house."

She hobbled to the bed and sank down on the edge, wondering why, after their mutual understanding, though an unspoken one, he would want to get rid of her? Or was she reading too much into what had passed between them, because she wanted his love again so badly?

CHAPTER ELEVEN

THROUGHOUT HISTORY women have waited for their men to come home from the sea. They wait for their men to come home from wars. Women seem to spend half their time waiting.

Shannon waited for Ash.

Curled up in a corner of the big leather couch in the library, she thumbed through photograph albums. Since the invention of cameras, the Bartlets had kept a pictorial diary of their lives. She reckoned there must be at least sixty of the specially made, leather-bound, gold and green embossed books on the shelves.

The two she had spread out around her were the last in the line, ones she'd never seen. Ten years crammed into two thick tomes. Years of Ash's life she'd had no part in. She was enjoying her browsing until she came upon his wedding photographs. After studying his ex-wife, she quickly turned the pages. He had never talked about her or his marriage, only that it hadn't worked out and he was to blame. Maybe he was right. He and Shannon were destined to destroy anyone who came between them. She felt guilty, but there was some hope underlying her feelings too. If that were so, then maybe they were fated to be together.

She absently turned another page in the last book and found herself looking at Jeri and Paula on a Paris street she immediately recognized. This must have been their recent trip of a couple months back. Neither of them looked as if they were enjoying themselves in the cold weather that had all but paralyzed France and brought the country to a standstill.

She was just about to close the book when the edge of a glossy picture came loose from its tiny black corner sticker. As she tried to slip the edge back under the mounting, another picture, carefully trimmed and placed beneath the first, slid down the page and landed in her lap, staring up at her.

Her eyes widened, first in amazement, then in growing revulsion. Dean stood with his arm around Paula. There was something putrid about the photograph, something evil in his face as he gazed into the camera. There was too much savage pleasure in his eyes, as if he'd just committed the ultimate violation against her. Had he and Paula had an affair? Nausea brought the bitter sting of bile to the back of her throat.

She recognized that expression. She'd seen it too many times, heard the coarse laughter when he would taunt her with his conquests. Immoral, degenerate, totally corrupt—it was all there in the face staring back at her. It would have been just like Dean to seduce Paula to get back in some way at Ash. There was nothing she wouldn't put past him.

Shannon slammed the album shut, but for some unexplainable reason she kept the picture of Paula and Dean out, picked it up between the tips of her fingers and laid it on the edge of the coffee table. Her gaze moved from the picture to the window. Streams of sunlight filtered through the sheers and made a strange, wavering pattern on the polished oak floor.

There was a humming in her ears as the wind, cold and biting, whipped her hair around her face and into her eyes. A strong gust pushed at her back, hard, making her step closer to the edge of Devil's Leap. But it wasn't the wind. It was Dean.

She quickly stooped to pick up something, something long and cold from the ground. When she looked up, Dean was no longer behind her, but standing in front of her, his face twisted with hatred.

He was screaming, yet the words kept slipping away on the frozen wind. A blast of snow, as thick as a curtain, blinded her.

Terror sapped her strength, biting deep into her bones, paralyzing her. Dean was going to kill her.

She couldn't breathe.

Not with Dean's hands wrapped around her neck, his fingers digging deeper into her flesh. She could see the uncontrolled wildness in his eyes, feel his breath hot on her face as he slowly tightened his grip and whispered in her ear, "You're not going to leave me. I'll kill you before I'll let Ash have you."

Her arm rose, the weapon held ready, when suddenly he let her go and she staggered backward, gasping for air. The wind howled louder, like an animal denied its prey.

There came a deafening roar, and when she looked up it was to see Dean's mouth working like a mime. Snowflakes stung her eyes, and her vision blurred. She couldn't make out what was happening, but Dean seemed to be standing unnaturally stiff. Then, as if in slow motion, he collapsed into himself and tumbled backward over the edge of Devil's Leap.

He was suddenly gone from sight, but not before she'd seen the red stain that seeped through his shirt. Trancelike, she lifted her arm and stared at the weapon she held....

Trembling violently, Shannon fought the undertow of her memory. God, what had she done?

She lowered her head, closed her eyes and tried to regain her composure and calm her ragged breathing. It wasn't true! She couldn't remember all of what had happened, just disjointed fragments that didn't make any sense. Surely she had dreamed this, and somehow had transformed it into that hideous picture.

Paula stepped into the library and stopped, the corners of her mouth pulling tight as she spotted Shannon. The cinnamon chamois slacks and multihued silk blouse in black, brown, crimson and a touch of burnt orange that Shannon was wearing were definitely Valentino. She'd seen the outfit in *Town and Country* magazine only last month. It wasn't fair. *She* should be wearing designer clothes.

Shannon lifted her head, her eyes meeting Paula's across the room. When the older woman turned to go, she said, "I didn't realize you and Jeri saw Dean when you were in Paris recently."

"We didn't."

Snatching the photograph from the table, Shannon held it up. "What's this then?"

Paula walked a little closer then stiffened as she saw the picture. "Oh, that. Where did you get it?" Then she saw the photo albums spread out and shrugged as she ran a shaky hand through her limp blond hair. "That was on a trip a couple of years ago."

"Is that so?"

"Yes, Jeri was dating the American ambassador's son and he was on some kind of diplomatic trip for his father and asked us to meet him in Paris. Or was it the time I'd been to the Bircher-Benner clinic in Zurich to lose a few pounds and regain my sanity after an endless season of parties in Washington? That must be it."

"You're a liar, Paula."

"And your loss of memory must be playing tricks on you. I tell you that was a couple of years ago. Jeri met me in Paris and we ran into Dean by accident. He was with a very lovely model."

Shannon shook her head, wondering why she felt as if Paula was a deadly viper poised to strike. "No, Paula. That full-length sable coat Dean's wearing was a gift from his grandmother. A Christmas gift of only a few months when this picture was taken."

"I tell you you're crazy." Paula spun around and was about to stomp out when she found her way blocked by Bridget.

"Himself won't like this, you're upsetting the girl, and you're lying, Mrs. Paula, just as surely as my name is Bridget O'Conner."

"Mind your own damn business," Paula snapped.

Bridget crossed her arms over her ample bosom, her sharp eyes taking in Paula's uncharacteristic attire; she never wore her housecoat this late in the day. Her lips puckered into a disapproving bud and her gray eyebrows met together in a puzzled frown. The woman wasn't right in the head today, she thought.

"Oh, all right. We ran into Dean on our last trip and he bought us lunch."

Bridget was still an immovable object blocking Paula's retreat.

Shannon decided she'd caused enough trouble in Ash's household. She didn't need him breathing down her neck because she'd upset his stepmother. "Bridget, is there an extra car or truck I could use? I'm going to my grandfather's."

"You can use my car," Paula offered, startling both women. "It's the blue Mercedes sedan in the garage. Are you sure you're able to drive with that foot?"

"It's the left one, Paula, it just sits there."

"Ash won't like this. You were supposed to wait for him," Bridget interrupted.

"Yes, and he said he'd take me this morning. It's now twelve-thirty and I'm tired of waiting."

Paula's eyes narrowed. "You're leaving for good?"

"If Happy will let me stay. But I'll be back later to pick up my luggage."

Bridget scowled and moved aside. "I still don't like it." Her gaze followed Paula as she walked past her and out of the room. "She never lets anyone drive that car."

"Maybe it's worth the worry to get rid of me."

Bridget's eyes darkened as a full-blown frown thundered across her brow. "There's something fishy going on here and I don't like it."

LANDMARKS from her childhood . . . the scenes of memories so indelibly imprinted on her heart it hurt to look at them through the car windows. Shannon tightened her grip on the steering wheel as heavy tears pooled in her eyes, forcing her to slow down to a crawl as the road wound precariously close to the edge of a steep ravine.

The Reed ranch, the Double R—a horse farm really, small in comparison to the Bar B and the Rocking W— sat between the two land moguls. The paternal peacemaker. It had been that way as far back as she could recall. She guessed she'd been the only Reed in history to upset the tradition; a troublemaking Reed. A wild wind they had labeled her, but she didn't care, not then.

Over the quiet purr of the engine she heard the river rushing through the ravine. A cold, dark, dangerous body of water that originated in the snowcapped mountains and gushed down the steep slopes, seeking a way out. It rushed past boulders and smooth stones, carrying the winter with it in a serpentine route to the large lake that sat behind the Reed place. There it fell gracefully over a waterfall and pooled beneath the warm sun, a dazzling mirror that reflected the sky.

As Shannon drove over the ridge she could see the lake surrounded by cherry trees. She longed to see them bloom and run through the groves as the petals floated like rain drops in a light breeze. The road took another twist and claimed her attention. Then suddenly she was there.

Home.

Her heart began to pound against her chest with excitement and dread. What if her grandfather wouldn't see her? What if he wouldn't forgive her? What if? Her mind went suddenly blank and her breath stuck in her throat as she pulled to a stop before the two-story, red cedar, log house. It had been built almost at the same time as the Bartlet house, and though she loved Ash's home, there was no place like her grandfather's house, so natural in its setting among the gigantic conifers, all green and smelling sharply of pine.

Before she lost her nerve she opened the door, grabbed her cane and got out. Her gaze was everywhere at once, and nowhere in particular, yet kept darting back to the front door. But it remained shut. The sun shone through the branches of the tall pines, and as she approached the front door she stepped into a patch of warm light and felt better, telling herself it was a good omen. When no one answered her knock, Shannon turned the brass knob, pushed the door open wide and stood perfectly still, just looking.

It was as if she'd never left.

Like walking into a dream or back in time.

She felt dizzy, disoriented and incredibly young. The past ten years had never happened, nor were they ever going to. She would wake up to a bright sunny morning and find Ash having coffee with Happy in the kitchen and making fun of her for being so grumpy. She would kiss her grandfather's leathery cheek at night and dream of her life together with Ash. She was a child again, young, wild and free.

Suddenly yelling her grandfather's name, she went limping through the house as fast as she could, looking for him, seeing the clean, worn shabbiness of the place without it really registering. She hobbled up the stairs and found herself outside her old bedroom. As she grasped the knob in excitement, a thought struck her and she paused and held her breath. What if the room was barren? She pushed the door open slowly.

Tears began to slide down her cheeks. A sob, deep and painful, forced its way past her lips. Nothing had changed. Even the framed photograph of her mother and father, parents she'd never known, was sitting among the bottles of perfume and knickknacks on her triple-mirror vanity. Everything was just as she'd left it; as if she could walk in and pick up her life as it had been before everything had fallen apart.

Wiping the tears from her eyes with a shaking hand, Shannon stepped over to the window. She touched the faded yellow-and-white-checked ruffled curtains almost reverently then pulled them back a little so she could see out. The big oak tree beside her window hadn't succumbed to age but stood strong and oddly inviting, its thick limbs strategically placed like a stairway leading up to her bedroom window. How many times had she climbed down to meet Ash and Dean? How many times had Ash climbed up, just to sit on the limb outside her window and talk for hours when she'd been sick with various childhood diseases.

How many times had she stood in that exact spot, gazing out over the neatly fenced paddocks, the two red brick horse barns and the sweet green of the land and the blue lake beyond? Too many to count.

Off toward the far side of the lake, through a forest near the edge of the mountain, was an enchanted place. A rare red cedar grove, the thick, twisted limbs and heavy foliage of the trees filtering the sunlight and turning everything, even the misty air, an eerie green. Yet it was oddly peaceful there, and so beautiful with a hot spring-fed waterfall that babbled quietly into a still brook.

A place of dreams where her knights slew dragons and rescued her from an evil wizard. And when she was older, it was a private place where she would lie among the soft ferns, as thick as an animal's fur, and dream away the hours with Ash beside her.

She felt alive for the first time in ten years, and it wasn't just the fact that she was home. It was Montana, the clear, big sky so close to heaven, the mountains . . . it was the land. Montana soil was a part of her, the sparkling water flowed in her blood and the scent of the trees and the earth were like breath to her. This was where she belonged. This was where she intended to stay.

"I knew someday you'd come home."

Shannon whirled around and froze. Happy Reed, a little older, a little grayer, stared back at her from the doorway. "Pops," she whispered, calling him by the name she had used through her childhood in times of emotional upheaval.

"I'm a foolish old man who doesn't have the brains to say I'm sorry."

She was in his open arms, like a baby bird snug in her nest, and when the old man began to tremble against her she sobbed louder and harder so she couldn't hear his own sounds of sorrow.

Happy Reed loosened his grip on his granddaughter and held her away from him, his eyes bright with moisture, his face wet as tears rolled unchecked and unashamed down his seamed cheeks. "Just look at you. My baby, a woman grown, and what a beauty—like your mother."

"I wrote you," she managed to say around the huge lump in her throat.

"Doesn't matter now. You're home."

"Every day for months."

"Hush."

"Dean stole the letters...he never mailed them for me."

"Bastard. I'll take great pleasure in horsewhipping him."

"I missed you, Pops."

"I love you, child."

"I'm never going back to him."

"Of course not."

"I'm getting a divorce."

"I'll see you do."

"I love you, Pops. I'm sorry I disappointed you."

"I'm a foolish old coot with too much pride."

"Me, too."

They both began to chuckle, then were hugging each other again.

Shannon released her grandfather and stepped back, putting too much weight on her sore ankle. Happy wrapped his arm around her shoulders and urged her out of the room, down the stairs and into the kitchen.

"Sit down and let me have a look at that foot."

"Doc..."

"Doc's a pill pusher. He doesn't know beans about sore muscles and sprains like I do."

She watched him with amusement as he squatted down, unwrapped the elastic bandage and probed her ankle. The thick gray-haired head was so close and so dear she couldn't resist a gentle touch.

Happy glanced up, and his usual stern expression broke into a beaming smile. "Looks okay to me. A few more days and you'll be as good as new."

For the first time she noticed he had a doozie of a black eye and jokingly asked, "Who'd you tangle with, Pops?"

He gingerly touched the darkening area and gave her a sheepish smile tinged with masculine pride. "With a no-account, low-down snake in the grass! Believe me, he got the worst of it." He placed his gnarled hands on his thighs and pushed himself up, then stuffed his hands into his baggy jeans pockets in a stance that said he didn't wish to discuss the matter further. "We need to talk, Shannon, about the past, about what happened. To clear the air."

"I know." Curiosity about his black eye made her grin, but she knew better than to question him; he'd tell her in his own good time. As he turned away and pulled two mugs from the cabinet, she glanced around the kitchen, sadly noting the signs of age.

"What are you thinking?"

She tried to smile around the flood of memories that overwhelmed her. Happy had always let his work come first, but even at times when she'd childishly felt a ne-

glect, he'd always been free with his love for her. "I was
remembering how many times we used to sit here, just
like this, discussing our day. It seems like only yesterday in some ways and a hundred years in others."

"Time is our worst enemy when we pass childhood,
my dear. We shouldn't waste a second. I wasn't always
there for you when you were young. But I wanted you to
have everything, to make up for you losing your parents, I guess. It wasn't easy for an old man, but I loved
you dearly then, still do."

"I knew that."

"But I failed you ten years ago and I can never forgive myself for that. I let that damnable Reed pride keep
you away, and at nights I'd lie awake and wonder if my
son and your mother had lived what they would have
done."

"Please, Pops, don't."

"No, let me say it. I should have given you a chance
instead of condemning you out of hand. Dammit, I
should have known it was Dean's fault."

That shocked her, and as she accepted the mug of hot
coffee, she asked, "What do you mean?"

Happy sat down opposite her, wrapped his work-worn
hands around the mug, then cleared his throat. "Dean
deliberately caused the accident that killed Ashland's
Fire. He bragged to Clyde, that weak-kneed sissy of a
foreman, if he couldn't have you he'd rather see you
dead than married to Ash. It was just his luck that Ash's
horse died and everyone blamed and turned on you.
Luck of the devil, I guess. Then, before anyone realized
what was happening, you were gone and we were all too
proud to make the first step to get you back."

"You're saying Dean planned everything? That he
was trying to kill me? Oh, Pops, that can't be right. I

could expect something of that nature now, but we were all so young then."

"Not him! He was born sly and dangerous. Why did you think I would never let you go anywhere with him alone? I made sure Ash was always along. An evil piece of work was Dean Wayne."

"But..."

Happy reached over and captured one of her hands and held it firmly between his. "I only found out most of this this morning."

She opened her mouth to ask how, then clamped her lips together as she saw his bushy gray eyebrows come together. Some things one never forgets, she mused. And that expression was one not to be interrupted.

"I told Dean when his dad shipped him Dictator from France that the animal was a killer. I've never come across more viciousness in my day. I advised him on more than one occasion to have the beast put down, that he'd never be able to ride him with other horses. Dictator liked to fight. I checked into his background and gave Dean the proof that the horse was a crazy killer. He injured three horses so badly they had to be shot, and he crippled one of his trainers. But Dean wouldn't listen. He knew, Shannon, what that animal would try to do when he dared you to race. He planned it."

"He hated me that much even then?" She shook her head in disbelief, yet she never doubted what her grandfather had told her.

"No, he loved you in a strange, warped sort of way. A destructive, obsessive love that would destroy sooner or later. But that's not all." When she made to pull her hand from his, he tightened his grip. "All those years you were gone and he'd come back three, four times a year to check up on the Rocking W, the rumors and stories about you would run rampant. He paid Clyde to keep them going."

"What kind of stories, Pops?"

He shook his head. "You don't want to know, child."

"Yes, I do. I have to if I'm ever going to be free of him. Please, tell me."

"There were stories of your wild behavior in Europe, of drugs and parties, orgies, I think they call them, and lots of men."

"I can't believe it. They're not true. I swear, Pops." She thought of the embarrassment and humiliation her proud grandfather must have felt when he walked into a store in town and overheard some of his friends gossiping about her. "Why? Why would he do that?"

"To keep us, especially Ash, from ever wanting to come get you. To keep us apart so he could have you to himself and privately gloat over his victory over Ash."

"I'm so ashamed." She stared down at the table.

"Why?" her grandfather demanded. "We were all pawns in Dean's destructive games."

"I still feel as if it was all my fault. None of this would have happened if I hadn't let Dean talk me into leaving so fast. Oh, Pops. I wish . . ."

"Now you stop it. The past is best forgotten. I never cared a hoot what those pissant, tiny-minded townspeople thought or said. I know my girl."

Tears filled her eyes and it was her turn to clasp his hands as she gave him a very edited version of what had happened over the past ten years.

"I'd like to meet this Lilith even though she was part conspirator in keeping you with that maniac grandson of hers. She finally saw what he was and took care of you. You say you went to college?"

"I'm a veterinarian, Pops," she said proudly. "I'll have to see what I have to do about transferring my license to Montana." She leaned forward eagerly. "Just think, Pops, I can work with you." When he didn't respond or show surprise or pleasure, her own excitement began to wane. Then he grinned, a sly little smile she was all too familiar with. "You knew!" she exclaimed.

"I didn't want to spoil the telling, but yes, Ash told me this morning."

"He was here? He told you?"

"Couldn't keep the secret, he was so excited for you."

The back screen door opened and Ash strolled in. "One of the reasons I never got back to the ranch when I said I would was because I had to bail Happy out of jail this morning."

Shannon spun around in her chair. "Just how long have you been out there? And what do you mean you bailed him out of jail?"

Both men grinned at each other then Ash reached for a mug in the cabinet, poured himself some coffee, pulled out a chair, turned it around backward and straddled it, resting his elbows along the back. "I've been sitting outside since you and Happy came downstairs. I didn't want to interrupt the reunion."

She glanced from one man to the other, noting their smug expressions. "Which one of you is going to tell me what's up?"

"Inquisitive as ever, isn't she, Happy?"

"Always was nosy, couldn't stand it when something was going on and she didn't know every detail. Curious as a cat."

As she sat at the kitchen table with her grandfather and Ash bantering back and forth, a strange sensation of déjà vu stole over her. She shivered, not unpleas-

antly, but with an inner happiness. "Okay, you two—
stop teasing and tell me." She tore her gaze from Ash
and glanced back at her grandfather. "How in heaven's
name did you get thrown in jail? You of all people,
Happy?"

"Wasn't very hard." Happy touched his sore black
eye. "Jeff asked me to have a little chat with that big
mouthed, gossip monger Chester about all the stories he
was continually spreading about you. He said Chester
wasn't smart enough to think them up by himself. Jeff
felt someone was feeding him things to say. I just cornered the old busybody at the Cattleman's Café and
when I asked him nicely..."

Ash and Shannon burst out laughing, knowing there
had been nothing polite in Happy's asking. He and
Chester had been enemies for more years than they could
remember.

"Anyway, he chose that particular morning to be sly
and secretive, so I dragged him out on the sidewalk and
beat the hell out of him. He talked then. Squawked like
a chicken with his head cut off after I got through with
him. The lying bastard. Dean's foreman was being paid
to keep the stories going, and Clyde paid Chester to
help." He stopped, rubbing his leathery cheeks and
trying not to laugh as he remembered the fun he'd had
that morning. "We attracted quite a crowd in town, including Jeff's deputy. Old Chester, thinking he was safe
with the deputy present, started bad mouthing you again
and I took in after him, hit him for the lying scum he is.
I guess Bob figured the only way to break us up and keep
me from killing him was to arrest us."

She couldn't believe it. Her proper, dignified grandfather brawling on the main street of Bartlet with just

about everyone watching. She was torn between shock and amusement, and laughter won out. "Happy!"

"Felt damn good." The old man beamed at them. "Might do it again, too, just for the satisfaction of getting even with that worthless excuse for a man for fouling the air with your good name." He chuckled. "I bet the town is buzzing like a disturbed bee hive today." Happy's expression sobered as he stared at Shannon, inspecting the dark bruises around her neck and on her face for the first time. "I promise you, Dean's going to answer to me, too, when he turns up."

"Like a bad penny, Pops, Dean always shows up."

Ash and her grandfather exchanged a look that made her nervous. She brought the mug to her lips and took a hefty gulp, wanting desperately to ask what was going on, but not daring to, knowing it had something to do with Dean. If she couldn't forget him entirely, at least she didn't have to think of him while she was with her grandfather.

"You still don't remember anything, child?"

"No." The happiness faded from her face and shadows of fear and doubt clouded her eyes.

Happy gave a slow nod. "Well, it should be cleared up soon anyway."

Ash rose quickly, the legs of the chair scraping the floor. He wasn't ready to have Shannon know Jeff had gone up the mountain in search for Dean. Better to wait until they all knew what had happened. He touched Shannon's shoulder. "We'd best be getting back to the ranch."

Her head snapped around. "What do you mean? I thought you wanted me to stay here?"

"What gave you that idea?"

"You did last night . . ."

"I said I would drive you over. I didn't say you were to stay. As usual, you jumped the gun. By the way, why didn't you wait for me?"

Her skin tingled where Ash's hand had rested on her shoulder. She fought the urge to rub her cheek against the spot. "I hate waiting, you know that. Besides..." She remembered her grandfather's presence and said, "Never mind. But since I'm here, maybe I ought to stay. I've disrupted your household enough. Paula and Jeri are at each other's throats. They hate having me there and Bridget and Paula have had more than a couple of words because of me."

"Tough! You're coming back with me."

"Pops..." She glanced at him and caught his smug expression of satisfaction before he sobered.

"You best go, Shannon. I have work to do and you'll be alone here in the house. Ash can protect you better at the Bar B than I can here."

She felt as if something loathsome had crawled over her. "What do you mean, protect?" The two men shared a look again, and the feeling of foreboding that had been with her ever since that morning increased.

"If Dean shows up, we want to make sure he can't get to you," Happy said too quickly. "I'm an old man. Ash can take care of you better than me."

He was a poor liar, too. They were both hiding something from her and she didn't like it. But Ash had removed the coffee mug from her hand and was lifting her out of the chair, then guiding her toward the front door, stopping only long enough to allow her to kiss and hug her grandfather goodbye.

"We'll return Paula's car and I'll send one of the men over for my truck later."

Somewhat against her will, Shannon found herself seated in the car and waving a little sadly to her grandfather as they pulled away.

"He'll be over for dinner tonight, Daffy."

It was the use of her old nickname that brought a shine to her eyes. She rapidly blinked the moisture away and twisted around in the soft leather seat. Her amber eyes sparkled like a cat's caught in a beam of light. "Now. What's this about protecting me? Happy's worried, so are you. Have you heard something about Dean? Has he shown up somewhere?"

"Do you know in all the years I've known your grandfather, I've never seen him smile so much."

"Don't change the subject."

Ash flashed her a lopsided grin as he steered the car from the lane onto the winding road. "You should have seen him this morning. He was in one cell, Chester in the other. But that didn't stop his threats. Jeff's deputy was at his wit's end as to how to handle the two old men. I thought he was going to kiss me when I sprung Happy. Then Chester started yelling about false arrest and suing the county and Happy. Your grandfather was so angry he wanted to post bail for Chester so he could beat him up all over again. I tell you, I laughed till my sides hurt."

Shannon touched the button and the window beside her glided down. Fresh air fanned her face and cooled her angry red cheeks. Ash didn't intend to answer her question. They were hiding things from her.

She glared out the window, about to tell him exactly what she thought of his secrets, when she saw the hairpin turn ahead. Old habits never die. She automatically shut her mouth. The turn was treacherous enough without having her distracting him.

Ash's attention was diverted from the road for only a second as he looked over at Shannon. It was comforting to know some things never changed at all. When Shannon was angry her cheeks would flush red and she'd clam up. People who didn't know her well might think she was sulking. Shannon never sulked. She was only contemplating her next remark, sharpening her wit with a sarcastic edge for a comeback. He waited, anticipating the verbal combat he'd missed so much.

Ash shot her another quick, amused glance before his attention returned to the road and he started to slow down to navigate the turn. Suddenly there was a loud pop, the sound ricocheting off the trees as one of the tires blew out. The wheel jerked violently then it was wrenched from Ash's hands before he realized what was happening.

Shannon screamed as the edge of the road seemed to jump in front on her. "Ash!" she screamed again as the hood of the car, then the front wheels nosed over the side of the road and seemed to hang there, rocking back and forth like a child's teeter-totter on a playground. It seemed a lifetime before it slipped over and she could clearly see the dark rushing water at the bottom of the ravine. She wound her hands around the heavy shoulder strap and squeezed her eyes shut.

"Hold on, sweetheart."

The car rode the steep slope sideways down the ravine. Metal crunched against rocks, outcroppings of bushes were uprooted and small trees splintered as the Mercedes picked up momentum.

Realizing the futility of trying to steer, Ash let go of the wheel and braced himself for the shock of the crash and the freezing, churning water below. His one and only thought was to save Shannon—to get her out of the car and the icy water as quickly as possible.

CHAPTER TWELVE

THE CAR never made it to the water. Instead it crashed into a small stand of trees growing from a cluster of boulders and came to a jarring, ear-screeching stop.

"Shannon! Shannon, are you all right?" Ash's fingers shook as he wrestled with the clasp of his seat belt. When the stubborn mechanism finally released him, he lunged for her, his hands feeling, touching, searching for broken bones.

Shannon giggled, a nervous reaction of relief, which only made Ash curse. He was still turning the air in the car blue with his colorful vocabulary as he tried to unbuckle her. "Are you hurt, Ash?"

"No. Come on, we have to get out of here. I don't know how long those poor excuses for trees will hold the car."

"What happened?" She was a little dazed, but swatted his hands away as he fumbled with her seat belt.

"Blowout, I think." Ash reached across Shannon and unlocked the door, holding it open as he crawled over her and out onto the ground. "Come on, Shannon, stop fussing with your clothes." He slid his arms in, one under her legs and the other behind her shoulders, and pulled her out. Her weight and the slant of the slope made him stagger a few feet before he regained his footing. "Quit grinning like a jackass, we were almost drowned."

"But we weren't." She wrapped her arms around his neck and smiled into his fierce expression. "Ash, we're okay. Don't be such a grouch."

His only answer was a grunt of irritation as he positioned himself at an angle to the slope, inching upward as best he could. In a few seconds he was out of breath. He spotted a sizable pine tree and headed toward it. "Here, lean against this while I go back to the car and get your things and my hat."

He set her down, making sure she was securely propped against the tree, and started to walk away when she grasped his arm. "Ash. Why are you so angry?"

"Why!" He stopped and scowled. "Dammit, Daffy, we could have been killed." Then he was holding her, his body pressing her into the rough bark of the tree, his mouth on hers as hunger radiated from him like heat from a blazing fire. When he pulled away, he placed his face against her hair and whispered, "God, I love you. Nothing has ever been the same since you left. I've missed your smile, your frowns, your laughter and your temper. Most of all I've missed you at night, missed holding you in my arms." He kissed her again. "Don't leave me. Never leave me again." His mouth captured hers, the passion and loneliness and love of ten years in his kiss. "I couldn't bear it if you left me again."

His plea, though spoken in hushed tones, was like the roar of a wounded lion. If it took a near fatal accident to make him realize he loved her then she was glad it had happened. "I love you, Ash, and I promise I'll never leave you. Say you love me again."

He seemed to have realized what he'd said and started to back away. Wasn't this the very thing he was trying to avoid until they found out about Dean? Until she was free? But he couldn't deny what he'd said or that he'd meant every word of it as long as he was looking down into her lovely face so full of happiness. "I've always loved you, Shannon. Even when, for the sake of my sanity, I thought I hated you—I loved you."

Ash put temptation away from him by setting her back against the tree. "Now be a good girl for once and stay put while I go take a look at the car and figure out what we need to do." He carefully planned each step, sinking the heel of his boot into the ground where it was soft, grabbing hold of bushes and rocks where his footing was precarious, as he began making his way back down the slope. When he finally got to the car, he opened the door and pulled out Shannon's purse, cane and his Stetson, which had been knocked off. He placed the hat on his head and the rest on the ground before making his way around to the front of the car.

Almost falling over in his haste, he grabbed the bumper and squatted down for a good look at the tire. When he glanced up and scanned the land around, his expression was murderous. He'd been almost positive he'd seen a glint, a flash of sunlight on metal before the car had gone out of control. And just as the steering wheel was jerked from his hands, he would have sworn he'd heard the sound of a rifle shot. Now he was sure, his feeling confirmed the puncture hole in the thick rubber. Someone had taken a shot at them. No, that was wrong. No one knew he was going to be at Happy's or that he would be driving the car back.

The bullet was meant for Shannon.

Someone wanted her dead. But who? Dean was the only person he could think of, and no one was sure whether he was alive or not. If not Dean...

"Ash, what's taking so long?"

His sharp gaze swept the far reaches of the ravine, and seeing nothing out of the ordinary, he climbed up to her, but his skin crawled when he turned his back on the opposite bank.

"Paula's going to kill me when she sees her car."

Ash winced. "Here." He handed her her purse, watching while she slipped the strap over her head and through one arm, then slung it around to her back.

She looked up at him expectantly, her eyes twinkling, and smiled. "Piggyback?"

"Piggyback."

Once in position, her legs locked around his waist and her arms around his neck, she handed him the cane. "This might be helpful." Then she was quiet as he struggled up the slope, holding her breath at times when he slipped or his footing seemed unsure. When they finally made it up to the road, both were out of breath and damp with perspiration.

Ash squatted down to let Shannon get off, then slowly stood, stretching his cramped leg muscles. The breeze was cool but the spring sun beat down on them relentlessly. Ash pulled off his hat, wiped his forehead with his shirt sleeve and eyed the road in both directions.

"Are we going back to Happy's?" Shannon asked.

He put his Stetson back on his head and glanced at her. She was standing on one leg. "How's the ankle?"

"Better. I can at least put my heel on the ground without too much pain. Which way, Ash?"

"We're halfway between both places. Let's go on to the Bar B." He turned around and hunkered down. All she had to do was step close so he could grab hold of her legs and hoist her up on his back, but nothing happened and he looked over his shoulder. "What the hell are you doing?"

Shannon was pulling her shirt from the waist of her slacks, unbuttoning the cuffs and rolling up the sleeves. She gave Ash a slanted look from beneath her lashes. "It's going to be a little warm."

Ash snorted, thinking it was going to be a damn lot hotter than she knew, having her so close. "Come on, Shannon, we don't have all day."

"Yessir, just a minute. Hold on to me for a second. No, around the waist," Strong hands grasped her sides and she bent down and quickly rolled up her slacks to the knees.

She was pressed against him, her firm rounded bottom an enticing invitation for the palm of his hand.

"Don't even think it, Ash Bartlet," She raised herself up and twisted around in his arms. "Now I'm ready." Her voice grew husky as she leaned into him.

"I've been ready since I walked into the line shack and had to strip you naked." A seductive gurgle of laughter drew his eyes to her mouth, but he resisted the temptation. "Let's go." He presented her with his back once more.

She climbed on, disappointment and confusion dimming her happiness. Why was he being so... careful, so determined to keep everything on a nonpersonal level after he'd already admitted that he loved her? The brim of his hat kept bumping her in the nose and chin so she snatched it off and set it on her head. "Seems like we've done this before, doesn't it?" She put her lips close to his ear and grinned when he shivered.

"At least a hundred times. Why was it, Shannon, that you were always hurting yourself and I had to cart you around on my back like some slave?"

"I wasn't always hurt, you know. I just liked being in your arms, even when I was too young to realize what it was I wanted."

Ash slowed, hoisted her up higher and said, "You'd think after all those times you'd learn that I have to breathe. Loosen your death grip from around my neck."

The sun had warmed and turned his hair a molten gold. She wanted to run her fingers through it, play with the waves and the tiny curls around his neck. "Do you remember when you were about twelve and I talked you into letting me roll your hair?"

He almost choked. "No! I never did."

"How soon we forget. Oh, yes, little pink and blue rollers all over your head, and when I combed it out you looked like a Greek god from a book I'd seen."

"For heaven's sake, don't dare tell anyone that, will you?"

She brought her lips closer to his ear, her tongue darting out to tease the shape.

"That's not fair, Shannon. Stop it now."

"Right."

"And if we're going to reminisce...do you remember the time I found you sunbathing naked by Willow Falls?"

"No." But she did, and tried to put her hand over his mouth.

"You were getting acquainted with your body, so to speak."

"Ash! You watched? How could you?"

"It was the most disturbing and exotic thing I've ever seen."

She buried her flaming face in his shoulder. "I was only sixteen."

"And a real beauty."

Their memories carried them to the Bar B with laughter and a fair share of embarrassment on both sides. But one name was deliberately never mentioned.

IT WAS WITH A GREAT SIGH of relief that Ash pushed open the back door of the ranch house and walked in. Bridget and Tom, sitting at the kitchen table, glanced around and fell silent as he lowered Shannon to her feet. He handed her the cane. "Why don't you go up and rest—have a bath, put your foot up. I have some things to take care of."

She didn't protest. Heat and the way her foot had bounced around had brought on a throbbing pain. She leaned heavily on the cane and hobbled out of the quiet kitchen.

Bridget and her husband watched Shannon leave, careful not to speak until she was out of hearing distance. Bridget asked the question first. "What in the name of the saints happened to you?"

"I wish to hell I knew. Tom, take some men and the truck to the sharp turn in the road leading to Happy's. You know the one?"

"Sure, Ash. But why?"

"You'll find Paula's car near the bottom of the ravine."

"God preserve us." Bridget crossed herself. "What's going to happen next?"

But Ash wasn't paying any attention to his housekeeper. "Also have one of the men check out the opposite side of the ravine. Look for a spent rifle cartridge. We didn't have a blowout. Someone took a shot at Shannon, and I just happened to be along for the ride."

Bridget sat down heavily in a chair. "Deliberate, it was?"

"Oh, yes, very deliberate. Tom, check to see if anyone here was gone this morning."

"Someone from the Bar B, Ash?" Bridget asked, her bright eyes wide with horror. "Surely not."

"Quiet, woman," Tom scolded his wife. "Let the boss finish."

Ash threw his foreman a grateful look. "Where's Paula and Jeri? I want to have a talk with them, see if they mentioned to anyone this morning about Shannon going to see her grandfather?"

Tom glared at his wife when she gave him a stubborn look. "Speak up, Bridget O'Conner. Now that the man's asked you a question you can answer, don't let your pride get in the way."

"Paula rode over to Maybella's this morning to see about a new saddle she wanted to buy from her. And Jeri left right after her mother. She said she was going to town. Speaking of town, Ash, Jeff called and said when you came in to come to his office as soon as possible."

Ash didn't wait to hear her next question but sprinted out the door, yelling over his shoulder that he was going to borrow Tom's truck. Once on the road he let himself relax, and a chill seemed to take hold of him, shaking him to his very core.

His heart pounded like a jackhammer in his chest. His breath came deep and hard as if he were a long distance runner at the end of a marathon.

He tried to control his fears, but dread gripped his guts, twisting them into knots with the feeling of impending disaster. Yet he tried not to think, forcing himself to keep his mind a complete blank as he pushed the gas pedal to the floorboard.

As he sped through town he saw small groups of people standing in front of stores, and as he passed them they broke off their conversations and watched him drive by. Still, he wouldn't allow himself to think about what Jeff had found out. Surely life wouldn't be so cruel and take Shannon away from him after he'd waited and loved her for so long?

He pulled the truck to a tire-screeching stop in front of the sheriff's office and was out of it before the engine had time to die. He shoved open the door. His gaze searched the small room, ignoring the deputy and the radio operator, and he headed directly for Jeff's office. Without bothering to knock, he walked in and slammed the door behind him. Jeff looked like death warmed over. The macabre turn of his thoughts made him grimace.

Jeff rubbed the heavy stubble on his cheeks, glanced up then back down at his hands, folded on the desk top. "We brought him down a little while ago."

"Dead?"

"Yes. Doc's doing the autopsy."

"How? What happened?"

"One shot through the heart with a 30-.06, his own rifle by the way."

Ash sagged against the door. "Everything's all right then. Shannon only hunts with a bow. She stopped using a rifle years before she left."

"We found the bow. We found everything. Ash, the camp was torn apart, like a madman had been turned loose."

Ash wasn't listening, but went on as if Jeff had never spoken. "I wish to hell he was alive. It would explain what's been happening since you left." He told him about the bull being set on Shannon and of the attempt on her life that morning.

"Could be coincidence. Has she remembered anything yet?"

Ash shook his head and patted his pockets. "Got a cigarette?"

"I quit yesterday after I ran out." With all the worry and emotional upheaval in his life lately, and utter exhaustion from his trip, Jeff felt like an arthritic old man as he rose slowly to his feet, unfolding joint by creaking joint. "Another thing. I found Shannon's coat up there, near the ledge. The front was smeared with blood. My gut feeling tells me it's not animal either, but human." He took a few steps around the desk, leaving Ash staring off into space while he opened the door and bellowed for someone to go get him a carton of cigarettes.

"But you're not sure it was Dean's blood?"

Jeff gave a tired, sad sigh. "No, not yet. Just don't place any bets against my instincts, though." He watched Ash's jaw harden and his eyes flash, then the light of battle died and he only nodded. The evidence against Shannon was beginning to pile up.

"Did Bob tell you about Happy and Chester?"

"Yes."

"Dean and Clyde have been behind all the stories about Shannon. For what reason I'll never know."

"It's a nasty business all around, Ash." Jeff studied his friend for a second, feeling a deep sense of pity. Ash needed time to realize the implications of what he'd been told. Jeff knew there was no way he was going to be able to convince his friend that Shannon was a murderer.

The door opened a crack and a carton of cigarettes flew across the room. From habit, Jeff caught it easily and tore it open. He hadn't realized how much this mess had affected him until he saw his hands shaking. He tapped out a cigarette for Ash, shrugged, then lit one for himself.

Ash dug into his jeans pocket and pulled out the worn silver lighter Shannon had given him on his twentieth birthday. "She didn't do it, Jeff. Shannon is not capable of murder."

"Not even in self-defense? Come on, Ash, with those bruises on her neck, Dean was trying to kill her. She's only human. She would have protected herself. It will be a good defense. I'll testify about the bruises."

Ash inhaled deeply then blew out a steady stream of smoke. "I still say she didn't do it. Why the attempts on her life?"

"Maybe Clyde somehow found out about Dean's death and is upset he won't be getting any more money. Hell, how do I know! One of your newer ranch hands could have been one of Dean's plants. Anyone could have let the bull loose. Anyone could have ridden out and hidden till the Mercedes came by. Ash, everyone around here rides, tracks and can shoot. Hell, man, even Paula and Jeri are experts on horseback and with guns."

Ash nodded. "She didn't do it, Jeff."

"Ham knows, Ash, and he's going to be breathing down my neck for a murder charge just as soon as the Doc makes his report."

"How long?"

Jeff shrugged. "Ham's probably already talking to the governor and the press."

Ash surged to his feet and paced the small confines of the office. He stopped long enough to crush out his cigarette, then immediately lit another one. "I won't let Shannon go to jail. I won't let that political peacock use the woman I love as his stepladder. If necessary, Jeff, I'll sell off some Bartlet land and hire her the best defense attorney in the United States."

Shock showed easily on Jeff's tired face. A Bartlet selling off land. It was unheard of. "You love her then?"

Ash stopped his pacing. "Was there ever any doubt?"

"No. Just in your mind. Ash, you better prepare her for the ordeal to come. The press is going to be all over this in a day or so. And you can bet your ass that Ham's going to tie the Bartlet name in with this. A love triangle, my man, makes for good reading." Jeff reached in his desk drawer and pulled out a half-empty bottle of bourbon and two glasses.

Ash eyed the depleted bottle and raised his eyebrows.

"Jeri was by this morning." When Ash closed his eyes Jeff quickly went on. "We didn't talk. I didn't tell her anything. She doesn't know about Dean yet. Then I had to call Dean's grandmother in Paris and notify her of his death and explain what we know so far." He took a sip of the bourbon. "She guessed right away something bad had happened, wasn't even surprised when she learned the truth, said she'd been expecting it . . . that Dean had been acting strange."

"Why the hell didn't she warn Shannon?"

"She did. She encouraged Shannon to come to Montana then immediately leave Dean. The old lady really loves Shannon and I think she finally realized what Dean must have turned into."

Ash sat down heavily in the chair, rested his elbows on his knees and put his face in his hands. When at last he looked up he said, "Help me, Jeff."

"Anything, name it."

"Time. We need a few days. Can you get Doc to slow down on his autopsy? Just a few days, Jeff. Enough time to keep Ham away till the cause of death is officially declared. He won't dare make a move until then, not with the weight the Bartlet and Wayne names carry."

Without asking any questions, Jeff picked up the telephone and called the doctor. When he hung up he looked at Ash. "Forty-eight hours is all he can give us. Now do you want to tell me what you have in mind?"

Reaching across the desk, Ash grabbed the bottle and poured himself some more bourbon and lit another cigarette. "How do you feel about making another trip up the mountain?"

"Not very enthusiastic. Why?"

"Just the three of us, Jeff. You, me and Shannon. If she can't remember here, or won't, maybe the scene where everything happened will jar her memory."

"You're betting on a long shot."

"You with me?"

"Damn right."

"If it doesn't work, Jeff, it could be your job."

"Hell, Ash, if the law can't bend a little for the innocent then what's the use of being a lawman?"

Ash reached across the desk, grabbed the bottle and poured them both a shot. He raised his glass. "To friends."

They drank deeply and were silent for a few minutes, then began to make plans.

"We'll leave at first light in the morning."

Ash set down his glass and turned to leave, but Jeff's next words stopped him cold.

"When are you going to tell Shannon about Dean and our plan?"

Ash didn't turn around, he didn't want Jeff to see the anguish he knew was in his face. "Tonight. Tonight, after dinner."

Jeff watched him go, thinking of the old adage about the condemned eating a hearty meal. He didn't envy his friend his task.

JERI FOUND HER MOTHER in the big greenhouse. The heavy door eased quietly shut behind her, locking her in the tomb of blossoming flowers, their fragrance overpowering. Warm, humid air, a direct contrast with the cool breeze outside, caused her to shiver violently. Normally she loved working with the flowers, digging in the special blended soil, so spongy and pungent, but today the flowers made her faintly sick, reminding her of funerals.

The bright profusion of colors assaulted her sensitive eyes like a strobe light, forcing her to blink a couple of times to regain her equilibrium. When the feeling of sickness passed she began to walk toward the back, passing beds of multicolored roses from deep bloodred to pale pink, gardenias as white as virgin snow, lilies, yellow daffodils as bright as the sun, tresses of honeysuckle, violets so purple they looked blue, and her mother's prize orchids. Her stomach turned over at the mingled scents and she had to stop a second until her insides righted once again.

A familiar noise drew her attention, and she turned the corner of one of the rose beds to find Paula sitting on the cement floor, digging furiously in an empty bed. She stopped a few feet behind her mother and watched a second while a deep frown began to crinkle her forehead. "Mother."

Paula jumped, screamed and jerked around, her dirty hand clutching at her heart. "Dammit, Jeri. Are you trying to scare me to death?"

Jeri's expression changed from puzzlement to real concern. Her mother looked dreadful. Her blond hair, usually so neat, hung in limp strands; her face was gaunt with sunken hollows under her cheeks; and her lips were devoid of all color. They stared at each other, then Jeri cleared her throat. "Mother, someone tried to kill Shannon this morning. They took a shot at your car and it went off into a ravine. Ash was driving, and it was the only thing that probably saved her life." She searched her mother's face for some sign, some emotion. When nothing changed she asked hoarsely, "Mother, where did you go this morning? Bridget told me you left before Shannon."

Paula rose slowly to her feet and faced her daughter. "What are you implying, Jeri?"

"Nothing. Nothing. Mother, what's happening around here?"

Paula ignored the question and asked one of her own. "Where were you this morning, Jeri? You left early, too. Bridget made a point of telling me. Where did you go? What did you do?"

"Mother!" she sobbed. "Surely you don't think...?"

"Just what don't I think?"

Jeri's mouth dropped open, then snapped shut as she got hold of herself. "I just drove around for a while."

"Can you prove it?"

"Stop it, Mother. I drove around then went to town to see Jeff."

"Ahh. And have you made up with your sheriff?"

"I was going to tell him about Europe, Mother, about what you talked me into."

"But you were the one who did it, not I. And if you tell that upstanding pillar of law and order, you're crazier than I thought. He'll never forgive you."

"He kicked me out of his office without even talking to me. Oh, Mummy, he wouldn't even take the time to listen to me. She began to cry in earnest, tears streaming down her pale cheeks. When her mother only stood there staring at her, she wiped her wet face with the sleeve of her blouse. "I can't go on feeling this way, loving him and knowing what he'll think of me when he finds out. And he's bound to find out. We won't be able to hide the truth much longer. Everything is falling apart. The truth will come out sooner or later, especially now."

"You're a fool if you tell him. And what do you mean, especially now?"

Jeri wiped her sweaty palms on her jeans, then crossed her arms over her breast and hugged herself to stop the shaking that had suddenly come over her. "Dean's dead, Mother. He was murdered, shot. Jeff found his body at the bottom of Devil's Leap."

Paula's eyes took on a distant look. "I figured when he didn't show up something was wrong. But if Jeff didn't talk to you, how did you find out?"

"I ran into Mr. Watts, the D.A., coming out of the sheriff's office. He was gloating, Mother. He said this was one thing the Bartlets weren't going to get away with. He's out for blood. Ours. You know how he is. He'll dig up every piece of evidence." She was becoming hysterical and couldn't seem to control her voice as it grew louder and higher. "He'll find out, Mother. I know he will, then he'll drag us into the scandal."

The sound of a palm striking a tender cheek echoed around the hushed greenhouse. "Get hold of yourself, Jeri. Nothing will happen if you keep your mouth shut. That means don't tell your precious Jeff about Europe.

Do you hear me, Jeri? You can never tell Jeff, no matter how guilty you feel."

Jeri nodded, her hand on her cheek as she stared at her mother. "Does my own happiness mean nothing to you?"

"Of course. Everything I've done has always been for you. Now be a good girl and go back to the house and let me think."

Jeri nodded again and began to turn away, realizing Jeff was lost to her forever. She bowed her head, but her mother's next question brought it up with a snap.

"Did the D.A. say when he was going to arrest Shannon for Dean's murder?"

"No, Mother."

"Does she know?"

Jeri's heart felt as if someone was squeezing the life out of her, and it hurt to breathe. Her mother's questions were asked with entirely too much enthusiasm. Suddenly she felt dead inside. "I don't think Shannon knows yet, and I'm certainly not going to be the one to tell her."

"Of course not." Paula looked at her daughter, her grin as friendly as a shark scenting a stream of blood. "We'll let Ash do the honors. It should be an interesting evening, wouldn't you say?"

Jeri shook her head and walked away, feeling sorry for Ash and Shannon and herself. How had everything become so vile and sordid?

CHAPTER THIRTEEN

SOMETHING was terribly wrong.

The evening should have been festive. Ash loved her. Her grandfather had welcomed her back with open arms. Yet there seemed to be a cloud hanging over the house, a sense of doom she couldn't comprehend.

Earlier in the afternoon, after Ash had left and she'd bathed and rested, she'd roamed the house trying to figure out what was causing the drastically changed atmosphere of the house. When she'd entered the kitchen, Bridget and Tom had immediately halted their heated conversation. Instinct told her they'd been discussing her. But why stop? Bridget had always been open and forthright with her, never hesitating to speak her mind.

Now at the dinner table, where the conversation should have been gay, there seemed to be a brooding, brittle quality to the mood, as if the wrongly spoken word would shatter the room into a million pieces.

Ash sat silently, talking in monosyllables, and then only when spoken to. Happy talked nonstop, chattering like a magpie, something so totally out of character it set off warning bells in her head.

Jeri moped, pushing her food around on her plate with a total disregard for Bridget's culinary efforts. Shannon thought at any minute the housekeeper, who hovered between the dining room and kitchen checking on their needs, would yank Jeri up by the scruff of her expensive silk blouse and shake her like a terrier shaking a rat.

Paula's mood defied description. With her face bare of makeup and her blond hair scraped back into a tight bun, she looked every day of her fifty-four years and then some.

The malevolent glance Paula had given her, when she stepped into the library for predinner drinks in her black-and-white herringbone Carolina Herrera dress, was enough to send goosebumps dancing over her bare arms. She didn't know what was going on but concluded that Paula was ill—and not necessarily physically, either. The woman was obsessed with money.

"Eat your dinner," Bridget urged her over her shoulder. "Would you like some more lamb? New potatoes in cream sauce? English peas?"

"Bridget." She threw a look of laughter mingled with impatience over her shoulder. "Don't nag. I've still got a plateful."

"Get another bottle of wine, Bridget," Paula ordered.

Ash stiffened. "Don't use that tone of voice on her, Paula. And I think you've had enough to drink tonight."

Shannon watched, knowing better than to interfere when Ash and his stepmother were in the midst of an argument.

"I'm sorry, Bridget. But please get another bottle of wine. And why don't you bring Shannon a glass? After all, this is a celebration of sorts, isn't it?"

"Paula!"

"Well, it is, Ash."

"Shut up."

"It's not every day that a woman is joyously made a widow, and a very rich one I would imagine."

It was as if the very air had been sucked out of the room and everyone struggled for breath.

Shannon's eyes widened, her head turned slowly to the other end of the table, catching the look of anguish and anger on Ash's face. "What's she talking about, Ash? What does she mean, widow?"

"Well, dear..."

"Shut your goddamn mouth," Ash roared. He was the only one to move; the only one who could. He shoved back his chair, uncaring as the antique toppled over backward and crashed to the floor.

But Paula wouldn't be quiet. "Why, I thought that's what this celebration was all about. You mean Ash hasn't told you yet? Jeff found Dean's body and brought it back down from the mountain. He was shot through the heart. Murdered in fact." She picked up her half-empty wineglass and finished off the contents in one gulp. "Surely you could have thought of a better and less scandalous way to get rid of your rich husband, Shannon?"

"No!" Shannon whispered brokenly.

The wind screeched in her head. Dean's face was before her, twisted with a mixture of lust and murderous hate.

She stooped to pick up something, something long and cold in her hand.

He was screaming at her, spittle forming at the corners of his mouth. She couldn't hear what he was saying over the roar of the wind and the blood pounding through her head. Then his hands were on her neck, squeezing hard, cutting off her breath, making bright spots of light dance crazily before her eyes. Terror, con-

*fusion, hate, fear—they lent her nothing, no strength to
fight back.*

Her arm rose, the weapon ready.

*The wind was as shrill as a woman's scream in her
ears. Or was it she who was screaming? She couldn't tell.
Suddenly she was free, staring at Dean and the small red
spot on his shirt that was spreading all too quickly.*

*Then he was gone. Tumbling backward over the ledge,
falling into darkness.*

"No, no, no." Shannon felt the room begin to spin.
Her head ached unbearably and she was sick with the
knowledge of Paula's revelation. Like Ash, she pushed
back her chair, and before anyone could react she darted
from the room, up the stairs, through her bedroom and
to the bathroom, where she leaned over the porcelain
bowl as her stomach gave up its contents.

Her worst nightmare had come true. For days, as her
memory returned bit by bit, she'd lived in fear of the
truth. Yet she'd refused to voice those fears, thinking
that by speaking aloud, by sharing her thoughts, they
would somehow become unbearably real. So she had
hidden them from herself and Ash, quietly praying that
Dean would show up.

Dean was never going to come back. Dean was dead.

"Are you through? Here." Ash held out a small cup
filled with mouthwash. He had to help her hold the cup
to keep the contents from sloshing over as her trembling fingers tried to grasp it. When she was through, he
set the cup down and stood watching her closely. Her
shoulders began to shake as choking sobs racked her
body. He grabbed her arms to fold her in his embrace
but she wouldn't let him.

She didn't want to be touched and she fought him. "I
killed him. God, I did it, didn't I?"

"No!"

She slapped at his hands. "The dreams weren't dreams, they were real."

"Stop it, Shannon. Dammit, I'm trying to help. Be still, Daffy."

"I did it," she screamed. "I must have."

He finally captured her flailing arms and jerked her to him, holding her tightly against him until her knees sagged and she began to cry. A noise behind him made him turn slightly, and he shook his head in warning at her grandfather. He waited until the old man left the room and the door closed, then pried her now clinging arms from around his back.

"Stop crying and listen to me." He cupped her face, wiping the tears from her cheeks with his thumbs. The haunted look in her amber eyes was like that of a trapped fawn. The expression disturbed him deeply. He loved her so much it was tearing him apart to see her suffering. "Are you listening?"

Shannon bit her lip to keep from crying, but her tears seemed never ending.

"You do remember something?"

She nodded.

"Do you actually remember picking up a rifle, taking aim and killing him?"

"No. But I must have. What's going to happen? Oh, Ash, what are we going to do?"

"First of all you're going to get it through your head that you didn't kill Dean."

"But—"

He shut her up with his mouth on hers, and she clung to him as a drowning man would a lifeline.

"I had to have done it." She couldn't look at him, though the expression in his eyes proclaimed her innocence. She rested her forehead on his chest. "I hated him so much. I can't count the times I wished him dead." Lifting her head, she finally stared into his green eyes, so dear and so close. "Who would, or could, have done it but me?"

Shannon pulled away from him, and though he was loath to release her, he knew they both needed some distance to work out what they had to do. "You didn't kill Dean, Shannon. I know you too well."

"People change, Ash. It's been ten years, ten miserable years."

"People change. Ten years is a long time. Could she have done it in self-defense?" Those were Jeff's words. He couldn't give them credence then or now. "You didn't do it."

"I wish I had as much faith in myself." She limped from the bathroom on shaky legs. With the support of furniture, she made her way to the bed and sat down heavily on the edge, putting her face in her hands.

"Tell me everything you remember. Start from the beginning, when you and Dean left the ranch. Don't leave anything out."

"I only remember fragments, bits and pieces. But they're enough, Ash, to make me believe I did it."

"Why don't you let me be the judge of that?"

She told him what she could, her face still hidden from his probing eyes. At last she looked up, her cheeks pale and bloodless, and was shocked into silence when she saw him smiling. For a moment the thought crossed her mind this was his revenge—that he would watch her be convicted of murder without raising a hand to help her, and be happy to see her go. Then the moment passed and she was deeply ashamed of herself. Ash loved her. Surely in a world suddenly gone crazy it was the one hope she could cling to.

"You really don't remember anything. They're just disjointed fragments of scenes you probably put together in the wrong sequence. Or maybe what happened up there is too terrifying for you to want to remember."

"Yes. Like shooting Dean."

He ignored her and went on. "You were running blindly off the mountain, sweetheart. That's not like you to panic in a tight situation. You know the wilderness and how to survive. But this time you were so scared of something that you completely forgot all your survival instincts. Did you ever consider that if you didn't do it, and I say you didn't, there had to be someone else there? A third party, Shannon. Do you remember running into anyone?"

A couple of steps brought Ash directly before her. He crouched down, pulled her hands away from her face then grabbed her shoulders and shook her hard. "You listen to me. You didn't kill that bastard. Oh, I won't deny you wanted to, but you couldn't do it, Shannon, it's not your nature. I believe that with all my heart. Jeff believes it too and we have a plan."

"I want to believe you, Ash."

"Then do, it's that simple. I know we have a lot of problems to work out, but trust me, Shannon."

A knock on the bedroom door startled them both, and before Ash could yell at whoever it was to go away, Happy walked in carrying a cup.

"Bridget sent you some of her herbal tea to settle your stomach."

Ash clasped Shannon's hand and rose. "Where the hell is Paula?" His anger at his stepmother radiated from him in waves.

"She left a few minutes ago after I tore into her," Happy told him. "Said she was going to go over to some friend's house, that she wanted to totally disassociate herself from the scandal that was sure to arise from all this."

"Bitch," Ash growled. "She knew very well I didn't want anyone leaving the ranch and taking the chance of running into any reporters."

Shannon choked on the hot tea. "Reporters? My God," she moaned. "How have they found out so fast?" She set the cup down on the bedside table, put her elbows on her knees and dropped her face into her hands. "It's going to be a front-page, three-ring circus, isn't it?"

Happy sat down beside her, wrapped an arm around her shoulders and held her. "The D.A. has let the cat out of the bag prematurely, so to speak. We've had to take the phone off the hook and some of the ranch hands are patrolling our place and the Bar B."

Shannon's voice shook. "When is Jeff going to arrest me?"

Ash and Happy exchanged a look.

"You haven't told her?" Happy asked.

"Not yet."

"Told me what?" She leaned farther into her grandfather's comforting embrace, dividing her gaze between both men.

With his free hand, Happy smoothed back her hair from her damp forehead as Ash pulled up a chair and sat down. "That's what we were all talking about in the library before dinner. Poor child, you knew something was wrong when everyone stopped talking as you walked in, didn't you?'' She nodded, and he gave her a gentle squeeze.

"Ash says I didn't do it, Pops. I don't know if I believe him or not."

"Child, I've never lied to you and I have no doubts whatsoever that you couldn't have done it. The thing is, it looks bad for you. You're sure you don't remember seeing anyone else up on Devil's Hump with you?"

"No, Pops, no one."

"But you were terrified, weren't you? To put yourself in danger the way you did and come off the mountain instead of finding shelter?"

She closed her eyes, remembering the terror that had stalked her down the side of the mountain; the urgency that kept her moving, the feeling of panic to get away, for no reason she could remember. And fear...she'd been almost paralyzed at times with fear. As if, she suddenly realized, she were a hunted animal fleeing for her life. She told Ash and her grandfather her recollections and they nodded with approval.

"But that doesn't mean anything. I can't remember anyone being there."

"It means more than you think, child."

She still didn't completely believe their line of reasoning. Somewhere, not too far from the surface, lay her conviction that she might have actually killed Dean. Even if it was self-defense, how would she be able to prove it? Her mind tried to shy away from thoughts of a trial and prison, but the reality and horror of the situation would not go away. She hung her head as a feeling of weakness washed over her. The image of being locked away was more than she could bear.

As if reading her mind, Ash said, "Shannon, Jeff and I have come up with a plan that may help you remember."

She looked up, hope relieving her tightly clenched jaw and the grim line of her lips. A little color flushed her cheeks pink. "What?"

"Jeff and I are going to take you back up on the mountain to the campsite and see if that will jog your memory. We think it will work. Doc agrees. He says your block is not physical but mental, and you have to face your fears about whatever happened up there."

Shannon stiffened automatically in fear at the thought of going back up to Devil's Leap. She was quiet for a long time, thinking over the pros and cons, then relaxed. It was her only hope. Turning her head she stared at her grandfather, then lightly kissed his leathery cheek. "You agree with them, don't you?"

"Yes."

"You're coming with us?"

"No, child. Jeff wants me to quietly keep an eye on Clyde. There's a chance that if he and Dean were lovers at some time, as you've said, there could have been enough hard feelings about Dean bringing you here to set Clyde off. Maybe he killed Dean."

"I wish you'd come."

Happy rose, kissed the top of her head and straightened. "I'm going to leave you in Ash and Jeff's care. They're younger and can take the ride up the mountain better than I'm able to." Hating to leave her, Happy leaned down and hugged her hard. "I must go. There are supplies I promised Jeff I'd get together for your ride tomorrow. Take care of yourself, child." He was at the door, his back to her, when he added, "I love you, Shannon. No matter what happens this time, I'll be there, standing beside you. I've always loved you even though I've had trouble showing it."

He was gone before she could form a reply. Tears leaked from the corners of her eyes and she wiped them away and took a deep breath before turning her attention to Ash. "What if I don't remember anything once we get up there? Oh, God. Ash, hold me." She was in his arms, then on his lap, feeling the strength of him and wishing she could stay that way forever. Her dreams had turned into a nightmare, the nightmare into a horrible reality. "I don't know what to do now. Help me, Ash."

"Haven't I always?" His lips touched her fragrant hair then her forehead. "When we were young and got into trouble, who always got you out?"

"You did," she whispered and closed her eyes, wishing they were those crazy kids again. His warmth seeped into her cold body and she began to relax, the tension melting away as she listened to the rumble of his voice so close to her ear.

"When you couldn't swim and jumped into the creek anyway to show me how brave you were, who pulled you out?"

"You."

"When old Mr. MacGregor caught you sitting in his prize cherry tree eating his cherries, who talked him out of telling Happy you'd skipped school to do it?"

"You. But only because he was going to tell on you too. Besides, you had to spend two days after school picking those damn things for him."

"Yes, but you didn't. And he never told your grandfather."

She nodded sleepily, a tiny smile teasing the corners of her mouth.

"And when Hamilton Watts tried to kiss you at the fair, who gave him a black eye and put the fear of God in him?"

"You. But I don't think you did it just to help me. You were jealous."

"Damn right."

The evening sun sank lower in the sky, throwing long shadows across the room. Ash reached out to turn on the lamp, but Shannon caught his arm.

"No, please. There's something comforting and peaceful about being in the dark, and in your arms."

Ash leaned his head back and his eyelids drooped, only to pop open again when he heard her soft chuckle. "What's so funny?"

"I was thinking of the other times you were helpful."

"Such as."

"Oh, the time you tied me to the snow sled because I kept falling off, then pushed it down Runway Slope. I broke my arm over that one. Or the time we read *Tom Sawyer* together then built a raft. You told me I had to hold onto the ropes in the front, that I was your figurehead, and we shot the rapids. I nearly drowned then."

Ash began to laugh quietly. "What about the time you talked me into raiding Miss Lanshire's honeybees? Or the night we stole my dad's new car and went for a joyride? Dad, Happy and the sheriff thought a couple of hours in jail would stop some of our escapades. You talked his deputy into calling Stella at the café to bring us some dinner, except you wouldn't share it with me."

"Only because you'd been so mean and arrogant and wouldn't let me drive."

They fell silent for a long time, taking comfort in each other's arms and the good memories from their childhood.

. "Ash," she whispered, "I'm scared."

He didn't want to tell her that he was, too. Their future balanced on a hunch—and a long shot, at that.

Shannon pulled away from the security of his arms and gazed steadily into his eyes, trying to read his thoughts. But Ash had carefully masked his feelings with a smile. As she continued to stare, the smile faded, replaced with a look of tenderness and love that stole her breath. She felt his hand travel up the center of her back and tangle in her hair as he drew her lips toward his. His mouth slanted across hers and the hand that had rested around her waist slid to her hip, her thigh, smoothing out the wrinkles of her dress before it moved on to her knee, her calf, then back again. Except this time his fingers slipped under the hem of the dress and began to massage her stocking-covered thigh.

"Woman's armor," he sighed against her lips. "I want you more than I thought it possible to want anyone." A mental picture of Shannon stretched out naked on the crisp white sheets sent a jolt of passion through him that was hard to control.

"There should be a better word than love," she said. "It's so small and simple and inadequate for what I feel for you. The thought of you, my memories, my love, kept me sane throughout the years. I think it drove Dean crazy," she added sadly. "But I couldn't help or change the way I felt."

"Shh." Ash kissed her quick and hard. "We won't speak of him tonight. After this mess is cleared up, and it will be, Shannon, we'll do what we should have done ten years ago. We'll get married."

A lump too big to swallow formed in her throat. "Will it ever be the same? Can we go back to what we once had?'' She wanted to believe that dreams could come true. She'd clung to them for so many years.

"Shannon, the only thing that's changed is that we're older and maybe wiser. We'll find what we lost, given time, and we'll make it even better."

He'd given her back love and hope, a gift more precious than he would ever know. If things went wrong, if justice didn't prevail, she could still face anything just knowing that with Ash's love and forgiveness she was whole again. "Make love to me, Ash." There was desperation in her voice, an urgency in the way she kissed him, a hunger that refused to be denied. If she had no others, she'd have this *one* night to remember, to savor.

Milky shafts of moonlight spilled into the room, illuminating the dark shadows to a soft pearl gray. Ash got up, taking Shannon with him, then gently lowered her feet to the floor. With slow deliberation he began to undress her, taking his time as he kissed her neck, the hollow in her shoulder, and the curve of her arm. When her bra floated to the floor like a wispy white cloud, he touched her breasts, tracing the visible blue veins that snaked like rivers under the surface of her pale skin.

"It has always amazed me that as tall as you are, you always look so small and frail." He lifted her hand, his fingers wrapping around the delicate bones, then he kissed the inside of her wrist. She was magnificent in her nakedness, proud, erect. The young girl he once knew was gone. Shannon was all woman now. But some things never changed. He watched the play of emotions slip across her face, the way her amber eyes darkened, and the rapid rise and fall of her breast.

Shannon's eyes had closed at his touch, and she reveled in the way his fingers set her skin tingling like a fire flaming into life too quickly. Her eyelids fluttered open when he moved away from her, and before her mind could frame a protest, before her lips could form the words, Ash had shucked his clothes and stepped farther back so she could see him fully and note the changes from a youth to a man full grown.

She reached out to touch his chest. Where there had once been only smooth tan flesh, blond hair now glistened in the moonlight like an armor of bright shining gold. She let the tip of one finger trace the darkening line downward, then grasped him firmly, feeling the strength of his desire pulsing in her hand. A soft hiss of his breath told her more than any words what her touch had done. "How beautiful you are, Ash."

"Not I, love, it's you who takes my breath away."

"Is this a dream? I won't wake to find I've imagined it and you're gone. Please tell me it's real?"

Ash's hand covered hers and squeezed, then he chuckled. "Does that feel like a dream? I'm as real as you are."

She sighed and limped a step closer, her body lightly brushing against his. Then she wrapped her arms around his waist and her palms splayed out against the broad back. "Hold me close just for a minute so I'll know for sure this is no dream."

Ash pressed her cheek to his chest, holding her tightly as he rested his chin on the top of her head and rocked her gently back and forth as he would a small hurt child. His throat worked spasmodically, the muscles contracting painfully as he tried to swallow the love and tenderness that gripped him. Moisture filled his eyes and blurred his vision. He buried his face in her hair lest she see.

Shannon dropped her arms and clasped his hand. Tugging him along behind her, she took the last few necessary steps to the bed. When resistance met her efforts, she looked over her shoulder and frowned in confusion.

Ash threw back his head and laughed, then he scooped her up in his arms and twirled her around in the moonlit room. "Just like old times, you always leading me astray, shameless hussy."

Breathless, both laughing, they fell across the bed.

"I remember the first time we made love. You were an intoxicating mixture of shy virgin and sly woman. You led me then, too, when I balked over a sudden sense of morality and fear of your grandfather."

She ruffled his hair, loving the silky feel of it between her fingers. "You didn't hesitate long, though."

They fell silent, each remembering the sweet, young passion of their youth.

Ash rolled over, taking her with him so she lay full length against him. "You were a gangly, budding wildcat and I agonized over taking you."

"Yeah, that bothered you all of two seconds," she whispered as she slid farther up his body so she could reach his mouth. With a fingertip that trembled slightly, she traced the lines and grooves of his face, coming to a stop at his lips. She replaced her finger with her mouth and kissed him hungrily.

She squirmed, and Ash squeezed his eyes shut, fighting for control. "Shannon."

"Yes."

She wiggled.

"Damn you," he chuckled softly. "I want to make tonight special for you. But I'll never last if…" Her hand found him and suddenly he was buried in her as she straddled him.

"I've waited ten years. I've dreamed and fantasized about this. I don't need hours of foreplay. I want you now."

Ash grasped her shoulders, shifted his weight and flipped her over, following her as she slid beneath him.

Control was a phantom. They came together in wild abandon, clutching each other in need and passion. When she called to him, his name a breathless scream, he cried back, letting reality slip away and fall over the edge of the world.

She watched him in wonder, awed by the way the hardness and tension melted away from his features, leaving him looking years younger. When Ash finally opened his eyes to gaze down at her, his face blurred and she realized tears had pooled in her eyes. And when he raised up on his elbows she felt the splash of his own tears on her cheeks. Her heart ceased to beat, then began to hammer against her ribs again as she gathered him into her arms, soothing his shaking shoulders with her hands. She'd seen Ash convulsed with laughter, coolly angry, in a rage and sad, but she'd never seen him cry. She too wanted to cry and laugh at the same time. She wanted to speak words of comfort, understanding and love. Yet she wisely kept quiet, even though it left a painful ache in her chest.

Ash raised his head, heedless of the tears on his face, and met her gaze. Her eyes told him she knew the depth of his need for her, and that he had finally let go of all the emotions he had held back for ten years. Maybe in the next ten years he would be able to make up for the hell she'd been put through because of his damnable pride and lack of trust.

"What are you thinking about?" she asked.

Ash rolled over, taking her with him. He brushed at a few damp strands of dark hair that clung to her forehead and cheek. "Oh, just imagining how you'll look old and gray, with false teeth and wrinkled like a prune."

"Ashland Bartlet!" She knew what he was doing. The bombardment of emotions and the physical release had left them both shell-shocked. She snuggled closer, resting her head on his shoulder, and sighed, content with the world for the first time in years. The quiet room, his even breathing and the sound of his heart slowing to a normal beat worked like a drug. Her eyes fluttered shut. She was willing to follow his lead and keep things light or they would both end up a wreck, wallowing in a sentimental puddle. "Tell me when you've recovered and you're ready to play again. I know what advanced age does to the male libido." The rumble next to her ear made her smile.

"I deserved that."

As the night advanced the room grew darker, taking away the light, making shadows dance like fairies in the corners until they too disappeared into the blackness.

Shannon lay still in Ash's arms, her breathing steady and even, lest the slightest movement wake him. With her eyes adjusted to the shadows, she studied his face. Fear had awakened her. So much rode on her memory returning that she felt scared. What if she couldn't remember anything? What if they returned to the campsite and nothing came back to her? What then?

At some point during the night she aroused him and tried to discuss the possibility, but Ash wouldn't listen to her. Instead he silenced her by making slow, delicious love to her again.

Ash was convinced of her innocence.

She wasn't so sure. There was still that niggling doubt in the back of her mind.

Could she have killed Dean? The answer lay like the night, quiet and shrouded in darkness.

CHAPTER FOURTEEN

THE WIND WAILED, surrounding her like some living thing, the icy blasts sucking the air from her lungs. The snow, raw and wet, carried by the wild fury, stung her skin with needle sharpness and plastered tendrils of hair to her face. Crystals of snow gathered on her eyelashes and blurred her vision.

Dean was coming toward her, stalking her, forcing her back. She threw a frantic glance over her shoulder. Step by step she was getting closer to Devil's Leap.

The storm captured his words and swept them away, allowing her to snatch only a few phrases from the wind. Her fear made her hot then trembling with cold. She strained to hear over the roaring in her ears, but it was his eyes she watched. The icy blue irises were hard and glinting, the pupils wide and round and as black as licorice.

Death dogged each carefully placed step. She could see it in the rage of Dean's face. She stumbled over something, righted herself and glanced at the ground, then quickly picked up the weapon, knowing she was about to fight for her life.

Laughter mocked the wind. Dean's laughter—the exhilaration of a hunt finally over and the prey cornered for the kill. She was screaming at him, straining to be heard over the storm, but he only laughed again.

Suddenly everything happened at once. He was on her, his hands wrapped around her throat. Like a death dance, a ballet of violence, they switched places and his back was to the ledge. She couldn't breathe. Bright dots of light played before her eyes.

She raised her weapon.

Shannon opened her mouth to scream, but no sound came. She bolted out of her nightmare, sat up and blinked, the wind and the unearthly scream still echoing in her head as she tried to recapture the scene. What had she remembered? But the picture wouldn't come again, and trying to force it only left the residue of a throbbing ache behind her eyes. She moved closer to Ash's warmth and laid her hand on his arm to reassure herself he was real. What were they going to do if she couldn't remember? What was going to happen to her?

Not until Ash's hand covered hers did she realize her fingers were wrapped around his arm, and she'd been squeezing so hard she'd awakened him.

"A nightmare?" his husky voice, still half asleep, asked.

"Yes. I almost had it, Ash, but it slipped away."

Ash sat up and gathered her close against him. "What slipped away?"

"Dean. Damn! Why can't I remember? Will it ever come back to me? Ash..."

"Hush. Once we get up to the campsite you'll remember."

She snuggled closer, burying her face in the curve of his shoulder. "I wish I had as much faith in me as you seem to have." In truth, the nearer it came to morning the less she believed the trip was going to work.

The room seemed so peaceful in the darkness, yet fear began to gnaw at her insides, knotting her stomach. She didn't want to go up that mountain, yet at the same time she knew she had to. For Ash. For Ash she would go anywhere, and take the consequences no matter what they were.

Shannon closed her eyes and said a prayer, a plea for help and guidance.

"Come on, lazybones, don't go back to sleep. We have to get up."

"What time is it?"

"About four."

Shannon groaned. "No, Ash. I can't think this early." She tightened her arms around him.

"You don't need to think, just ride a horse." He chuckled. "Hell, I've seen you ride for miles sound asleep on the back of a horse."

Before she could form an answer, he was up and out of the bed, pulling her with him.

She stood shivering with cold and dread as Ash leaned around her and flicked on the bedside lamp. The soft glow scattered shadows to the far corners of the room, but goosebumps slid over her skin and she clutched her arms to her body.

"Are your knees shaking from the temperature in here or are you just scared?"

Ash's eyes smiled at her and she felt warm inside. "Both." A grin twitched the edges of her lips as she took in the display of desire he was neither trying to hide nor doing anything about. She glanced up then back down. "You're sure you want to get up?"

"Don't tempt me." He grasped her hand and whirled around, leading her to the bathroom. "How's the foot?"

Limping along behind him, distracted as her gaze roamed over his wide shoulders, smooth back and long legs, she said, "I can put my heel down a little. Ash, how in the world am I going to get my boots on?"

He turned on the shower. Thick steam began to fill up the room, driving away the chill from the tiled floor and walls with clouds of white vapor. "Happy and I discussed it. I'm going to double wrap your ankle and you'll wear your running shoes. Come on, Shannon." He held the shower door open. "Let's get moving. Jeff will be here soon."

"What happened to that romantic, insatiable man from last night?" she grumbled as she stepped under the hot jet spray.

Ash patted her wet behind and shut the door. "Right here."

When they finally walked into the kitchen an hour later, Bridget gave them a knowing, pleased glance and set their breakfast before them without a comment.

Shannon bit her lip to keep a straight face, knowing the housekeeper was bursting with curiosity—eager to know if they'd worked out their problems. She slid a sideways look at Ash, caught his eye and smiled into her coffee mug. The sound of a skillet banging down on the counter top jerked their heads up.

Bridget jammed her fists on her hips and glowered at them. "Well!"

Ash laid down his fork, picked up his napkin from his lap and wiped his mouth, taking his time. "Well what, woman?"

Bridget's cheeks puffed out and her sharp blue eyes narrowed. "Don't you start that with me this morning. Are you two gonna get hitched? Have you made up?"

"Did you ever doubt it, Bridget?"

"Not for a second, Ash Bartlet. Though, mind you, I know how bullheaded you can be." She beamed at them, her eyes filling with tears before she whipped around in an effort to hide her relief and happiness. "Jeff's here," she said gruffly.

Ash rose from the table, then placed his hand on Shannon's shoulder as she started to get up also. "There's no need for you to come out and get cold. I'll call you when we're ready to leave. Bridget, did you pack the provisions?"

"Don't I always? Bob's loading them on the pack-horse."

Shannon quietly watched him go, waiting until the door closed behind him before she swallowed the lump that began to clog her throat. "Oh, Bridget, if I can't remember, if I can't prove I didn't shoot Dean, what then?"

"Don't you dare start thinking that way. I won't have it, do you hear me? Not one word." She left the sink and picked up a bundle from her rocking chair by the big fireplace. "Here. Your grandfather brought this over a little while ago."

Shannon grabbed onto her old sheepskin coat like a long lost friend. She clutched it to her chest and inhaled its many memories. "Is Happy still here?"

"No. He and one of Jeff's deputies are going to take turns watching the Rocking W and Clyde. Now put your coat on and get out of my kitchen. I'm sure the men can find something for you to do. Go supervise their work, it will keep your mind busy and you out of my hair."

Shannon smiled and was on her way toward the door when Bridget reached her.

"I'll be wishing you good luck here." She hesitated then grabbed Shannon and crushed her to her ample bosom. "Don't worry your head—everything will work out."

Shannon returned the bear hug and whispered, "I hope so." She let Bridget go and grasped the doorknob, then stopped. With her back to the other woman, she said, "If the trip doesn't turn out the way we hope... promise me you'll take care of him." She heard a strangled sound but refused to turn around. "Promise me, Bridget."

"Aye. That I'll do."

"God bless you, Bridget."

"And you, Shannon."

The encroaching dawn had left the sky a pearl gray. A cold breeze stirred dark wisps of hair around her face and tugged at the intricate shoulder-length French braid. Feeling hot and flushed, she scraped her damp palms against her jeans and unbuttoned her coat. Her throat was bone dry and ached, and her knees trembled slightly. Fear gripped her like a tight fist, reminding her once again that if Ash's idea didn't work, she could be charged with murder.

Her eyes swept the land, taking in every detail as if to permanently fix a picture in her mind. She looked north toward Devil's Hump and her eyes narrowed as if they could penetrate the gloom of the morning and see beyond the dark shadow of the mountain; past the boulders and rocks, the trees and brush, back in time to when she had camped with Dean. She could recall nothing, and the deep sense of dread that had dogged her every thought increased.

Car lights fractured the dawn off to her right and diverted her. She followed the brightness like a moth to a flame. Male voices raised in conversation and laughter lifted the feeling of doom and she limped a little faster toward the human sounds in hopes of escaping the inner voice that kept reminding her of the trip to come.

The jangle of metal bits, the squeak of leather, the rumble of voices and the stamping and snorting of the horses worked like a balm on her ragged nerves and slowed the quick pounding of her heart. The fear had been chased away at the sight and sound of so much familiar activity. Ash stood at the side of a big, black-and-beige-spotted paint, his Stetson pulled low over his forehead as he listened to Jeff's deep voice. It wasn't until she drew closer, unseen, that she heard what the sheriff was saying.

"Hell no, Ash. I didn't clear this trip with the D.A. He's too hot-to-trot to file charges without Doc's report as it is. I wish the bastard would, then when Shannon tells us what actually happened it would publicly embarrass him for jumping the gun. Sawed off little twirp."

"And what if I don't remember?"

Both men spun around, startled. Jeff yanked off his hat and held it in his big hands, rolling it by the brim. "Morning, Shannon."

"You didn't answer me, Jeff. What could Ham do to you about this unorthodox trip?"

"Demand my resignation."

She swallowed hard. So much rode on her recovering her memory, so many lives were going to be affected. "Maybe I should just—"

"Absolutely not," Ash shouted as he walked over to her and wrapped an arm around her shoulder.

His nearness gave her more than warmth, it gave her strength.

"In this country you're still innocent until proven guilty." Jeff shifted his weight from one foot to the other, then set his hat firmly on his head. "We're going to prove you're innocent, one way or the other." He stepped in front of her, his eyes searching her anxious face. "Don't worry about me *or* Ham. I've beaten that little bastard at all his games. Besides, everything doesn't ride on your remembering. I have a few ideas to work on."

"Like what?" Ash demanded as he tightened his grip on Shannon.

"For one. The rifle that killed Dean had no fingerprints. Not even Dean's, and it was his. In the condition Shannon was in I don't think she would have taken the time to wipe the rifle clean. There's a few other things my men are checking out. Some possibilities."

The morning sun was gently lifting the dawn's mist, highlighting everything in a golden haze, making the dew-covered ground shine as if it had been covered in a layer of silver gauze.

Shannon noticed that somewhere in Jeff's speech his gaze had wandered, drawn away from them. His face had paled, making the thin, pink scars on the side of his cheek stand out starkly. She glanced over her shoulder and followed the direction of his eyes. Jeri, dressed in jeans, boots and a heavy coat, was obviously ready for a long ride. Shannon looked at Jeff and saw his sad, hungry expression before he was able to mask his feelings. He nodded politely to Jeri as she stood beside them. A strained silence followed her arrival as if each person was waiting for the next to say something. "Good morning, Jeri," Shannon said, but Jeri ignored her and Ash. Her eyes were glued to Jeff's.

"I'm going with you."

"No, you're not." It was Ash who answered. "This is not a picnic or a social outing. We're going to be riding hard and fast."

"I'm as good a rider as her." She tore her gaze from Jeff and looked at Shannon. "I'll keep up."

"No." This time it was Jeff who responded.

A little embarrassed, Shannon watched as Jeri reached out and clasped Jeff's hand, but Jeff shook off her hold.

"Please, Jeff. I have to talk to you."

"For the past two years you've treated our affair like a yo-yo. You've had me so strung out I don't know which way to turn. First you want me, then you don't. You love me, you say, then you're not sure. You promised to stand up to your mother and tell her about us. And just when I think you mean it, you let her talk you into that damn trip and everything changes again. What do you think I'm made of, stone?"

"Please," she pleaded. "There's some things I haven't told you, things that happened in Europe."

"I damn well don't want to hear it, Jeri. Not now." Jeff spun around, strolled back to his horse and began tightening the cinch and adjusting the saddle more firmly on the animal's back.

But Jeri wasn't about to give up. She turned a very determined, pleading look on her stepbrother. "Ash?"

"No, Jeri, Jeff's right. And now is not the time to push him with your personal problems. He's under as much pressure as we are. Wait until we get back."

"I don't want to wait . . . I can't wait. You don't understand," she wailed, losing her composure.

"No, you're right, I don't understand," he yelled. "You and your mother have been acting crazy ever since Shannon came back. Do you really think Shannon wants your sullen sarcasm on this trip? After the way you've treated her?"

For the first time Shannon noticed the lines of strain bracketing Ash's mouth, the haunted look in his green eyes, the set of his mouth. Though he tried not to show it, he was as worried as she. Fear rode his thoughts with a heavy hand, and that fear was making him unusually harsh with Jeri.

The blood had drained away from Jeri's face and Shannon gripped Ash's arm tightly. "Stop it, Ash. She can come."

"I said no. We've got enough on our hands as it is. By the way, Jeri, where the hell is Paula anyway?"

"I don't know. She didn't come home last night, said she wanted to stay as far away from the scandal as possible." She shot a quick look at Jeff's back then turned to Ash and Shannon. "You won't reconsider and take me along?"

Ash shook his head.

Shannon watched as the young woman whirled around and sprinted off, realizing she was the only one who caught the softly mumbled words, "Happy will take me." Jeri was running toward the garage and a few minutes later an engine roared into life and car headlights bathed them in brightness for a second as the car turned the curve onto the lane.

"You were rough on her, Ash."

"It's time she grew up and learned she can't always get her way."

Shannon smiled cryptically. "I have a feeling she'll get it anyway." She remembered how Jeri could wrap Happy around her finger when she was a little girl. She didn't imagine the situation had changed much in that respect.

"What..." Ash didn't get to finish his sentence as Jeff's shout caught their attention.

"Two riders coming in."

They followed the direction of his pointing hand. Two riders were indeed heading for the ranch, except they weren't riding together. It looked to Shannon as if one was trying to intercept the other, galloping fast and at a direct angle.

As the horses drew closer, Ash began to curse.

Jeff grunted with irritation then started to laugh.

Shannon strained to see who the rider was that seemed to be having a difficult time staying on his horse. Then she realized that the he was a she, dressed in a loud, shocking-pink blouse and with brassy blond hair that stood out against the brightening sky like a sore thumb. "Who is she?"

"The *Bartlet Star*'s ace reporter and resident man-eater." Jeff grinned. "It looks like Sally Roland has finally met her match in that horse."

Ash's mouth tightened. "The other clown trying to catch up with the lady, and I use that term loosely, is young Bob. I'll have his hide."

Both horses nearly collided as they shot through the gate. Gravel from the lane flew out in all directions under skidding hooves as they pulled up to a stop.

Bob flew off his mount, yelling as he ran toward Ash. "She came from the Douglas place, Boss. We were guarding the front gate when I spotted her. Damn fool wouldn't stop even when I fired a warning shot."

"Will someone help me off this goddamn, stiff-legged beast? My ass is bruised to the bone. I've bitten my tongue twice and my head hurts like the devil. Well!"

Jeff assisted her down, stepping quickly away as Sally's hands lingered on his broad shoulders.

"You're trespassing, Roland," Ash growled. "I've guards posted just for the purpose of keeping your kind out."

"How unkind," Sally drawled.

"Get back on that worthless excuse for a horse you borrowed from the Douglases and get the hell off my property."

"Now, Ash, darling. Don't be that way. I've known you too long—" she batted her heavily mascaraed eyes at him "—for you to treat me like this."

Shannon stiffened. She suddenly remembered the Roland woman and her unsavory reputation with men.

"Out!"

Sally rubbed her backside, caught Shannon's glance and grimaced. "I thought *I* was the only person this hick town liked to talk about, but, honey, you top me by a wide margin." Ash growled again and she threw him a sly smile. "Knowing how gossip gets started here, I only took what was said about you with a grain of salt." She shook off Ash's hands as he reached for her and walked over to stand in front of Shannon. "You didn't shoot that husband of yours, did you?"

"No," she whispered, none too convincingly.

"Well, hell. You don't sound too sure of that." From her shirt pocket she pulled out a small spiral pad and a stubby pencil.

"Sally," Ash warned as he and Jeff insinuated themselves between the two women.

"Come on, you two. Give me a break, an exclusive interview and I won't warn our esteemed D.A. that you're about to hightail it out of the county. That is what Jeff is helping you do, isn't it?" Her hand poised over the pad, she glanced up and frowned. She didn't like either man's expression.

"Bob," Ash called, and the young man was immediately at his side. "Take Miss Roland to the tack room and lock her in."

"Now just wait one damn minute."

"And keep her there for a couple of hours."

Bob grinned, his boyish face lighting up like a roman candle on the Fourth of July. "Yes, sir." He grabbed hold of Sally's arm and began to lead her forcefully away.

"You can't do this to me, Ash Bartlet," she protested "I'm a newspaper reporter. I have a right to write the truth. Jeff, damn you, you're the sheriff, stop this. Jeff—*Jeff*..."

Ash and Jeff grinned at each other.

Jeff turned, picked up a saddle from the ground and pitched it onto the back of the black horse. "That's one of our headaches out of the way. But we better hurry before the others start finding ingenious ways to get in."

Shannon watched as the men hurriedly finished saddling the horses and checking the packhorse. "What others, Jeff?"

"You tell her, Ash, I'm going to pull my car and trailer around to the back so it's not spotted."

"Ash?"

"Reporters, sweetheart. Seems that Ham leaked the story of Dean's death to the press. Late yesterday they were swarming all over the town and our front gate."

Shannon squeezed her eyes shut. So much trouble. Lately that's all she'd managed to cause in the lives of the people she loved. She felt Ash's hands on her face and she opened her eyes, gazing into his with a stricken look.

"Don't do this to yourself."

"I can't help it, Ash." She moved her head, loving the feel of his touch, the way it soothed her and made her warm inside. "None of this would have happened if I hadn't come back."

"And we wouldn't be together, either."

"I just hope, when it's all over, that you don't end up hating me."

"How could you think that?"

She laughed a little shakily. "Easy. I could end up in jail. Your life has been torn apart. The scandal will hurt everyone. Jeff has put his job and future on the line for me. Happy's too old to have to be put through this."

"Hush." He kissed her softly, his lips barely touching hers to take away the words that were forming there. "We'll work everything out. Trust me, Shannon. Let me, let everyone, show you we're willing to stand beside you no matter what because we believe in you and love you."

She wrapped her arms around his waist and laid her cheek against his chest. "So much faith. Where did it all come from so suddenly?"

Ash took hold of her shoulders and pushed her away from him so he could look into her amber eyes, so dark and turbulent with doubts. "I don't think faith has anything to do with it, it's love, Shannon. We all love you." He kissed her again. "Some more than others, that's all."

"Ash—Ash Bartlet," Bridget yelled as she trotted down the walkway toward them. "You let go of that girl and quit making love to her in broad daylight for everyone to see." She spotted Jeff coming around the corner of the garage and motioned frantically for him to hurry up. "Here, you might need this." She handed Shannon a rather beat-up gray felt Stetson. "It's one of yours I found in the attic. Smells a bit, but it'll keep your head warm. And this." She pushed a silver thermos into Shannon's other hand. "Some of my herbal tea with a touch of brandy to keep the chill from your bones. Gets damn cold up on the mountain at night."

Bridget looked at Jeff, a frown puckering her mouth, her expression fierce. "And why the devil are you standing around? Stella called from the café to tell me that Hamilton Watts found out you were here. He just left, headed this way with the intention of making you arrest Shannon. He's not going to wait for Doc's autopsy report."

Ash plucked the hat from Shannon's hand and jammed it on her head. "Come on. It's way past time we moved out." He tucked the thermos into the saddlebag on her gray horse, locked his fingers together and held them out. "No, not your foot. I don't want any pressure on it. Put your knee there and I'll heave you up."

Her mouth had gone dry, and her heart began to pound. "Ash."

There was a desperate plea in her voice and it brought his head up. He smiled, deliberately making light of the situation. "Don't back out on me now. We ride together or not at all."

She took a deep breath, placed her knee in his hands and was hoisted up in the saddle. "What's her name?" Letting the horse sidestep and prance away from the others, she quickly brought her under control, settled down into the saddle and pulled her hat firmly on her head.

"She's King's Lady."

Shannon reached out and gave the horse a few reassuring pats on the neck. None of the four horses were the spindly legged Thoroughbreds that stocked Ash's stalls. These were a mixed breed of wild mustang and a stouter stock, bred for hunting and for their surefootedness on the rocky mountain paths. They were strong, even-tempered beasts, with big hearts and a mule-headed de-

termination to keep their footing. They wanted their
riders on their backs, not down some gorge or ravine.

Bridget watched them ride out of the yard, through
the gate, then line up abreast of one another with the
pack horse tied to Jeff's saddle and trailing behind. She
sighed and said a quick, silent prayer.

The morning sun had crept up a little higher in the sky,
bathing their faces in a pink glow as they rode between
the white fences then suddenly burst out into the open
pasture. Shannon glanced from one man to the other
then began to laugh. It was so much like old times that
for a few minutes she forgot everything that had happened and reveled in the pleasure of the memories that
flooded her mind.

Ash and Jeff must have felt the same pull back to their
childhood because they were laughing, too. Then all
three were leaning low over their saddles, challenging
one another. She could have gone on forever, chasing the
wind, but as they raced toward the dark shadow that
Devil's Hump threw across the land, her lighthearted-
ness seeped away. She pulled up her mount and let the
men continue. They too must have felt a sense of foreboding and slowed down, circling around and trotting
back to her.

Once more, lined up abreast of each other, they rode
on in silence.

Shannon shivered.

It was more than the quiet or the looming mountain
that caused the deeply felt chill. As much as she wanted
to remember, she deliberately blanked out her mind. To
remember was to face the fear and horror that had
haunted her sleep for days. She felt like a child again,
wanting to confront the threatening monster, yet also

wanting to hide her head under the covers until the morning light chased it away.

But she wasn't a child. She was a woman and possibly the instrument of Dean's death. How could she live with herself if it were true?

How could Ash?

SHADOWS LENGTHENED across the land, reaching from tree to tree, traveling from rock formation to high stacked boulders to leafless shrubs, connecting them all in a growing darkness that sent Jeff on ahead in search of a sheltered campsite for the night. A light, icy breeze whispered off the higher snowcapped mountains beyond, slicing through their clothing, stinging already reddened cheeks and frosting their breath in fogged clouds.

Shannon drooped visibly in the saddle. She was bone tired, cold, and her ankle ached.

Ash, riding ahead of Shannon, pulled back and let her catch up with him. His eyes searched her strained face and his mouth tightened. "Hold on, Daffy. Jeff's scouting for a place. Soon you'll be warm and with some hot food you'll feel like a new woman."

She was too exhausted to answer and only nodded.

"How's the ankle?"

"Fine."

"Liar. It hurts like hell." He reached over and caressed her cheek, pleased to see that the bruises there and on her neck were beginning to fade.

A long series of whistles split the evening, a signal that Ash immediately recognized, and he turned his mount toward the sound.

Shannon gritted her teeth and followed. Now that relief from the jarring ride was nearly there, she felt her aches more keenly. They rode under a canopy of towering pines, the air pungent with their sharp fragrance, then they weaved around outcrops of boulders, and just when she thought she couldn't stand another minute, she smelled smoke and the mingling scents of coffee and food. Kicking the side of her horse, she winced as her ankle protested, but managed to catch up with Ash.

The campsite, the warm glow of a roaring fire, had never looked so good. Before she could slow down, Ash was off his mount and striding back to her. She dropped the reins and fell into his waiting arms with a gusty sigh. Suddenly she was being taken care of. Ash set her down on soft bedding, gently pulled off her sneaker and began unwrapping the elastic bandage.

Jeff collected handfuls of snow still left in small pockets dotting the dark base of the trees. He helped Ash pack the ice around her puffy ankle, then handed her a hot cup of coffee and a plate of steaming stew with thick gravy and big chunks of beef and potatoes. He whipped out a thermal blanket and watched as Ash tucked it around her like a cocoon. They worked fast, silently, with the sole purpose of easing her pain, cold and hunger.

Once she was warm and her ankle had stopped throbbing and the coffee had filled the empty pit in her stomach, she leaned back to watch as Ash and Jeff finished their dinner.

"With all this special treatment, which one of you is going to pull out a guitar and serenade me?" The question, she could see, had stumped them for a second. Then they began to laugh. She eyed the men over the rim of the tin cup and smiled. She loved them both for what they were trying to do, as obvious as it was. Ever since they'd reached camp their conversation had been focussed on their childhood, stories of their friends, ranching—they'd even covered some of the less pleasant aspects of Jeff's job. The two men talked nonstop, including Shannon, yet never forcing her to contribute unless she wanted to.

Ash and Jeff were taxing themselves to keep her mind off tomorrow.

She set her cup aside, snuggled down into the warm sleeping bag and let their deep voices flow over her. High above her head, the thick overhanging limbs of the trees tried to stamp out the sky, but she found an opening where the stars peeked through. This was her sky, her land. She felt a part of it and the life that went on around her in the dark, as familiar as her own heartbeat. And Ash.

She shifted her gaze to him, watching through slitted eyelids as the glow of the fire danced over his features, throwing shadows across the sharp planes of his cheekbones, making the blond hair turn golden in the light. Their voices had lowered to a murmur, and though she couldn't hear the words, she knew they were discussing what would happen the following day.

Her whole life could change tomorrow.

Shannon squeezed her eyes shut, playing possum, knowing she'd never sleep that night, not with the morning looming before her like the nightmare of her dreams.

CHAPTER FIFTEEN

A FICKLE MOTHER NATURE seemed to take delight in mocking her the next morning.

The sky boasted only a few dusty-gray clouds, chasing each other across the heaven. The sun shone bright, burning off some of the intense cold of the high mountain air. Birds chirped and small animals scurried playfully back and forth along the trail.

The ringing thud of the horses' hooves against the rocky path hammered out questions to plague her sanity. The closer they came to the plateau of the mountain, the more insistent the questions became.

Why had Dean tried to strangle her?

Shannon turned in her saddle and looked back at Ash riding silently behind her, hoping he might read her mind and give her the answer. But Ash was as lost in his own world—or hell, she supposed—as she was.

Had she hated Dean so much?

Her horse stumbled, and for a second she thought she was going to lose her seat and end up sliding down the side of the steep cliff. Once she'd righted herself and her heart had resumed a more normal beat, she fought to erase the nagging questions from her mind. But they wouldn't leave her.

Could she have taken a human life? Was she a murderer?

Her soul-searching was of no use. The answers just weren't there. Whole days had been erased from her memory. She couldn't account for them no matter how hard she tried.

The thick stands of trees began to thin out the closer they got to the top. Her hand holding the reins began to tremble. They were almost there, close to the campsite where the course of her life and that of her loved ones had changed. She wanted to squeeze her eyes shut and wish herself away, back to the peace and comfort of home. There was a humming in her ears. She could feel the wet bite of driving snow against her skin, stinging her eyes, blurring her vision.

Shannon shook her head like a dazed animal and looked around. The wind was a gentle breeze, the sun hot on her face. She felt sick inside, numb.

Ash and Jeff pushed on relentlessly, stoic sentinels, keeping her between them as they rode up the mountain, over the treacherous trails, around outcroppings that took them too close to the edge of the path and the sheer drop over the cliff beside them. She hated them. She loved them.

Dear God. She wanted to go home.

Jeff disappeared around a bend and she followed blindly, recognizing where they were. He would take another turn and another trail, then go up a steep incline that would lead them to the plateau of Devil's Hump and the deserted campsite that lay like a ghost, beckoning them upward with the false, sweet promise of the truth.

Run! Leave now. Ride away, be wild and free like the Montana wind.

As Shannon's horse took the steep slope, she was forced to lean forward, the saddle horn digging into her stomach. When the ground leveled out she sat up, and her horse slowed to a walk, following the lead of Jeff's mount. She gazed around with wide knowing eyes at the flat ground and the stunted trees along the edge of the timberline that were twisted in grotesque shapes by the fierce wind that blew from the higher snowcapped peaks beyond. Shrubs, naked of foliage, grew from odd rock formations, boulders that had tumbled down from the cliffs millions of years ago. Sprigs of brown grass fought for life among the cold, hard-packed earth.

An eerie hush surrounded them. The birds, as if sensing a storm, had flown away. The small animals scurried to their holes and treetops to watch. The air had turned colder and felt chilly on her skin, yet she was suddenly hot inside, her mouth sawdust dry, palms damp.

The noise of the wind slapping the corner of a collapsed tent against the ground made her jerk her eyes in that direction. The campsite. Their provisions, carried away by the wind and curious, hungry animals, littered the area.

Shannon sat straight and tense on her horse, ignoring the men as they dismounted and talked to each other. Then Ash was at her side. His hands were around her waist, and before she could fight the inevitable she was in his arms, her feet firmly on the ground as he held her close to his chest.

"It's time, Daffy."

"Yes," she whispered through stiff lips.

"Do you remember anything?"

"No."

"Give her time, Ash." Jeff patted her shoulder. "Let go, man. Give her some breathing room. Let her look around and see what happens."

Ash shot Jeff a hard glance, sighed, nodded and reluctantly dropped his arms. "How's the ankle?"

Shannon answered his question by gingerly putting weight on her foot, then she smiled shakily. "Better," she mumbled. But she didn't move from the safety of Ash's side.

Both men stared at her like two dogs guarding a bone, waiting to see which one would make the first move.

"Go on, walk around. Maybe something will come back." Ash gave her a nudge.

Shannon nodded, but still didn't move. She raised a panic-stricken face to them. "What if I can't? What happens then?"

Ash gave her a reassuring smile, one he had to force. "Just try." God, she looked sick, ready to collapse at any moment. The trip had been too much for her; the pressure and the mental anguish too taxing. He wanted to help but didn't know how. He wanted to take her away, but couldn't. He'd promised himself he would never hurt her, yet he was. His hands were tied until they played out this scene. He could only love her.

Grasping Shannon by the shoulders, he turned her, holding her in front of him. "Listen to me." Her face was so white, her amber eyes so big and haunted. He took her hat off and handed it to Jeff, then smoothed a few wisps of hair from her cheeks. He tugged at the shoulder-length braid to make her look into his eyes. The sun bounced off her jet-black hair and sparkled as if it had been sprinkled with diamond dust. He could feel her trembling under his hands and ached for her. "I love you, Shannon. More now than I've ever loved you. No matter what happens, I'll always be there. I trust and know you. Whatever happened up here was not of your doing, or your fault. But you must try to remember."

"For you, Ash?"

"No, Daffy, for us." He kissed her cold lips, his heart aching for her.

Shannon gave him a weak smile and limped slowly toward the campsite.

Ash and Jeff were at her heels.

Her eyes passed over the area, searching for a sign, a clue to the nightmare locked away in her mind. Nothing. The toe of her sneaker bumped a solid object, and she glanced down at a canvas-covered, army-green canteen. She shook her head.

Right behind her Ash stiffened. "Do you remember something?"

"No."

She walked on, panic beginning to eat away at her insides. Her gaze touched a spoon half hidden by a rock, the end scratched with the small teeth marks of some night creature.

"Anything?" Ash mumbled.

"Nothing." A fine sheen of perspiration dampened her forehead. A leather guncase lay ripped open, its white cotton padding spilling onto the ground like down from a torn pillow. Still nothing.

"That's Dean's, isn't it?"

"Yes."

Ash growled, "Well!"

"No."

He sighed and she wanted to scream. Thick crystal tears flooded her eyes and she blinked them away.

Shannon had been walking the perimeters of the camp. When the sun caught on something bright and made it wink, she held her breath and stepped inside the imaginary circle her mind had set up as a boundary. Leaning down, she saw a foil package of powered orange juice and picked it up, then dropped it as if it had burned her fingers.

"Anything?"

She shook her head. "It's useless, Ash. I just don't remember. Everything looks familiar, yet strange."

"Keep trying," Jeff put in, then grabbed hold of Ash's arm to warn him away. But Ash shook him off and followed Shannon to the center of the camp and the remains of a fire.

A skillet lay partially buried among the cold gray ashes. She squatted and stared, rubbing her temples, straining to remember. She must have cooked dinner? Lunch? Something, but what? She glanced right then left, exploring the ground until she spotted a metal coffee pot. Nothing. A soft moan escaped her lips.

"You remembered something?" Ash crouched down beside her. "What?"

"Nothing...nothing...nothing. Not one damn thing!"

There was an edge of hysteria in her voice and he tried to calm her down. "Take it easy."

Jeff grumbled behind him and Ash threw him a killing glance over his shoulder. "You're trying to force it, Shannon," Ash told her. "Just relax."

Jeff snorted and mumbled under his breath.

"What's your problem, Jeff?" Ash snapped, then lowered his voice. "Relax, Shannon. Try to remember back to the Rocking W when you and Dean left on the hunt. Take it a step at a time."

She looked at him then, the tears she'd tried so hard to keep back snaking a wet path down her cheeks. "There's nothing there, Ash. I've tried."

"Not enough. Dammit, don't give up."

Jeff coughed.

Ash ignored him. "Try again. Look around." His hand swept a wide arc. "These things must be familiar to you."

"Of course they are," she snapped, and quickly rose to her feet. "I've hunted and camped out all my life. I've used every item here hundreds of times. I just don't remember and don't think I'm going to—ever." She wiped her cheeks with the soft suede of her coat sleeve. "Maybe Jeff had better arrest me and take me back to town."

"Now you listen to me. I don't want to hear talk like that. It's my life you're throwing away too with this self-pity. Think. Remember."

"That's enough," Jeff roared, grabbing Ash and yanking him to his feet. They faced each other like warriors ready to do battle. "Ash, stop hounding her for God's sake. How do you expect her to remember her own name with you breathing down her neck like a dragon? Hell, man, you've distracted and irritated me till I don't think I could remember what I had for breakfast."

"Go to hell."

"Yeah, sure. You want to hit me, don't you? Go ahead. Maybe it will get rid of some of that anger you're feeling. Go on, take a swing."

Shannon watched, openmouthed and stunned.

"But our fighting won't help anything," Jeff went on. "Come with me and leave her alone. I want you to take a look at the ledge."

Ash felt like a complete ass, grinned and went with Jeff.

Relief that they'd left her alone was short-lived for Shannon. The inner trembling started again. She turned her back on them and gazed down into the dark ashes of the fire.

She blinked.

Intense heat warmed her legs through the heavy jeans as blue and yellow flames danced in the wind. Panic squeezed at her heart, making it difficult to breathe, and she threw a frantic glance toward Ash and Jeff. They were standing close to Devil's Leap, looking at her, yet she realized they didn't see anything unusual. Maybe she'd just imagined it. She glanced down again. The fire had come to life, hot and bright, and only she could see it.

"Dean, we have to get out of here, there's a bad storm coming."

"How blessed it must be to be able to divine the weather. Do you have a direct line to God?"

"Don't be funny, you fool. All any sane person has to do is look at the sky."

Shannon shut her eyes, then opened them. No flames. No heat. The fire lay dead and cold at her feet. She wrapped her arms around herself and quickly moved away, looking back only once to verify that the fire was indeed gone.

Ash knew something was happening. Shannon was acting strange, dead still one moment, then fidgeting the next. "I think it's beginning to come back," he whispered to Jeff.

She sat down on a smooth slab of rock, the hard surface reassuring, telling her she wasn't hallucinating. She stared at the ground, trying to figure out what was going on. The wind began to hum in her head. Cold and icy it made her ears hurt, and she cupped her hands over them.

"I'm leaving you, Dean. I mean it."

"I'll never let you do that. Never!"

"You won't have any say in it. I'm home now."

Shannon dropped her hands to her lap. The breeze was light and warm, caressing her face, the sun hot on the top of her bare head. She surged to her feet and limped a few steps, then stopped.

"You think Happy will help you? Or Ash?"

"Yes."

Laughter, mean and mocking, touched her and she trembled.

"They think you're a whore, a slut. I've seen to that. They'll treat you like a leper."

The wind increased, growing colder and slicing through her coat like the sharp edge of a knife. The sky darkened as clouds gathered above her.

"I took you from Ash once. I'll do it again."

"I never loved you. You knew that from the beginning. I never loved you, dammit."

She tilted her head and squinted from the glare. The sky was cloudless and the air warm.

"There was always a third person in bed with us—Ash. I was forced to share you and I don't share. He was there with you day after day, night after night. Always in your thoughts. God, how I hate him—and you."

She walked over to the horses tethered to a row of pickets. Her mount butted her with his cold, wet nose and she patted his neck, then reached down and grabbed the saddle by the horn and hoisted it onto his back.

"Look around you, Dean. We have to go, now, or we won't make it down the mountain."

"I'll never let you go to Ash, Shannon. He won't have you, not the way I have."

"You're sick and disgusting and I'm leaving."

There was nothing in her hands; no saddle, its leather stiff and cold; no horse to warm her touch. Nothing but empty space. She shivered. What was she doing? What was happening?

Ash and Jeff recognized her movements, fascinated by her pantomine.

Ash took a step forward. He didn't know whether to go to her and help or to stop her.

Jeff held him back. "Let her play it out—all of it."

"Look at her. It's as if she's walking in her sleep, but it's broad daylight and she's wide awake." He felt sick inside yet excited by the thought that maybe it would all be over soon.

Shannon spun around and hurried away from the ghost horses, feeling foolish and scared. At the center of the camp she paused, changed direction and took a few steps toward Devil's Leap. Then she halted. The steel point of an arrow caught her eye, one of her arrows. She leaned down and picked it up. The slick wood shaft had been broken near the end. A snowflake settled like a butterfly on the back of her hand and she dropped the arrow as she watched the snow melt. Another flake fluttered against her cheek, leaving a cold, wet spot.

"He'll never caress that luscious body, or kiss your lips, or die that little death of ecstasy. Ash will only have his memories—like me. I'll kill you before I let him touch you again."

"You're crazy."

"Am I, sweets?"

"You'll never get away with it."

"Won't I? A hunting accident, they'll say."

The wild fury of the wind buffeted her. Snow stung her face and hands with needle sharpness.

Shannon shook her head, dazed. The sun warmed her and she inhaled the sweet mountain air. Suddenly she couldn't breathe, and she gasped as if something had hit her hard. "Ash, Ash . . . Ash help me."

"A fall over the ledge, maybe."

Jeering laughter scoffed at her attempts to escape him.

"Ash, he's coming toward me, stalking me, forcing me back." She was no longer silent in her nightmare, but was loudly describing to her two spectators what had happened. "He's crazy."

The wind wailed around her, sucking the vile words away so she could only make out half of them. "I can't hear him." A rush of fear nearly paralyzed her, but the sight of Dean's face, twisted and ugly with hate, his blue eyes glinting strangely, the pupils big and round and black as death, kept her moving slowly backward.

"He's really going to kill me." Terror and hysteria punctuated the shock she felt.

Ash watched her stumble over a patch of smooth ground, right herself, look down then pick something up. But there was nothing in her hands. He glanced at Jeff and held his breath.

She raised her arm and brandished her invisible weapon. "He's laughing at me, telling me I won't use it. But I will, I will if he comes any closer." She swung around slowly, facing the two men standing so still near the ledge as her eyes followed the ghost of her living nightmare, watching him, trying to calculate his next move so she could make her first strike count. The intense cold was sapping her strength, the blowing snow like a white blindfold across her line of vision. She blinked wet flakes from her eyelashes and Dean took advantage of her distraction and made his move.

Shannon dropped her arm limply to her side, her next words a hoarse rasp. "I couldn't breathe." She was drifting in and out of reality, shifting from the past to the present. Once again she saw the uncontrolled wildness in Dean's eyes, felt his breath hot on her cheek and heard his mad whisper, "I'll kill you before I let Ash have you." She remembered the awful pressure around her neck and how it had increased. She saw the bright dots of light again as they danced before her eyes. She was going to die.

"I knew if I didn't do something he was going to choke me to death or push me over the ledge. We were already too close to the edge as it was. Then for no reason Dean stopped and just let go of me, as if he'd changed his mind. He was staring over my shoulder with the most peculiar expression on his face." She lifted her hand and rubbed her eyes, then stood very still, concentrating on the imaginary weapon in that same hand.

"Even though he'd let go, I was still terrified, too scared to move. I was fighting to get my breath back." Once again she looked at her empty hand. "Ash," she breathed his name like a prayer, "I didn't kill Dean." Holding her hands before her, still doubting her own statement, Shannon inspected each finger, one by one. There had been blood on her hands once, now they were clean. She glanced up at the two watching her so closely and was stunned to see the bright shine in Ash's eyes. Her own tears ran unchecked down her cheeks.

"I didn't kill him. I'd only picked up a broken tree limb, not his rifle."

Ash made a move toward her. Jeff clamped hold of his arm in a grip that wasn't to be broken.

"What happened next, Shannon? Who shot Dean?"

The relief she'd felt at realizing she was innocent quickly faded with Jeff's question. Taut with tension, she glanced from one man to the other, then back to Jeff with a pleading look. When Jeff shook his head she knew he had a good idea what she was trying to hide.

"Finish telling us what happened. Everything, Shannon," he said sadly.

"You know how fierce the wind can get up here in a storm? Deafening, the way it bangs tree branches together and moans. Or how it can whistle through holes in the rocks and make sounds that are almost human. I thought I heard a high pitched scream, but I wasn't sure because I was pretty dazed and terrified. I must have sagged to my knees, Dean was standing over me. Then I heard a loud cracking noise, like the sound of a dead tree being snapped in half by the wind.

"When I looked up Dean moved. He'd stepped backward with a jerk. He was just standing there very still and with a rather surprised look on his face. He tried to say something and it was then that I saw the red stain on the center of his chest. He seemed to hang there forever, then like a puppet with his strings suddenly cut he began to collapse backward. I knew he was going over the edge and I reached out to grab him. I don't think I really realized what was happening until just before he fell and I touched the spreading stain and my hand came away wet and sticky with blood."

She looked down at her hands, remembering the feel of the warm blood on her cold hands and the revulsion she'd felt. She'd frantically wiped the sticky stuff on the front of her coat, then, sickened further by the sweet, tinny odor, she'd ripped the coat off and thrown it on the freezing ground.

"When I glanced back to the spot where Dean was, he was gone as if he'd never been there. I crawled to the edge of the ledge." Shannon shuddered. She'd never forget the shock and horror of the wide empty panorama, the wind tearing and sucking at her, trying to shove her over into that bottomless dark pit below.

Gritting his teeth, Ash yanked his arm from Jeff's death grip and gathered Shannon into his arms. "Who, Shannon? Who shot Dean?"

The name stuck in her throat like a thorn. "When I backed away from the edge and turned, I realized I was in as much danger then as I had been from Dean. All I could think was to run—and I did."

"Who?"

The silence that followed was abruptly broken by the sound of someone's heavy step, a boot snapping a small tree limb. Then a shot reverberated through the hushed mountain air. All three spun in that direction.

As had happened in the preceding days, Shannon felt the grip of terror once more. Her blood ran cold and the urge to flee was so strong she tried to yank free of Ash, but he only tightened his arms around her. She waited, sick with dread and fear, knowing that what was to come was somehow her fault.

The sound of snapping twigs came again.

Jeff's hand eased down past his waist and under his coat to the regulation automatic strapped to his hip. He winced as the snap on the leather holster popped open.

"I didn't mean to kill him." A voice carried through the chilly mountain air from the direction of a stand of grotesquely twisted trees. "He promised me he'd get rid of her, but I'd been watching and listening and knew he was only trying to scare her so badly she wouldn't dare leave him. He was a coward and he lied. So I was going to do it for him. I aimed at her, but she moved."

The voice no longer rushed at them like an evil mountain ghost, but the speaker stepped out from the shelter of the trees into the brightness of the day. The long barrel of a rifle caught the sun and glinted wickedly as it rose slowly in steady hands and took careful aim at Shannon.

"Now I can finish what I started."

CHAPTER SIXTEEN

"PAULA!" Ash whispered. He closed his eyes in agony then opened them and yelled, "No!" as he watched, horrified, while she lifted the rifle to her shoulder and sighted down the barrel. "No!" he screamed, and pulled Shannon behind him.

Jeff lunged beside his friend, using his body as a shield. "Put the gun down—*now*, Paula."

He should have known something was wrong, Ash berated himself. But he'd been so angry, confused, then gloriously happy Shannon was back and still loved him that he hadn't taken the time to see what was going on in his own home.

He reached around, grasped Shannon's hand and squeezed it to reassure himself she was still there. He should have paid more attention to Paula's irrational behavior, her changing moods, the way she'd let herself deteriorate. She'd acted strange from the moment he'd brought Shannon off the mountain. Dammit, he should have guessed. But murder!

"Jeff, she's not rational, don't make any suspicious moves. She's liable to pull the trigger. Let me talk to her. Stay behind me, Shannon, and for God's sake don't open your mouth."

All her life she'd been fearless, taking chances and flirting with danger. She'd made it off the mountain in a blinding snowstorm with all the odds against her and

she'd faced the past, Ash and her grandfather with a
singleminded determination and strength. But in the last
few minutes her courage had completely deserted her.
She was more than willing to let Ash handle Paula.
Reaching under his coat, she grabbed his wide leather
belt and held on to it like a lifeline. Many a time she'd
seen Ash talk a wild, enraged stallion to a trembling
standstill. He was using that same smooth, persuasive
voice on Paula. She prayed it would work.

"Do as Jeff says, Paula, and lay the rifle down nice
and easy. You really don't want to hurt anyone else.
Come on, everything will be okay. We'll work it out."
He couldn't believe what was happening, what she'd
done. "Why did you do it, Paula? What has Shannon
ever done to you?"

Jeff began to edge away from his friends.

"She took Dean away from my baby."

Jeff froze. "Jeeze," he groaned.

Ash's back muscles tightened. "From Jeri, Paula?
You're not making sense."

"Ask her about Europe, Ash," Shannon whispered
fiercely and peeked around his shoulder. She remembered the photograph of Paula and Dean together and
how ill she'd felt by his expression; a lascivious look of
lust and sexual triumph. Now she realized that the look
was directed not at Paula but at the person holding the
camera—Jeri.

A wave of nausea washed over her and she rested her
forehead against Ash's back and swallowed audibly.
Sweet, gullible Jeri. Always overruled by her mother's
demands. Somehow Dean had played a part in Paula's
driving obsession that her daughter marry the right man,
a person with power and money.

But how Dean had fitted into Paula's plan was a mystery. Or was it Paula's plan? Now, even in death, Dean promised to destroy those she loved with his hatred. He was reaching out from the grave to finish his last sworn act of revenge.

Paula walked out farther from the stand of weirdly twisted trees, the rifle still aimed at them. She moved along the narrow path near the edge of the cliff and motioned them with the barrel to the center of the ravaged campsite. When Jeff refused to budge, she commanded in a voice gilded with ice, *"Now."*

Unwilling to take any chances, Ash kept Shannon behind him and backed slowly in the direction she wanted. "What are you going to do, Paula, kill all three of us? Be reasonable." He saw a momentary flicker of confusion in her haggard features and was relieved, then her expression swiftly became determined again and he felt weak with dread.

"It's all *her* fault. Step away from her, Ash. Don't move again, Jeff."

The light breeze tugged at the lank blond hair hanging in ribbons around her head and Ash could see the extent of her physical deterioration. Her blouse was wrinkled, a small tear at one shoulder. Her jeans were dirty, and there were smudges on her face and leaves in her hair. She'd ridden harder than they had and had managed to camp out on the mountain. Her determination scared the hell out of him.

He glanced around searching for shelter, a place to hide, where he could secure Shannon while he tried to get a rational explanation of what was going on from Paula. But there was nowhere to go. He had to stall her until either he or Jeff could come up with a plan. He caught Jeff's eye and read the message there. *Keep her*

alking, reason with her. You're the only one she'll lis-
en to until we think of something. Ash nodded, then
umped, his heart hammering in his chest when Shan-
on whispered close to his ear. He should have known
he would be on the same wavelength as he and Jeff.

"The path, Ash. We could make it. The rocks will
hield us, but we need a diversion to distract her."

"I thought I told you to move away from her, Ash,"
aula called to him. "Now. Please. Don't make me hurt
ou, too."

This soft, reasonable voice scared him more now than
er earlier passionate outbursts. Paula was going to kill
hannon if she had to send a bullet through him to do it.
"Paula, we've never been particularly close, and I re-
ret that. Dad loved you and Jeri. He just didn't have the
ash to leave you so you could live the way you wanted.
Listen, I'm willing to sell some Bartlet land and hire the
est defense attorney in Montana to get you through
his. Let me help you now, please."

Confusion had softened her features, then muscles in
er face hardened and he knew the mention of money
ad been a big mistake. It only added fuel to her hatred
f Shannon. Money was Paula's passion and her ob-
ession.

Before Ash could think of something to smooth over
what he'd just said, the sound of horses' hooves racing
angerously up the path drew everyone's attention. A
urefooted mountain pinto came flying around the bend
n the trail, then skidded to a stop on its hind legs. Jeri
umped from her mount's back before the animal could
ight itself.

Happy, equally as reckless, was not far behind, his
lismount as quick, but with more finesse.

"Mother, no!"

Like a hunter with too many targets, Paula froze, then the rifle barrel jerked back and forth, finally settling o Ash and Shannon again. "Stay where you are, Jeri."

"Mother, are you mad?"

Shannon sucked in a frightened breath.

Ash winced.

Jeff groaned and moved so fast in the hush that fol lowed Jeri's question that no one even saw him. He pu himself in front of Jeri. "This has gone on lon enough." His next angry words were cut off as chips o rock and dirt dusted his boots and lower legs. Paula ha put a bullet only a fraction of an inch from his feet.

Everyone froze—except Jeri. She stepped around Jef and began walking toward her mother. "You kille Dean, didn't you?"

"I didn't mean to, darling. Don't come any closer." Jeri stopped. "It was an accident. Please forgive me."

"Forgive you? I'm glad he's dead. Do you hear me" I hated him after..." Her voice trailed off and she sho an agonized look over her shoulder at Jeff.

"You don't mean that, dear. You loved him."

"I despised him, Mother. You were the one wh planned everything. You pushed and pushed and neve considered my feelings or what kind of man Dean was I think I hate you as much as I hated him."

"I wish to hell I knew what was going on," As whispered.

"I believe we'll soon find out," Shannon whispere back. "By the look on Jeri's face, I don't think Jeff going to like it, though." She glanced at her grandfa ther, who ignored the weapon now aimed at him an walked over to stand beside Ash and Shannon.

"It's a nasty tale. That's how Jeri got me to bring her up here. She told me everything that happened in Europe and at the ranch."

"Europe? The ranch? What's he talking about, Shannon?" Ash didn't wait for an answer but pulled Happy in front of Shannon and moved up beside Jeff and Jeri. "Will someone tell me what's going on?"

Jeri's shoulders slumped and she began to cry. "Are you going to tell them, Mother, or am I?"

Paula shrugged and lowered the rifle but still kept it aimed in Shannon's direction. "It doesn't matter now, does it, baby. He's gone and all his promises were lies."

"Of course they were, Mother. He made fools out of us all." She wiped her cheeks with her sleeve. "Mother and I ran into Dean in Paris. He played tour guide and entertained us lavishly. He wined and dined us and even bought us both mink coats. Believe me, he knew Mother and how she was obsessed with money and finding me a rich husband. All the time he was making advances at me and she encouraged him." Jeri dropped her head and stared at the ground.

"But he loved you, darling. He told me over and over if it weren't for Shannon and her greed he'd be a free man and would marry you in a minute."

"And take care of you, Mother? He said he'd set you up in the style you deserved, didn't he?"

"Well, yes. I'm your mother after all. He knew how close we were, that I couldn't bear to be away from you. After all, as his wife you would need me to show you how to go on in society."

Jeri couldn't raise her head, too ashamed to look at anyone. "Sometimes I wonder just who you are, Mother. You let Dean seduce me, you pushed me to go to bed with him." Her head jerked up and she swung

around to face Jeff. His vacant eyes made her insides
wither and she wanted to curl up and die. But she'd gone
this far and wasn't going to back down now. Jeff deserved to know what she'd done. "Dean promised
Mother, one way or the other, he would get rid of Shannon and marry me. I was confused and, yes, flattered.
But I didn't really know what he was like. Jeff, I never
intended to sleep with him. I know it's no excuse. It just
happened."

Jeff stared at her, his face as hard as stone.

"Please understand. He kept talking about Shannon
and how she'd ruined his life, and hadn't things changed
since she left Montana the way she had. He was right.
Ash was not like he used to be, nothing was. Jeff, don't
look away from me."

Shannon shivered and took comfort in her grandfather's presence. Damn Dean to hell.

"For the first time in my life I'm trying to grow up
and face what I've done. Please hear me out." When
Jeff swung back around she went on. "I know it sounds
crazy," she burst out, "but he made me feel as if going
to bed with him would be getting back at Shannon for
the chaos she'd caused in our lives. I know it's no excuse for what I did, but I did it, and afterward I wanted
to die. No one knows what he was like." She looked over
at her onetime idol, the woman she had wanted to imi-
tate in every way. "Just you and I know, don't we,
Shannon?" Then she covered her face and began to cry,
deep racking sobs that shook her body.

"You see, baby, it was all *her* fault." Paula raised the
rifle to her shoulder once more. "Step aside, old man.
You've protected her all her life, you can't anymore."

"But *I* can." Ash walked into the line of fire. "You're not going to kill Shannon or anyone else. Give me the gun, Paula."

Shannon held her breath. Fear raced through her. She could sense the change in him—from confusion and sorrow over what his stepmother had done, to a burning anger.

Ash took another careful step. Jeff followed.

Paula waved the rifle at them and moved back a tiny step.

"Now, goddamn you, tell me what went on at the ranch," Ash demanded. "What else did you do?"

"Get back! I'll shoot, I swear I will."

"Tell them, Mother. Tell Ash how you gave Shannon her medicine and deliberately didn't inform me so I'd give her a double dose. Tell them how you opened the gate for the bull to get in the same pen with her, hoping he'd gore her. Then tell Ash how you rode out the other morning with that very same rifle and waited across the ravine for Shannon to leave Happy's. You didn't know Ash was with her and you almost killed them both."

Ash roared like an enraged animal and lunged.

Shannon screamed as Happy shoved her to the ground. The breath was knocked out of her, and as she struggled for air she kept her eyes riveted on the scene before her. From her level she saw what neither man could.

When Ash roared out his anger and he and Jeff rushed Paula, she stepped back closer to the soft edge of the cliff. She stumbled and at the same time tried to raise the rifle more securely to her shoulder. But astonishment at their surprise assault and her precarious footing had thrown her off balance. She aimed the rifle over the men's heads and in her struggle to gain control pulled the trigger. The rifle recoiled with a forceful jolt that cata-pulted Paula backward, over the edge of the cliff.

With a sickening feeling of déjà vu, Shannon realized she'd already played this scene out with different char-acters. Her scream mingled with Jeri's and she closed her eyes. Too many tragedies in so short a time, and all her fault.

Happy was helping her to her feet, talking to her, but she couldn't hear what he was saying. She felt numb and tired and sad. Guilt began to creep upon her with each passing second. If only she hadn't come home.

"Shannon." Ash gathered her into his arms. "Are you okay?"

She lied, her words coming out clipped. "Fine. Is Paula...? Jeri? How's Jeri?"

"Jeff's taking care of her. It's you I'm worried about. None of this is your fault, you know." He captured her face between his hands and gazed down into the dark-ened amber eyes. His thumbs wiped at the tears streak-ing her pale cheeks. "I know you, Daffy. You're not going to blame yourself for this one."

He didn't seem to notice that she'd made no reply. Both became aware of Jeri's heart-wrenching sobs, and Shannon pulled out of Ash's arms. "She needs me, Ash. Jeff's too wrapped up in his own pain to help her."

Assured that Shannon was all right, but still deeply shaken by what had happened, Ash stumbled off to join the men at the cliff's edge. He felt as if he'd aged twenty years in a matter of minutes.

Shannon watched him go, then went to the young woman standing pitifully alone in her misery. When Jeri raised her head, Shannon saw the glazed eyes and with-out hesitation gathered her in her arms. Jeri's legs buckled and the sudden dead weight brought them both to their knees on the hard-packed ground. Shannon rocked the distraught girl, trying to give her some comfort.

"These past few weeks I've hated mother so much. At times, alone at night, I've even wished her dead. But I didn't mean it, really I didn't."

Shannon knew the hazards of wishing someone dead. How many times over the past ten years had she done the same? Like Jeri, she'd learned the hard way that destructive wishes have a bad habit of coming true.

Jeri gulped and began to talk again, half sobbing and a little incoherently. "All these years I've blamed you for everything that's gone wrong. I love Ash as if he were my real brother and his withdrawal hurt. Happy changed and didn't have time for me. I laid that at your door, too. But it wasn't you, was it, Shannon? It was me. I didn't want to grow up and face life and I resented the changes going on around me. Mother raised me in a fairy-tale world and I wanted to stay there."

She raised her red-rimmed eyes to meet Shannon's. "You were right. I thought of you as a kind of second mother and you left me, hurting everyone when you did—just like my father. Mother was always leaving me with friends for days or weeks to go off to some party. Even after she married the senator and I thought I'd have a real home, they were always traveling somewhere. But I had Ash and he loved me. And I had you. Yet just when I needed you most to teach me to stand up to Mother, you left. I couldn't fight her on my own, she was always too strong for me, too overpowering. That was my fault, not yours though, but I had to blame someone for my weakness." She sniffed and tried to force a smile. "I'm sorry for all the things I said about you. You're the strongest, most wonderful person I've ever known and I do love you, Shannon." She grabbed Shannon's hand. "Please say you forgive me."

"Of course I do, Jeri. And don't be too hard on yourself about Dean. We both know what he was like, don't we?"

"Yes, yes, we do." She shuddered. "He was worse than an animal. Listen to me," she whispered desperately. "I never knew for sure what Mother had done. I only suspected it. I wasn't sure until I told Happy everything yesterday. Once it was all out in the open, he and I linked everything together. If I'd been thinking straight... I just should have guessed. But there was Jeff."

She glanced over her shoulder then turned back to Shannon. "I stood up to Mother too late. When we got back from Europe, I hated her and myself for what I had allowed her to talk me into doing. I wanted to tell Jeff. I tried, but Mother said he'd never forgive me. So I believed her and treated him badly. She was right. He can't even bear to look at me. He's never going to be able to forget."

Shannon helped Jeri to her feet. "Give him some time. Jeff has a great understanding of human nature and he knew how your mother was. He does still love you, I believe, and Jeff doesn't love lightly. He'll come around."

Jeri began to cry again.

"Shannon."

At the sound of her name, Shannon glanced over her shoulder. Ash looked pale beneath the shaded brim of his hat, and she tried to smile and let him know she and Jeri weren't falling completely apart on him. "What's wrong?"

"Paula's fall was broken by an outcropping of bushes and some kind of ledge. She's hanging precariously there and we think she's alive. Jeff and I are going down to bring her up. Happy's going to need your help though. Jeri—" he clasped his stepsister and turned her to face him "—we need your help, too. Are you up to it, Pumpkin?"

"Anything. Is . . . is she conscious, Ash?"

"No, and that's to our advantage."

They worked fast. Happy and Shannon stripped the equipment from the pack horse. Jeri was handed a hatchet to cut some strong pine limbs for poles.

Ash and Jeff attached ropes securely to the saddle horns, then quickly tied the ends into looped slings. They backed their mounts close to the ledge then stood there arguing about who was going over the edge of the cliff to rescue Paula.

"She's my stepmother and my responsibility."

"Yeah, but if something happens down there...if she comes to and panics and you lose her, you'll never forgive yourself."

"I'm going."

"Hardheaded son of a bitch. All right." Jeff smiled. "Be a hero, just be damn careful. I'll work the rope once you get it secured around her."

"Just don't suddenly get clumsy and fall over. You're too big to bring up this way."

"Crap! Man, don't joke."

Shannon listened to their bantering and gave Happy a strained smile. She knew it was useless to tell Ash not to go; he'd made up his mind and there was no changing it. But if anything happened to him . . .

Jeri came running up the path dragging two long, stripped limbs. She dropped them in the center of the camp and watched Jeff and Ash get ready. She wanted desperately to go to Jeff but held back. When Jeff called her name, she jumped like a frightened rabbit, then trotted quickly to his side.

"I want you and Shannon at the horses' heads, and when Happy tells you, I want both of you to start walking the animals slowly forward. Happy, you work Ash's rope and keep it from snagging on anything while I work Paula's."

With her heart pounding in her ears like a wild jungle drum, Shannon watched as Ash secured one rope around his waist, tucking in his thick coat so the pressure wouldn't bite into his flesh. Then he slipped the second rope over his head and through one arm so he could quickly remove it and attach it to Paula.

Ash wrapped the rope around his wrist and let it slide through his fingers as he began to back off the ledge. He stopped and glanced down the steep, rocky cliff, calculating it to be a couple of miles to the bottom. He tore his eyes from the compelling, almost hypnotic view and found Shannon's worried gaze. For a long minute he stared at her, then steadying his Stetson firmly on his head he slipped over the side and out of sight.

The leather from the bridle cut into Shannon's fingers as Ash disappeared from sight. The horse snorted and threw his head back at the restriction, so Shannon loosened her grip.

"He'll be okay," Jeri whispered beside her as she scratched her horse's jaw to keep him calm. "Remember years ago, you were baby-sitting me and I talked you into helping me to climb the old oak out by the horse barn? You got me to go to the very top, then I was too scared to come down and no amount of coaxing would make be budge an inch. You had to climb down and get

Ash. He couldn't talk me down either, and because the limbs near the top were too weak to support him, he had to lasso a branch near me and swing out from the barn roof. It was dangerous, but he made it.''

Shannon grinned, pleased to see some of the strain was gone from Jeri's face. "You couldn't sit down for a week and Ash wouldn't talk to me for days."

Jeri gave a watery chuckle. "Yes, but he did what had to be done. He's like that, brave, but levelheaded. Do you think he'll understand about Dean?''

"Ash? More than anyone, Jeri. He knew Dean's nature."

"Did you hate him very much?''

"Yes."

"Are you sorry he's dead? I'm not, just that Mother did it."

Shannon scratched the horse's ear. "I don't know. Maybe in time I'll feel differently and be able to forgive him. Right now I don't even want to think about him."

They fell silent and it seemed an hour before her grandfather alerted them.

"Get ready, you two. He has her."

They waited, the seconds stretching into eternity.

"Okay. Now!"

In unison, Shannon and Jeri began walking the two animals forward. When the ropes became taut the horses tried to stop, and Shannon clucked her tongue and tugged, talking, begging that her horse wouldn't come to a halt. She didn't want to think about what could happen if the horses began backing up fast. Ash could lose his footing and plunge far enough below to seriously injure himself.

"Keep going," Happy yelled. "Steady, steady... stop!''

She held the animal still until they were given the all clear, then quickly ran back to where Ash stood, breathless and dirty, untying the rope from around his waist.

He heard her approaching, recognized the distinct sound of her slight limp on the hard packed ground. But he could only stare down at Paula as Happy and Jeff attended to her. He reached out and stopped the two women as they drew near. "You don't want to look yet," he warned.

CHAPTER SEVENTEEN

"Is SHE ALIVE?" Jeri's voice was barely audible.

"She's breathing. I don't know the extent of her internal injuries, but she's hurt pretty badly." Ash held Jeri, waiting for her to fall apart, but she surprised him with her silent acceptance and a quick nod.

A whisper of a sound from Paula caused Jeri to break from Ash's hold. "Mother." She fell to the ground beside her and reached for her hand, but Jeff stopped her.

"That arm's shattered. Don't touch it."

Shannon turned her back to them and wrapped her arms around her waist to ward off a sudden chill. She had caught a brief glimpse of Paula and it had been enough to make the bile rise in the back of her throat. How could anyone live through such injuries? She wanted to close her ears to the pitifully weak voice laced with pain, but couldn't. She wouldn't want an animal to suffer the way Paula must be. Still, forgiveness would be slow in coming she knew, and wondered if Ash would be able to put this all behind him. So much had happened over such a short space of time. Once again she'd managed to tear his life apart and, as before, with the destruction had come death. Only this time two human lives were involved.

"Mother, don't talk."

"Must—love you. Forgive."

"Oh, mummy. Please hold on."

Jeff hoisted Jeri to her feet as Happy covered Paula with a blanket. "Where did you put the tree limbs you cut?"

She didn't hear him and continued to stare at her mother, lying like a broken porcelain doll on the ground.

Jeff gave her a little shake. "Pull yourself together," he said gruffly. "We're not through here yet."

Jeri shook her head and looked up. "In the center of the camp, Jeff?" She touched his arm to stop him from turning away. "I love you."

"Do you? I find that hard to believe just now."

"Can you forgive me?"

"This is not the time to discuss our problems. We have to get your mother medical help fast." He walked away, knowing he'd hurt her, wishing he didn't feel so empty inside.

Ash cut lengths of rope while Jeff laid out the long tree branches that Jeri had cut and stripped of foliage. They quickly lashed the ropes crosswise to the poles, fashioning a travois.

Shannon and Jeri worked frantically stuffing one sleeping bag with three others to make a soft mattress, while Happy eased Paula as gently as possible onto a blanket so they could carry her.

Once the travois was lashed to the packhorse, Shannon and the men each took a corner of the blanket and carried Paula to the litter, where Ash tied her down securely.

"I wish I could have strapped a litter between the two horses to cushion the ride but the paths are too narrow. It's going to be a helluva ride for her and a miracle if she even makes it." Ash pulled off his Stetson, wiped his damp brow with his sleeve, then shrugged. "We've done the best we can."

Jeff was repacking only the essentials they'd need for the trip down the mountain on his and Ash's horse. "We better go. If we can make it down to Willow Falls before nightfall the radio will be within range and I'll get the helicopter to pick us up."

Shannon put her arm around Jeri as she stood beside her mother. "Go with Ash and Jeff. Happy and I will clean up the campsite, repack what we need and follow."

Jeff scowled at them. "She can wait and come down with you, Shannon."

"No. That's my mother and I'm coming. Besides it might help her if she knew I was there." Jeri walked away from Jeff, leaving him with a deepening scowl as she mounted her horse.

"Jeff." Shannon touched his tense arm, waiting until she had his full attention. "Don't be too hard on her and end up like Ash and I, with ten wasted years and a lot of heartache between us. I've seen Dean in action when he set his mind on something he wanted, especially a woman. He could be charming and persuasive. With the added challenge of revenge to get back at me and Ash, she never had a chance."

He opened his mouth to say something then clamped it shut. The four thin white scars along his cheek turned pink as his face paled. Jeff nodded and walked off to check Jeri's saddle pack.

"Why aren't you coming with us?"

Ash's voice so near her shoulder made Shannon jump. "You need to concentrate all your efforts on Paula. If I'm there you'll worry about me." She held out her foot.

"My ankle's fine, see." She wiggled it around in a circle. "Just a little sore. Happy and I won't be far behind. It's for the best, Ash."

When he started to protest, she stopped him by covering his mouth with her hand. "Listen, you'll be at the hospital and there are going to be reporters crawling all over the place. If we're not together they can't feed on the scandal. It will help defuse it some."

She was right, but he didn't like it. Something was wrong. He could feel it. He kissed her hard and quick and walked to his horse.

Shannon and Happy stood side by side, watching them ride out. When the path led them around the bend and out of sight she shivered in the heat, feeling cold and lonely. She knew Ash felt her withdrawal from him and was puzzled by it, but she couldn't help it.

"You blame yourself, don't you?"

"Yes, Pops. If I hadn't come home..." That phrase had haunted her in the past couple of hours. *If only.* But she had come, and look what a mess she'd made.

"Child."

"No, Pops. When Ash has time to think things out, how's he going to feel? Ten years ago I wrecked his life, and now it's happened again. Only the results this time are far worse. Dean's dead. Paula's hurt, and if she makes it, she'll be charged with Dean's murder. If she doesn't pull through, there's another death. Because of me, Jeri and Jeff's lives are torn apart. The scandal—it won't die down that quickly. And you, Pops. Look at the pain I've caused you. The embarrassment of all those stories about me. You know half the people are going to believe them even if they're not true. Don't you know that everything will have to come out if there is a trial?

Maybe I'm jinxed." She gave a shaky laugh. "What will the next ten years bring?"

"You're not going to run this time, Shannon Reed."

"No, sir. I am not. But I don't know what's going to happen either and that's the killer."

THE SUN BEGAN to slip westward in the sky and the mountain air grew crisp with the oncoming night. Shadows lengthened on the ground, overlapping each other in the gloomy twilight. Happy called a halt and they made camp for the evening.

Tucked in her sleeping bag and propped on her side, Shannon stared into the blue-white flames of the fire. A movement opposite her snagged her attention and she looked at her grandfather across the wavering heat. Stretched out with his saddle at his back, a cup of coffee in his hands, the steam rising like a cloud around his face, she realized how contented he looked.

He knew her so well, she thought. Her need for quiet, a chance to think out her problems. For the first time in her life she acknowledged what he meant to her. Oh, she loved him dearly, but it wasn't until this moment that it occurred to her how hard it must have been on him, losing his son, then only a few months later his daughter-in-law, and forced to take a newborn baby into his busy life.

He hadn't farmed her out to the many willing hands as some thought he would. Instead he'd taken care of her himself. As an infant she'd traveled all over the United States with him as he cared for and trained the Thoroughbreds that others raced. When she became older and started school he'd stopped his travels, and the kings of the horse world brought their injured or unmanageable steeds to him. The lump in her throat thickened and she swallowed hard.

"What's worrying you, child?"

She laughed softly at the term *child*, then realized no matter how old she got, she'd always be his child, his baby. "You—you old fake."

"Figured me out finally, have you?"

"Not really, but it's okay. I love you, anyway." He nodded and took a sip of coffee, but she could see the brightness in his sharp eyes. "Pops, with Dean dead, I've inherited the Rocking W. Lilith made him change his will and leave it to me. What am I going to do with it?"

Happy jerked forward so suddenly that scalding coffee splashed over the rim of his cup and onto his chest. "Damn," he muttered and pulled the flannel material away from his skin until it cooled. "Are you serious? What about Dean's father? He's a shrewd Frenchman and I can't see him agreeing to that. Hell's fire, child, he married that bubbleheaded, flighty Helen Wentworth just to get the Rocking W. He needed an American investment to funnel French funds through."

"Dean's father had a massive stroke about six years ago. It was kept as quiet as possible because of his financial empire and investors. Dean took over and that's when Lilith made him sign over the Rocking W to me in the event of his death."

Happy whistled long and low. "The Rocking W. My, my. Its holdings are almost equal to the Bar B."

"Yes, but, Pops, what am I going to do with it?"

"Why, merge it with Bartlet land, of course. When I die you'll have my land. With the merger, the Bar B will far exceed the acreage of the King Ranch in Texas before the heirs started chopping it up."

"How do you think Ash will feel?"

"Like a hungry tick on a fat dog."

She grinned into the warm glow of the fire. "I don't know. He might resent it."

"Now don't start making more trouble for yourself. Go to sleep. We're breaking camp at daylight."

He was right, she had enough problems without adding to them. But still...

SHANNON AND HAPPY rode in the back way to the Reed ranch around noon. She knew her grandfather had taken the rough, grueling shortcut to make sure they'd miss any reporters hanging around the entrance.

The sun burned through her shirt and she was hot, sticky and mad as a hornet when they trotted toward the horse barn and Bartlet's only reporter stepped from the shadow of the building with her camera raised and clicking away.

Happy swung his leg over the saddle horn and slid smoothly to the ground, accosting Sally Roland before she knew what was happening. He yanked the camera from her hands, threw it down and stomped on it until it cracked in half.

"Mr. Reed, that's the paper's camera."

"I'll buy them a new one. Get! This is private property and you're trespassing, girl."

"Why thank you. No one's called me girl in years." She batted her eyelashes at the old man then turned to Shannon. "The town is swarming with reporters. Even a national television crew is there with the locals. I thought since I'm from Bartlet, you'd give me an exclusive."

"You thought wrong," Shannon snapped, but the woman was either deaf or just didn't want to hear.

"After all, I'll be a lot more sympathetic than any of those outsiders."

"No." Shannon dismounted and gave the reins to one of the hands who had come out of the barn to watch.

"Did you know that Paula is in critical condition? What happened on Devil's Hump? Is it true she killed your husband? Why?"

Shannon began walking away and the woman followed, making her wince with each rapid-fire question.

Sally would have matched steps with Shannon, but from the corner of her eye she saw Happy Reed's hand reaching for her. She quickly sidestepped. "Oh, no you don't. The last time I let one of your bunch touch me I was locked up in a smelly, hot tack room for two hours."

Happy scowled, trying not to laugh. "Then get, gal. I'm just liable to do the same, except I'll keep you there until Jeff comes to arrest you and that could be more than just a measly two hours. He's mighty busy these days."

"Yes, sir."

Shannon didn't hear the rest of what Happy had to say, but she imagined the woman got an earful. The cool shadows of the house enveloped her, then she was through the back door and standing in the peace of the deserted kitchen. She leaned against the counter, closed her eyes and moaned. The publicity had started; the scandal would feed headlines and news reporters for weeks. The humiliation Ash was going to be subjected to would be unbearable.

She pushed away from the counter and headed for the stairs, only to stop when she saw her luggage, which had been at Ash's, piled in the center of the entryway. With all his worries, he'd thought of her and her needs. She grabbed the handles and began to lug the cases up the stairs and into her room. A bouquet of gardenias sat on her vanity, the air sweet with their heady fragrance. She took a deep breath, dropped her suitcases and let the tears run freely down her cheeks.

NIGHT FELL QUICKLY in the mountain, shrouding the house in a darkness broken only by soft pools of light from the lamps.

Shannon finished washing the dinner dishes when the still of the night was broken by the sound of a car door slamming. "Not another reporter?"

Happy took the toothpick from his mouth, cocked his head and listened. "Nope. Sounds like Ash's truck to me."

She swung around, the dish towel clutched in her hands, and waited.

The back door rattled, stopped, then rattled again before Ash knocked.

She was suddenly scared and looked at her grandfather as he rose slowly to his feet and unlocked the door.

"Reporters been banging at our door all evening," he grumbled through the latched screen. "Come on in. Have a cup of coffee. You look like you need it."

Shannon already had a clean cup in her hands and was pouring the coffee before her grandfather finished his sentence. She swung around to face Ash. He looked so worn and tired her heart ached for him. He hadn't even been home long enough to bathe and change clothes. There was a paleness under his tan skin and a haunted look about his eyes that worried her. "How's Paula doing?"

Ash gulped the coffee down and held the cup out for a refill. "Doc doesn't think she's going to make the night. I tried to call you several times earlier, but the line was busy."

"Had to take the blasted thing off the hook," Happy said. "Reporters won't leave us alone."

"I know. They're at the hospital, too." He fell silent, his gaze searching the depths of the dark liquid in his hand. "Listen. I'm going to hold a press conference tomorrow to try to clear everything up."

"Ash, no!" Shannon felt the blood drain from her face.

"I have to, Shannon, or they'll never leave any of us alone. I would have done it this evening but...well, I wanted to wait and see if Paula pulled through. But there's not much hope. Doc said to go ahead and make arrangements."

Happy nodded. "Man knows his business. Do as he says. I'm real sorry for all your troubles."

She was sorry, too. After all, they'd been all brought on by her coming home. Ever since Ash had walked in she felt something was wrong. Now she realized what it was. He wouldn't look at her and she couldn't blame him. As she'd done earlier, he'd withdrawn from her. "How's Jeri taking it?"

"Better than anyone ever expected. Jeff's with her and they seem to be trying to patch things up."

"Good."

They fell silent, and Happy watched them both with troubled eyes.

"What time do you want me at the press conference?"

Ash looked at her for the first time. "I don't want you there."

"But, Ash."

"That's why I'm giving it, to keep them away from you."

She pulled out a chair and sat down heavily. "Ash, please."

"No, dammit. I wish there was some way you could go away. It's going to be bad enough as it is. The D.A.'s so hot he didn't get you or me, he's going after Paula with both guns."

"But she's—"

"Hell. He doesn't care. He was waiting for us when the helicopter set down at the hospital." His cup touched the table with a thud, then he raked both hands through his thick hair, leaving rows of finger tracks. "The ride to Willow Falls was pure hell. Paula was in and out of consciousness, then when we reached the hospital she seemed to rally some and made her confession to Jeff and the D.A. The damn bastard made Jeff officially charge her with Dean's murder so he could have it on record. Now he's hanging around like a vulture over picked bones, pestering Doc and the staff whether she's going to make it or not."

Ash leaned forward, put his elbows on his knees and rubbed his face. "Paula's confessed. A press conference will head off a public inquiry. It will keep your life with Dean and the past out of it and hopefully satisfy Ham's thirst a little. God, but I'm tired."

There was nothing she could do. She wanted to comfort him, hold him, but she knew he didn't want her, and the thought was more than she could bear. "I've made reservations to take Dean back to Paris. My plane leaves late tomorrow."

Ash's gaze lifted from his hands and he stared at her for a long time, his green eyes dark and worried.

"The D.A. won't try to stop me, will he?"

"If he knows, yes. But he doesn't, or he'd gloat over it and brag that he'd stopped you. You cleared it with Doc to release Dean's body?"

"Yes."

"What time does your flight leave?"

There was no "don't go," or "when will you be back," or "are you coming back at all?" "Six o'clock, but I'll be leaving earlier to catch the commuter to Great Falls." Her face felt unnaturally stiff, as if it would crack and break into a million pieces if she tried to smile. Her chest ached painfully and she wondered if people really did die of a broken heart. Surely hers was slowly breaking. There was so much she wanted to say. But the words just wouldn't come. If he rejected her it would kill her just as surely as if he put a gun to her head. So she just sat there, telling herself she wasn't going to give him the chance to hurt her.

The silence seemed loud in her ears and she clenched her teeth together.

"I'll put the press conference off until three o'clock."

Happy's gaze bounced back and forth, his mouth a tight line in his lined and leathery face.

Ash rose slowly. "I have to get back to the hospital and Jeri. I'll call you if there's any change, one way or the other."

He was gone as quickly as he'd come. Shannon shoved her chair back and started to rush from the room, but Happy's hand on her arm stopped her.

"You didn't tell me you were leaving tomorrow."

"I was going to tonight. Lilith was good to me, Pops, and I owe it to her to take Dean home. She wouldn't want him to be alone."

"He's upset, Shannon, walking around like a zombie. He's worried and completely worn out. He's just not thinking straight about what he's doing or saying."

"I know, Pops, but it doesn't make it any easier."

"No, child. I know. Remember, too, he's trying to protect you, and he has responsibilities. Once he's met them, then he'll come for you. You'll see."

"Will he? He didn't even ask if I was coming home."

She pulled her arm free then she too was gone, leaving the old man to stare off into space before he rose and went to the telephone.

THE NIGHT, like a sworn adversary, took its revenge, making Shannon toss and turn through the long hours, bolting awake at every little sound.

Dawn was a welcome relief.

She rose with the first light that cracked the dark sky. Knowing she had to keep busy, she set to work cleaning out stalls, grooming the horses her grandfather had boarded for training. She hauled buckets of water and grain; spread the clean stalls with new fresh hay. She worked until her back ached and her arms felt as if they were about to fall off. But the tasks hadn't been enough. Now she had time on her hands. Time to wait and think.

Seated before her bedroom window with the cool, sweet breeze twitching wisps of hair around her face, she sighed deeply as she heard her grandfather moving

around in his room down the hall. A light frown marred
her smooth brow as she stared blankly out the window,
thinking about his peculiar behavior. His silences and
hurt looks had weighed heavily on her conscience, and
just when she'd started to explain again why she had to
return to Paris, he'd smile rather slyly at her then leave
the room.

If she didn't know better, she'd think he was being
secretive. But Happy was a forthright man who liked to
speak his mind.

Shannon put her elbows on the windowsill, propped
her chin in her hands and gazed off blindly into space,
finally admitting to herself that she'd done everything
she could to keep from thinking about Ash. The physical work hadn't really helped, only tired her out. He'd
kept his promise and called around midnight to tell
Happy that Paula hadn't made it. From her grandfather's end of the conversation she realized Ash didn't
want her to change her plans. She was to leave town as
quickly and quietly as possible.

She felt like an outlaw—get out of town before noon
or else. If not an outlaw at least an outcast. God, how
she dreaded going back to Paris alone and facing the
memories there. If only he could come with her. A fluffy
brown squirrel began to chatter at her from the tree
outside the window and she managed a smile.

The tree, her tree. A symbol of her youth with its stair
step limbs that spiraled from her window to the ground
below. All at once a thousand memories came flooding
back. Ash climbing the tree, sitting out on a limb,
laughing, sympathetic and scornful, depending on the
trouble she was in. They'd been so happy then. The
idyllic days of youth, with dreams that grew as the years
went by. They'd come again, she told herself stoutly.

Somehow, when this trip was over and she was back, she and Ash would be together. Too much had happened to keep them apart. Maybe because she'd waited for Ash so long she wanted everything now. She expected too much too fast. She'd have to learn patience again.

A loud knock on her bedroom door startled her from her daydreams and she jerked around on the vanity stool. "I'll be right down." She rose shakily, straightened the butternut-yellow St. John knit dress over her slim hips and slipped her feet into the low heeled, black patent leather pumps. At least her grandfather had agreed to drive her to the airport, though he'd grumbled about her leaving for hours. Taking a quick look around, she swore to herself once again that she'd be back, nothing had changed.

Shannon picked up her garment bag and suitcase and walked slowly down the stairs, her eyes on the steps. When she was almost at the bottom, a cough made her look up and she froze.

"I ain't Ash, but I'll have to do."

Happy stood before her dressed in his one good black suit, his Sunday-go-to-church and weddings and funeral suit. A battered brown leather suitcase was in his hand and that sly grin on his face.

"What are you up to?" she demanded, her eyes narrowing.

He set the case down with a thud and crossed his arms over his chest. "I let you walk out of here once and I didn't see you again for ten years. This time I'm going with you to make damn sure you come home. Even if I have to drag you back by your hair."

"Oh, Pops." She let the garment bag slip from her arm and the suitcase drop to the floor as she rushed to him like a child. "I was dreading this trip."

"Figured you were."

She kissed his lined cheek and pulled back. "Thanks, Pops. I'll show you Paris before we come back."

"Just so long as you don't let any of those sexy French women get hold of me. I might like it and decide to send you back alone."

Shannon laughed as they picked up their luggage. She laced her arm through his and said, "Then let's go."

Happy managed the door. "Just don't get any funny idea about staying."

"No, sir."

"You have your life here to straighten out."

"Indeed I do."

"You're settled in your mind then?"

"I always was. I just got sidetracked a little."

Happy nodded.

"But this time, Pops, Ash is going to have to come for me. I don't know how I'll work it, but I will."

"Never doubted it, child. You're my granddaughter after all."

She'd taken courage in hand and come this far; she wasn't going to give up now.

CHAPTER EIGHTEEN

"SHE'S BACK!"

A gush of hot air rushed into the cool interior of the Cattleman's Café as Chester Fawnsworth pulled open the heavy glass door. He stepped quickly inside the yawning opening, then hopped an extra step to keep the door from hitting him in the backside as it was likely to do.

At the rear of the café, the monster juke box with its bubble lights flowing like a rainbow after a spring shower played a mournful country-western tune while the lunch crowd finished their meal.

"Shannon's back!"

Chester rushed in, hiked his scrawny frame on a high swivel stool and thumped the hard surface of the counter.

Before the old geezer could open his mouth to demand his usual, Stella Hopkins slid a steaming cup in front of him. "You got a chaw in your cheek, Chester?"

"Now, my beauty, you know I abide by your rules—no spitting, no drinking, no service." He scowled, poured some hot, dark liquid into the saucer, picked it up and blew a couple of breaths before he slurped the dish clean. "Did you hear what I said? Shannon's come back." He raised his voice a little and looked smugly at Stella. "She and that grandfather of hers got back late yesterday. Old Henderson was over at the drug store and saw them driving through town. He told Hally at the feed store when he went to pay his bill.''

"And she told you?''

"Naw, Goober was hanging around shooting the breeze with some of the boys and heard. He told me.''

"Chester, you're something else.'' Stella watched as the old man slurped more hot coffee from the saucer. "But didn't Happy Reed tell you he didn't want to hear you talking about his granddaughter?''

Chester looked hurt. "Lordy, no, Stella. He told me before he left for Par-ree that if I talked to any reporters he'd tear my tongue out with his bare hands. Well, them snoops left town, and I kept my lips sealed like the seams on a flour sack.''

There were a few chuckles about the room and Stella cast a bland glance to a nearby table, then shrugged helplessly.

"I wonder what's going to happen next? Ash Bartlet's been holed up since he buried that murdering stepmother of his.''

"Chester,'' Stella warned, but the old man had been silent too long. He was on a roll and not about to stop short of someone putting a gag on him.

"Can you believe, right here in this town, a murder? And I heard tell that Clyde out at the Rocking W has left town. A good thing too, I say. He downright lied to me, Stella. Fed me all those stories about the poor child so that husband of hers could get back at Ash.'' He loudly slurped some more of his coffee then looked up to see how his words were being taken. But the light of his life was not looking at him. She was staring off over his shoulder.

He sensed it then, the tightening of tension in the room, and the back of his neck felt as if it was on fire. He set the saucer down as if it were a fine piece of china, placed his gnarled hand on the edge of the counter and slowly pushed himself around. His eyes widened.

At first he didn't know who the young woman was. His old eyes began to twinkle with appreciation. A stranger and a real beauty to boot. Tall, with tight-fitting jeans and a white cotton western shirt that hugged all the right curves, curves he'd only dreamed of over the last some odd years. And that mass of shoulder-length, jet-black hair, as shiny as a newborn colt. He mentally rubbed his hands together. A new ear to tell tales to.

When amber eyes locked with his he felt a sinking sensation in the pit of his stomach. He knew those eyes—eyes full of mischief and laughter. The sudden recognition made him swallow a gulp of air. "Why it's…it's Shannon. My, if you ain't the prettiest gal I've ever laid these poor old eyes on in a long time."

Stella snorted. "Changing your tune real quick, aren't you, you old goat?"

Shannon walked to the counter, fished out some bills from her pocket and handed them to Stella, then she turned back to Chester and leaned forward and kissed him on the cheek. "Hello, Chester, it's good to see you." Then she walked out of the café.

"Did you see that? Stella, did you see what she did? She kissed me."

"You're lucky she didn't pick up that cup and pour hot coffee all over your besotted head, you old fool."

"Now, darling. Did I ever tell you how irresistible I was with the women? Why I had half the town chasing after me…."

Shannon stood on the curb outside the café, laughing at the expression on Chester's face. He'd expected her to chew him out for all the stories he told about her and was shocked speechless for once in his life when she kissed him. She shoved her hands in her back pockets and glanced up and down the street, looking for her grandfather's truck.

When she didn't see the familiar vehicle she frowned down at the tips of her boots, lost in thought. Happy had tried to talk her out of accompanying him to town, telling her she should stay home and rest. When she insisted, he'd grudgingly agreed, then he'd just dropped her off at the café with the grumbled words that he had important errands to run and he'd be back in an hour to pick her up. That had been almost two hours ago.

A horn honked and she glanced up, smiled and sprinted around the front of the truck. "You're late." She slammed the door to emphasize her irritation.

"Yep."

"I had lunch."

"That's good. I'll fix me something when we get home."

"Where did you go?"

"Here and there."

She blew out an exasperated breath and watched him closely. He wouldn't return her look. "Did you get my seeds?"

"Yep."

"All of them?"

"Shannon, I'm not senile—yet. You're sure you want to do all that flower planting today?"

"Of course. What's up, Pops? You've been jumpy all morning."

"Now, child, that's all in your head. I had errands, that's all."

"Okay, you're obviously not going to confide in me."

"I liked your Lilith."

He was deliberately, and not very subtly, changing the subject. "She liked you, too."

"Everything settled about the Rocking W? It's yours?"

"Hmm, yes." She watched the land speed by and suddenly felt free and almost happy. Her situation with Ash gnawed at her, though. She seemed to have developed a bad case of cowardice—worst of all, a lack of imagination—since she'd come back.

"Figured out a scheme to get Ash?"

She squirmed in the seat and twisted around. "I wouldn't call it scheming exactly, Pops. More like a master plan."

"Trickery, you mean?"

Why was he picking on her? "I'm too old for childish tricks." He roared with laughter, the first she'd heard in a long time, then he started to hum to himself. She glared and went back to watching the scenery fly by.

"You're going to be mighty tired and sore tomorrow if you dig out the beds and plant all those seeds today."

"Good, maybe I'll get a good night's sleep."

Happy chuckled and continued to hum off-key.

SOMEWHERE BETWEEN the hovering grasp of deep sleep and the elusive tug of awakening, a noise invaded her slumber. A well-known sound from times past, almost forgotten. She tried to ignore it to sink back into the peaceful darkness.

The sound came again, like a familiar old friend, and scratched at her dreams.

Childhood terrors seeped through her. Her heart
pounded. Her muscles seemed frozen, leaving her stiff
on the soft bed. Shannon opened her eyes a slit and the
gray shadows in the room took on the form of menac-
ing monsters. Then her eyes adjusted to the half-light of
dawn that chased away the imaginary creatures. She felt
foolish and rolled over, only to freeze once more as a
dark shadow oozed through the open window. Horrified, she watched it grow until it finally loomed over her
bedside.

She was going to scream, but when she tried, only a
gurgling sound came out before a rough hand clamped
over her mouth. Visions of Dean or Paula coming back
from the dead rushed through her mind. A warm breath
fanned her cheek.

This was no ghost! Not with the faint scent of tobacco on its breath. She'd never heard of a ghost that
smoked.

Shannon came alive, biting down hard on the hand
over her mouth and kicking out with all her strength
before her efforts were quailed by the heavyweight of
human body.

"Damn wildcat. Quit biting and scratching."

Ash! She groaned his name, undecided whether to be
angry or amused.

Laughter won out and the bed began to shake.

"Stop that. This is serious. I'm trying to be your
Prince Charming."

The bedside lamp clicked on and the light stabbed her
eyes, making her squeeze them shut. When she opened
them again, she found her gaze closely locked with
Ash's. She twisted her head, trying to jostle his hand free
of her mouth, but he only tightened it and she mumbled behind it. Then she realized what he was getting

ready to do and her eyes went round. Torn between fascination, bewilderment and excitement, she saw him pull out a tangle of men's ties from his back pocket. His weight pressed her deeper into the mattress and she began to wiggle.

"Be still." Ash shook out the knot of silk ties, grasping one before the others slid to the floor. "This was supposed to be easy. Damn near knocked myself out on a limb while climbing the tree. I almost lost my footing when I came face to face with an enraged squirrel who objected strongly to my invasion of his home. I skinned my shin on a broken branch and almost fell over backward when the window wouldn't open." He quickly removed his hand.

Shannon opened her mouth, only to have her words cut off by the gag he quickly fashioned. She growled. Had he lost his mind? Just what was he up to?

"No, I'm not crazy."

Her amber eyes began to dance with laughter.

"This is for your own good, though—and mine," he mumbled.

She tried to talk around the strip of silk but her efforts only made Ash chuckle.

"Hush. I can't make out a thing you're saying. Now give me your hands."

Shannon balked, her eyes narrowing into slits of brightness.

"You're going to make me do it the hard way, aren't you? Come on. I'm not into some weird new kind of sex." He chased her hands over the sheets and under her pillow until he finally caught them and quickly tied them in front of her. With a sigh of relief he heaved himself off her, stood up and yanked back the sheet, only to stop and stare down at her naked body. "Damn, I didn't plan on this, either. Why can't you wear clothes to be like any normal woman about to be kidnapped?" He glanced around a little nonplussed then began pulling drawers open and throwing out clothes.

Shannon scooted up into a sitting position and crossed her legs. He seemed oddly intent on his job. What he hoped to accomplish was beyond her, though.

"Don't you dare move."

She wasn't about to. Things had definitely become interesting. She grinned behind the gag.

Ash returned to the bed, carrying jeans and a shirt. Her eyebrows rose in an inquiring arch. "I can't carry you out of here buck naked. Think what the town gossips would do with that juicy tidbit." He held up the jeans.

Shannon shook her head and with her shackled hands mimed as if she were tugging at the waistband of her underpants.

"Crap." Ash dropped the clothes on the bed and rummaged through another drawer. When he returned, she touched her breast and he glared at her. "Forget it." He shook out the bikini panties, turning them this way and that, trying to figure out back from front. He shrugged, sat down on the side of the bed and picked up her locked ankles. "You're really going to make this difficult on me, aren't you?" She nodded and he scowled and pried her feet apart. A fine sheen of moisture dotted his forehead. "If your grandfather wasn't so close I'd forget this whole scheme and make love to you right now."

Shannon smiled behind the gag and wiggled her toes at him as he slipped the leg openings over her feet then up her calves. What started out as an impersonal touch turned slow and smooth. He made her skin tingle as he hooked his thumbs in the band and pulled the pants up, his fingers caressing her thighs.

"Lift your hips," he said gruffly, his eyes full of hunger. Ash swallowed, shook his head, and tried to clear his mind as he roughly yanked up the jeans. When he picked up the white shirt he'd found draped across the back of a chair, he paused and studied the situation for a second. "Okay, this is the way it's going to be. I'm going to untie you and you put your damn shirt on, then I'll retie your hands. Got it. No tricks. You're going out of here bound up like a Christmas turkey whether you like it or not."

The no-nonsense tone made her nod in agreement. When he began snapping the shirt closed, her eyes sparkled at the way his fingers lingered over her breast. She closed her eyes, savoring his touch, then opened them lazily to find him staring at her.

Ash cleared his throat. "Now comes the hard part." He rose, picked up her boots, stuffed socks in them then pitched them out the window. Back beside the bed, he looked down at her and scowled. "I'm going to carry you down the tree so I want you to be still."

Shannon's eyes widened and a long muffled 'no' issued from behind the gag. She glanced at the window then back at Ash, shaking her head and making a frantic gesture toward the door with her tied hands.

"Hell, no. I planned this this way and by heavens that's the way it's going to be. Where's your romantic soul? Your sense of adventure?" He clucked his tongue. "I'm afraid age has dulled your spirit."

Shannon squawked like a chicken as he lifted her and threw her over his shoulder. A firm pat on the backside made her growl threats he couldn't understand. She fell silent as another pat, harder this time, connected. Then as he started to move she grabbed hold of his belt and gasped as he stepped through the window onto the first thick tree limb.

Ash tightened one arm around Shannon and used the other to steady each foothold from limb to limb down the tree.

She held her breath with each move, praying silently, closing her eyes when he seemed to teeter. From her up side-down position the ground looked miles away. When Ash finally stood on solid ground, she sagged limply with relief. Maybe he had gone mad after all. Surely he'd put her down now, she thought, but he only heaved her slipping body higher on his shoulder with a quick movement that cut off her air supply for a second.

When Ash stopped and turned in the direction they'd just come, Shannon craned her neck around to see what had drawn his attention. Her grandfather was standing at his bedroom window giving Ash a thumbs-up signal of approval. Why that old conniver. He knew! He'd probably helped Ash plan this. She raised her red face and glared at him. Enough was enough, she wanted down, and began to kick and squawk once more.

Ash cursed and grabbed hold of her legs as she began to slide off his shoulder. He opened the passenger door of his truck and pitched her in with a grunt of relief.

Shannon bounced up into a sitting position and laid her head against the seat and began to laugh. This was her old Ash back. The wild, devil-may-care man of her youth. All the words in the world, the explanations, the recriminations didn't matter now. They could wait. What was important was that he'd come for her. She reached up to pull down the wet, soggy gag, but he stopped her.

"Not yet, you don't. Put your hands back in your lap." He buckled her seat belt, started the engine and set the four-wheel drive in gear.

They'd driven about thirty minutes over rough ground before she realized where they were headed. She yanked down the gag then reached over and turned off the ignition. The truck bumped along then stopped.

Ash turned in his seat to face her. "I guess you want a reason for my craziness?"

"No. I want you to untie me." She held out her hands. "Then I want you to kiss me."

He did as she asked, and when she pulled away, breathless and smiling, she said. "You forgot my boots, Ash."

He looked down and she wiggled her toes. "So I did. But believe me, you won't be needing them."

She tightened her arms around his neck and put her head on his shoulder and just held him close for a long moment. It was right, she told herself, the way she felt so peaceful inside. "We're going to the line shack, aren't we?"

He touched her face, caressing her soft cheek with tender, light strokes as if she had suddenly turned to porcelain. "Yes, where it all started for us. We were happy there once, weren't we, Shannon?"

"More than you'll ever know. Do you think we can go back to that time, after all that's happened?"

Ash started the engine. "We're going to damn well try."

She settled against the leather seat. "Why the elaborate production of climbing through my window and kidnapping me?"

Ash shot her a twinkling glance. "I thought you deserved to be taken in style. Actually, it was part Happy's idea. He told me this time I was going to have to come after you. I was wrong ten years ago. I should have flown to Paris and dragged you home. I hope that maybe this morning can help put the past behind us and we can start all over again.''

She placed her hand on his thigh and he covered it for a second with his.

The sun was beginning to set when they reached the line shack. The sunset fractured the darkening clouds in long streaks of light, making the sky look like a stained glass window.

Shannon stepped out of the truck, her bare feet sinking into the spongy spring grass. A cool breeze ruffled the thick new leaves on the trees with a whisper.

Ash came around to stand beside her for a minute before he urged her up the steps and through the door.

She had to blink to believe her eyes. Someone had worked long and hard to refurbish the place. The walls were painted white and flowers filled every available container. There was a big new bed with a floral down comforter folded neatly at the foot. Clean white sheets were turned back invitingly. One of her lacy nightgowns lay draped across a pillow.

"It's as close to heaven as I could take you without losing you again."

Tears brightened her eyes and she smiled through them as he took her in his arms. "I don't know what to say. It's lovely and I love you." She choked, then cleared her throat. Ash wasn't any steadier and he didn't need her bawling childishly. He needed a woman—he needed her.

"Come with me. I want to show you something." He led her out of the line shack, around the building and down the grassy slope to the lazy moving creek.

She saw it at once, the strange old tree that lay on the ground, wound itself in a hump then turned upward as it reached for the sky. Years ago, in their childhood, they'd dubbed it their lucky dragon tree because of its weird shape. But she was puzzled as to why he brought her here, now, when they could be back at the shack doing more interesting things. "Ash, what are you up to?"

He took hold of her arm and pulled her along behind him to the thick hump in the tree and pointed. "Do you remember those?"

Carved into the dark rough bark was a large heart pierced by an arrow and with their initials in the center. It took her a moment to catch her breath as memories came flooding back. "Yes, of course I remember. It was after the first time we made love. I was seventeen—a million years ago, yet only yesterday. I . . ." Her voice trailed off as she spotted a new carving under the very tip of the heart. She leaned forward and read, " 'Married.' Ash, it has tomorrow's date on it."

"Does it?"

"Don't joke. It says tomorrow."

"Why, yes. It does, doesn't it."

"Ashland Bartlet." She whirled around with her hands on her hips. "What's going on?" She was suddenly too scared to hope.

"Why, tomorrow about noon, Happy, Jeff, Jeri and Pastor Smith will be up here for a wedding."

She burst into tears. "Really?"

"Would I dare tease you about something as important as our wedding? I've waited ten long, lonely years for this."

"Me too. But how . . ."

"With Happy and Judge Davis's help."

She glanced at the new carving on the tree then back at Ash and flew into his arms. "You'll never regret marrying me, Ash."

"I know. I love you."

"I'll make you happy."

"You already do. You're the light in the darkness, Shannon."

"We'll have lots of children. I'm not too old yet."

Ash threw back his head and laughed. The sound seemed to bounce off the trees and echo back at them. "No, love, not too old."

"Well then..."

"You talk too much."

Ash wrapped his arms around her, lifted her off her feet and spun her around. They were as much a part of each other as the mountains and the land were of Montana. They were destined to be together forever.

Shannon was home!

MAIL-IN-OFFER

OFFER CERTIFICATE ✂

I have enclosed the required number of proofs of purchase from any specially marked "Gifts From The Heart" Harlequin romance book, plus cash register receipts and a check or money order payable to Harlequin Gifts From The Heart Offer, to cover postage and handling.

002

CHECK ONE	ITEM	# OF PROOFS OF PURCHASE	POSTAGE & HANDLING FEE
	01 Brass Picture Frame	2	$ 1.00
	02 Heart-Shaped Candle Holders with Candles	3	$ 1.00
	03 Heart-Shaped Keepsake Box	4	$ 1.00
	04 Gold-Plated Heart Pendant	5	$ 1.00
	05 Collectors' Doll Limited quantities available	12	$ 2.75

NAME _____

STREET ADDRESS _____ APT. # _____

CITY _____ STATE _____ ZIP _____

Mail this certificate, designated number of proofs of purchase (inside back page) and check or money order for postage and handling to:

Gifts From The Heart, P.O. Box 4814

Reidsville, N. Carolina 27322-4814

NOTE THIS IMPORTANT OFFER'S TERMS

Requests must be postmarked by May 31, 1988. Only proofs of purchase from specially marked "Gifts From The Heart" Harlequin books will be accepted. This certificate plus cash register receipts and a check or money order to cover postage and handling must accompany your request and may not be reproduced in any manner. Offer void where prohibited, taxed or restricted by law. LIMIT ONE REQUEST PER NAME, FAMILY, GROUP, ORGANIZATION OR ADDRESS. Please allow up to 8 weeks after receipt of order for shipment. Offer only good in the U.S.A. Hurry—Limited quantities of collectors' doll available. Collectors' dolls will be mailed to first 15,000 qualifying submitters. All other submitters will receive 12 free previously unpublished Harlequin books and a postage & handling refund.

OFFER-1RR

GIFTS FROM THE HEART
from *Harlequin*

FREE BY MAIL

With proofs of purchase plus postage and handling

A. **Hand-polished solid brass picture frame 1-5/8″ × 1-3/8″ with 2 proofs of purchase.**

B. **Individually handworked, pair of heart-shaped glass candle holders (2″ diameter), 6″ candles included, with 3 proofs of purchase.**

C. **Heart-shaped porcelain keepsake box (1″ high) with delicate flower motif with 4 proofs of purchase.**

D. **Radiant gold-plated heart pendant on 16″ chain with complimentary satin pouch with 5 proofs of purchase.**

E. **Beautiful collectors' doll with genuine porcelain face, hands and feet, and a charming heart appliqué on dress with 12 proofs of purchase. Limited quantities available. See offer terms.**

HERE IS HOW TO GET YOUR FREE GIFTS

Send us the required number of proofs of purchase (below) of specially marked ''Gifts From The Heart'' Harlequin books and cash register receipts with the Offer Certificate (available in the back pages) properly completed, plus a check or money order (do not send cash) payable to Harlequin Gifts From The Heart Offer. We'll RUSH you your specified gift. Hurry—Limited quantities of collectors' doll available. See offer terms.

501R

GIFTS FROM THE HEART
ONE PROOF OF PURCHASE

To collect your free gift by mail you must include the necessary number of proofs of purchase with order certificate.